Dark Spirit

Works by Kate Douglas

Paranormal Romances

DemonFire
HellFire
"Crystal Dreams" in *Nocturnal*
StarFire
CrystalFire

Erotic Romances

Wolf Tales
"Chanku Rising" in *Sexy Beast*
and as the ebook
Wolf Tales 1.5—Chanku Rising
Wolf Tales II
"Camille's Dawn" in *Wild Nights*
and as the ebook
Wolf Tales 2.5—Chanku Dawn
Wolf Tales III
"Chanku Fallen" in *Sexy Beast II*
and as the ebook
Wolf Tales 3.5—Chanku Fallen
Wolf Tales IV
"Chanku Journey" in *Sexy Beast III*
and as the ebook
Wolf Tales 4.5—Chanku Journey
Wolf Tales V
"Chanku Destiny" in *Sexy Beast IV*
and as the ebook
Wolf Tales 5.5—Chanku Destiny
Wolf Tales VI
"Chanku Wild" in *Sexy Beast V*
and as the ebook
Wolf Tales 6.5—Chanku Wild
Wolf Tales VII
"Chanku Honor" in *Sexy Beast VI*
and as the ebook

For a full list of all of Kate's books,
visit her website at www.katedouglas.com

Dark Spirit

Spirit Wild Series

KATE DOUGLAS

BEYOND THE PAGE
publishing

Beyond the Page Books
are published by
Beyond the Page Publishing
www.beyondthepagepub.com

Copyright © 2014 by Kate Douglas
Cover design by Dar Albert, Wicked Smart Designs
Cover background photo by Doug Moore

ISBN: 978-1-940846-00-2

This book is dedicated with much love and appreciation to my agent, Jessica Faust, for her amazing foresight and extreme patience. Thank you— there really are no words, though after all these years I imagine you've heard more than you wanted. Along with the excuses.

And to my editor, Bill Harris, who knows all too well just how many words I have. Thanks to Bill they're much better aligned for telling a good story.

Acknowledgments

I've got an absolutely terrific crew of beta readers who help me fine-tune my stories before they are ever seen by my editor. My sincere thanks and appreciation to Lynne Thomas, Ann Jacobs, Karen Woods, Lynn Sicoli, Kerry Parker, Jan Takane, Nicole Passante, Rhonda Wilson and Rose Toubbeh. I will never publicly admit some of the truly embarrassing things these amazing ladies have caught, but all my readers should be thankful they're so good at what they do!

I want to acknowledge the talented cover artist Dar Albert, who designed the perfect cover. It gives *Dark Spirit* just the right look for my Spirit Wild series. Thank you.

A very special thanks to Martin Biro, my editor at Kensington Publishing, for his sincere encouragement and a friendship that means a great deal to me. This business of writing can be a difficult journey at best, but the amazing people we get to meet along the way make every bit of it worthwhile.

To my husband~thank you so much.
Laughter really is the best medicine.

1

It was nothing more than a bare patch of earth littered with trash, but the grasses growing here were magic. And Romy knew she risked a beating for kneeling beside what had become, to her at least, a shrine. A shrine to both love and loss.

But it had been exactly twenty years ago today, and acknowledgment must be made.

Twenty long, lonely years, and if it meant a beating, kneeling beside this trash-strewn patch of dirt, well . . .

It wouldn't be her first.

She had no idea they planned to kill her.

First she heard the sound of gravel crunching beneath boots. Many boots. Then, before she had time to react, his voice. "I will make an example of you, Satan's bitch."

"What?" Spinning around, she leapt to her feet. "Reverend Ezekiel! What . . . ?"

"Do you dare question me? Question the voice of the Lord?"

His voice rose as if he spoke to the entire congregation. Meaty fingers wrapped around both her arms. Clamped down with bruising strength.

Romy turned away, but his spittle sprayed across her face. She tugged but she couldn't pull her arms free. This time, Ezekiel had plenty of help. The men she'd turned down over the years, every damned one of them laughing and making jokes, pulling her long hair, squeezing her unbound breasts through the loose-fitting dress, and then dragging her across the cornfield to the center of the compound.

Two bloodstained poles, planted firmly in the ground in the shape of an X.

Dear God! This would be no simple beating.

The men threw her roughly against the whipping post.

The women stood, heads bowed in prayer. Like that was going to help? Romy glared at them, all of them standing off to one side, eyes down, hands clasped demurely in front of their waists. So many of them pregnant because that's what women were for.

Their sole purpose in life, as mandated by God, according to Reverend Ezekiel, was to keep the men satisfied, to take their seed and produce more followers. All for the esteemed bastard and self-avowed reincarnation of one of the Lord's prophets, known to all who lived here in the compound as the Most Reverend Ezekiel, oracle of all things holy, and leader of the Glorious Salvation in Truth.

Bastards, all of them. A bunch of stupid women unwilling to want anything better than the horny old men who'd subjugated them through fear and ignorance. Women so cowed and terrified that not one of them would lift a finger to help one of their own. No, they'd ignored the terrified cries of a six-year-old child, and now they'd stand witness to her death twenty years later, thankful it wasn't one of them about to have their flesh stripped away.

To hell with them. They deserved their wretched lives!

But I don't, do I, Mama? I don't!

"Tighter. Don't want her breaking free. Samuel! Check those knots."

"Yes, Reverend."

She fought them. She knew she was strong—stronger than any of the other women—but Samuel, the little dick, tightened the bindings holding her wrists to the upper arms of the X. Not a cross for punishment. No, Ezekiel believed that sinners didn't deserve the same as the Christ, so the two polished beams had been planted in the ground in the shape of an X. As tall as she was, Romy's breasts were smashed in the top V, which was most likely the effect the good reverend wanted. He'd always liked looking at her breasts. Her arms were stretched overhead, extending outward, wrenching her shoulders.

She tugged at the ropes binding her wrists, glared at Samuel as he knelt to tie her legs to the lower section. When he grappled with her right leg, she kicked out, hard, cracking her bare toes against the softness between his legs. But he was hard, too. Erect and straining against his pants.

Romy laughed when he doubled over, screaming like a little girl. Screaming louder than she had when worse was done to her, but he was grabbing his crotch with both hands. She'd bet good money he wasn't hard now.

"Ahhhh . . . Bitch! You fucking bitch!"

Good. She knew she'd caught him hard in the balls, but he deserved it. No surprise that his dick had been hard. The jerk got off on what he knew was coming.

Sucking deep breaths, she dismissed the man whimpering in the dirt and stared wildly at the ones surrounding her. Were all of them hard? All erect, knowing she'd soon be naked, her back bleeding?

Strong arms wrapped around her thighs, holding them tight to the posts while others tightened the ropes lashed around her legs from her knees down. She felt their filthy hands reaching between her legs, invading her, and she cursed them, furious, twisting and struggling against the bindings holding her arms, against the arms trapping her legs. There were too many; she wasn't strong enough to fight them all. Eventually they had her, arms and legs spread wide, securely lashed to the smooth wood. She held her head high, no matter the strain on her neck, and stared at the forest surrounding the compound. Instead of the men celebrating her capture, Romy focused on the words she'd read just this morning, the words she read daily in her mother's diary. Thought of the magic she'd read about yet never mastered.

She knew there was a wolf inside her but she'd never been able to call it forth. She'd eaten the magic grasses, attracted to their sweet flavor, but her skin had never crawled with the sense of her other creature wanting free. Her vision hadn't changed.

No, only her dreams. Thank goodness she'd had her dreams. Running as a wolf through the deep woods, running beside her mother.

Except Mama was gone. For twenty long years she'd been gone. For twenty years, Romy had waited for the right time to escape, for the time when she could finally call on the wolf and run. Only then would she have a chance of surviving in a world she'd never seen. Not after a lifetime in the compound. A lifetime in bondage to the twisted beliefs of the one they called the oracle, the Reverend Ezekiel.

Romy sensed movement in front of her and raised her head. Her father stood there, glaring at her. He'd taken another wife, one who knew that Romy had been his unwilling bedmate all these years.

Was that the reason for this whole scene? From the way he glanced away when she tried to make eye contact, Romy figured she had her answer.

"Gee, Daddy. All you had to do was tell me you didn't want to fuck me anymore. I would have gladly stepped aside for your new whore. Isn't this taking things a little bit far?"

His hand flashed out before she had time to react, catching her across the left cheek hard enough to make her see stars. Romy's mouth filled with blood, but her father flushed a deep scarlet. It was worth the pain to know she'd pissed him off.

He turned to Reverend Ezekiel and drew in a breath deep enough to expand his skinny chest. "She has sinned and deserves no mercy. I renounce this harlot. She is no longer my daughter. She consorts with evil. Lures godly men to join her and follow the devil's path."

"Excellent, Brother Ephron. You may stay or leave. Whatever you choose."

"I choose to stay." He stepped closer. Close enough that Romy could see the tiny red lines in his bloodshot eyes. "You'll pay for your sins," he said. "And then you'll burn in hell."

He pulled out a knife and cut through the thin cotton fabric covering her. Down the front, along the sleeves, a ritualistic evisceration of the dress that had once belonged to her mother.

Romy had worn it today to mark the date.

Someone pulled the fabric away from her. She felt the heat of the afternoon sun caressing her bare back and buttocks, but she felt no shame. Neither did she feel fear. Raising her head again, she looked at the crowd in front of her. Men, women and children, standing silently, waiting for her punishment to begin.

The sense of anticipation sent a visceral pulse through her body, a sensual, sexual reaction that surprised her. After years of almost nightly rape by her father, she'd never felt anything remotely sexual. She'd merely been a receptacle for his seed.

A barren one, thank goodness.

She sensed Ezekiel moving into place, heard the soft hiss as he uncoiled the leather bullwhip. His voice rose in rhythmic cadence, as if he spoke to thousands rather than a few ragged followers practically salivating over the promise of Romy's punishment.

"You have been judged by the elders of this holy group and found guilty of consorting with the devil. Tempting your father with your whorish ways, and honoring your mother's death. Giving honor to a woman who sought the devil's attention is the same as honoring Satan. The only punishment is death by the lash. What say you, Romy Sarika, no longer the daughter of Ephron?"

"I say fuck you, Reverend Ezekiel." She smiled when the crowd gasped.

She made no sound when the lash left a trail of fire from her left shoulder to her right buttock, but she sucked a deep, startled breath of air.

Then slowly she let it out.

It hurt. Damn, the whip hurt more than she'd expected, but she'd die silently if it took everything she had. She wasn't going to give them the satisfaction of watching her scream or writhe in pain. She wrapped her hands around the poles in time for the next strike. Tightened her fingers at the crack of the whip and the slashing, burning pain.

Right shoulder, left buttock, fully aware of the split second when the newest stripe crossed the first.

The pain from the first slash sizzled into the second and then the third, and together they stole her breath. Romy clenched her jaw and went away in her mind. The way she'd had to do the night her mother died, when she was six and her father had shoved his big penis between her legs and made her bleed.

He hadn't cared that he hurt her at all, only that he had a warm cunt to fuck.

That's what he called her when no one else could hear. He'd called her a cunt and a whore, said she was just like her mother. But Romy remembered her mother as strong and beautiful, with a quick laugh that she shared with Romy but always hid from her husband.

Romy was proud to be just like her mother.

Then she thought of her mother's broken body—just bones, now—lying beneath the dirt and trash from the compound garbage dump. She'd tried to keep the unmarked grave cleared of debris at first, but then she feared that creating one noticeably clean spot in the midst of so much garbage would draw attention.

That was the last thing Romy wanted to do.

She'd given up trying to escape for the same reason. She couldn't do it as a woman, not on her own. Her few attempts had led to beatings, though none as severe as this one. The wolf, though. If she'd been able to find her wolf, no one could stop her. Her mother had said so.

Her life was all about staying out of the way, under the radar. Today she'd sat by her mother's unmarked grave chewing on a long stem of grass—Mama's magic grass—remembering. Her father screaming curses, her mother standing before him so tall and strong and beautiful. And then she'd suddenly stripped off her simple dark dress and changed. One minute she'd been Romy's mama, the next she'd been a huge, dark wolf, with sharp teeth and amber eyes. She'd growled, and then she'd lunged at her husband.

Romy hadn't feared the wolf at all but her father had run away, screaming. The wolf didn't chase him. She'd paced restlessly for a moment and then she was digging frantically beneath a shrub by the front porch, digging and pulling out a cloth bag and dropping the bag in front of Romy.

Romy remembered leaning over in front of the wolf, picking up the dirty bag and looking inside. It held a book—a cheap little diary no bigger than Romy's prayer book. Somehow she'd known to hide it, and she slipped it into her apron pocket before anyone could see.

She'd never forget the voice in her head—her mother's voice—the last time she'd heard her speak.

5

Good girl, baby. Hide it. Let no one read it, ever. It's for you, not for anyone else. Don't let them cage you. You and I are special, and it's time they learned to accept us. But just in case . . . just in case anything happens, remember I will always love you. The grasses in the forest are magic, Romy. You'll recognize them. They're our magic.

Her mother the wolf had turned to run, but she wasn't fast enough. Men from the compound were coming, running across the field of chest-high corn, when Reverend Ezekiel stopped, raised his rifle, and fired.

The beautiful dark wolf turned back into Romy's mama before her body hit the ground. The men had all gathered around, staring at her mother's naked body as her blood congealed in the dried grass. Her father never said a word, but he and the reverend and a couple of others had dragged the bloodied, naked body of her beautiful mother across the weed-covered field. Had dragged her to the garbage pit, where they threw her into the stinking pile of trash.

That night, while the men gathered at the chapel, Romy and one of the other grown women who had been her mother's friend had taken Mama's body out of the garbage. They'd found a place nearby and dug a shallow grave. Romy helped wrap her mother in a blanket off her own bed, and they'd quickly buried her and then scattered trash about to disguise the sinful thing they'd done.

No one could know. Only the one woman, and she would keep this secret, out of fear, if nothing else. No one disobeyed the men. That wasn't allowed. Ever. Romy was six years old, but she knew she would never be a child again. Not after what she'd seen. What she'd done.

That night, her father made sure her childhood ended. That was the first night he'd taken her to his bed and told his only child, his six-year-old daughter, what her new duties would be.

She surfaced for a moment, stunned by her reconnection to the blinding pain and the steady count as Reverend Ezekiel wielded his whip.

Seventy-three. Seventy-four.

Smiling, Romy went away again. Back to her memories. Into her mind, as far away from the pain as she could go.

• • •

Isn't she dead yet?

No. Still breathing after a hundred lashes. She's your daughter, Ephron. Do I finish her?

I don't know. Mary would rather she were gone.

Mary's a hot little number.

That she is. You know, Ezekiel . . . we have more young men than women. They are dissatisfied with celibacy.

It would be apropos, wouldn't it? Might humble the bitch.

(laughter) Nothing will humble her. She's just like her mother.

Is she, Ephron? Like her mother?

Romy held her breath, alert now, in spite of or because of the excruciating pain, waiting for her father's answer.

She has never become a wolf. I'm sure she's tried.

She could be worth good money to us, if she can change. I've had an offer. They actually want a breeding pair, but they'll still pay for a female. One who can change.

It's not happened. I think she would have run away if she could shift.

Probably true. I say we lock her in the small room off the chapel. Let the women care for her. If she lives, and when her wounds are no longer bleeding, we send the young men to her. It will give them something to look forward to.

Romy faded in and out of the conversation. They were talking about her. She knew that much. They were going to lock her up and give her to the same young men she'd been turning away all these years.

No. That was not acceptable. She tried to pull her arms free but the ropes still bound her to the whipping frame. A moment later someone untied her wrists and ankles.

Her body crumpled and the pain exploded, unchecked now, a fire burning from the top of her thighs to her shoulders. Rough hands threw her onto an even rougher blanket, but she bit her lips until they bled. She would not scream. Never would she scream.

Help me! Please, help me . . .

Her cry was silent, but she felt something.

Someone.

A voice in her head. A voice so much like her mother's, but not.

Shift, Romy. Like your mother. You are the wolf. Shift, and you can escape into the woods. I think you've had enough of the grasses. I'll help you.

But how? I don't know how!

Images flooded her mind. Perfect visuals of what she needed to do. It was simple. So very simple. The blanket was moving now. They were carrying her, using it like a stretcher, but she followed the instructions playing so vividly in her mind, reached for that other part of herself.

Reached . . . and found it. Strength flooded her, power like nothing she'd ever experienced. Power strengthened by anger, by pain, and by hope. Snarling, she lunged out of the blanket, snapping at the throat of the man in the back. He jerked away but her teeth caught him, leaving a bloody gash across his chest. Both men screamed. She twisted, finding even more power in this new and unfamiliar body, and took a desperate lunge at the one who was her father.

Snarling, jaws wide, she tore at his throat, ripping flesh, tasting his blood, relishing his frantic shriek and the silence that ended it. She stood over him long enough to know he would never hurt her again, that the other was on the ground, bleeding heavily but still alive. She heard shouts, the sound of men running, and knew there was no time to finish off the reverend. Instead, she raced for the fence, that barrier that had always stopped her, leapt it easily and then ran into the woods, running as far and fast as her lacerated body would allow.

She was a wolf, just like her mother. But unlike her mother, she was free of the bastards who'd hurt her. Free of the lying bastards and the Glorious Salvation in Truth.

Free to run as far and as fast as she was able.

But blood streamed across her back. Pain and bleeding from the deep lash marks in her shoulders, back, and hips would slow her down, make her easier to find.

She headed for the river, though it meant forcing her feet to move over the uneven ground with fire screaming over her back and flanks, but she made it, whimpering softly as the adrenaline wore off and pain rolled across her in waves. She practically fell into the slow-moving water, stumbled and lay in the muddy flow, gasping for breath. She couldn't stay here, not after leaving a trail of blood that even an idiot could follow, so she dragged herself forward, into deeper water.

It was cool against her flanks, almost soothing the deep slashes, though she knew she was weakening. Loss of blood and the trauma of the beating were quickly taking their toll. She struck out across the river, heading for the far side.

No. Bad idea. That's what they'd expect, once they realized she'd come this way. Fighting her growing weakness, she turned and headed east, swimming into the current, against the flow. This direction was more difficult, but she'd die before she'd quit. Romy knew she might not be able to go as far, but they wouldn't expect this of her.

No, they were men. Men who treated women like cattle, who thought women were stupid creatures, useful only for fucking and making babies. For waiting on them like servants. She'd show them. She had a good mind and a strong heart, and the strength and courage to win, no matter the cost.

The deep slashes across her back burned as her muscles bunched and stretched. Swimming as a wolf had come so naturally, just as running on four legs felt right. She thought of the dirty river water contaminating her wounds, but it was worth it, to risk death by infection or disease rather than submit to the future awaiting her at the compound.

A whore for the young men. Not quite the life she wanted, thank you very much. There was something out here, something better. She just had to live long enough to find it.

But who had helped her? And would she help Romy again?

A voice in her mind, images showing her how to shift. Was that how her mother had learned?

So many questions. So many unknowns.

Who was she? What was she? Definitely not an abomination. And what was Romy's wolf? Not something of Satan. Not a creature this perfect. This strong and this beautiful.

Struggling against the gentle current, Romy put her worries behind her and found a strong rhythm that had her making better progress than she'd hoped. If she could just get far enough away, they wouldn't know where to look. Finding one wolf in the forest would take trackers, experienced hunters.

None of the men at the compound had any skills at all, as far as she knew. A few of them hunted deer with big, heavy bows and sharp arrows, but they were stupid. Not experienced at finding, only in killing.

Ignoring the pain and the blood still dripping from her lacerated back, she swam for her life—swam for the first taste of freedom she'd ever sampled in all her twenty-six years.

2

Hey, Gabe . . . you about ready to call it a day?

Gabriel Cheval paused at the edge of the deep woods and glanced over his shoulder at the dark gray wolf with the striking black tips shading his thick coat. *What's the matter, Jace? You tired of havin' fun?* They'd covered close to a hundred miles over the past two days, but Gabe wasn't about to admit he was ready for a break.

It was a lot more entertaining, waiting for Jace to give in.

Instead of answering, Jace shifted, changing from dark wolf to tall, broad-shouldered, blonde-haired man in less than a heartbeat. The specially designed carry-all he'd worn around his neck as a wolf, the one, like Gabe's, that carried a compact emergency blanket, pants and a shirt, sandals and a cell phone, now hung loosely against his chest. He slipped it over his head and slung it across his shoulder, but kept his gaze on the river flowing sluggishly through a broad channel about a hundred yards north of them.

"Something's wrong, Gabe. I can't put my finger on it, but I feel like we need to check this area a little closer."

Gabe shifted as well, adjusting his pack as he caught up to his partner. Jace rarely alerted him for a false alarm. "Anything specific? The wolf pack that roams this area has been catalogued. There's no sign of any illegal trapping or hunting, and it's barely four o'clock. I thought you wanted to get closer to town. You know, the town with the bar? Where we might find a woman or two. Or three . . ."

Jace shook his head, but he was moving now, walking carefully through the dry grass, muscles rippling on his long, strong thighs and across his broad shoulders. He appeared to be focusing on the shoreline and the dark water. He paused a moment, shaded his eyes and gazed across the river. Then he threw his pack aside and raced into the water.

"What?" Gabe hung on to his pack but he followed Jace. They'd been friends since childhood and partners for the past ten years now, working summers together on the annual survey conducted by the Chanku pack of wild wolf packs roaming the American northwest. He'd follow Jace Wolf anywhere, even when he didn't have a clue where Jace might be leading him.

Jace was swimming hard now, strong overhand strokes that took him into the current and out into the middle of the river where a sandbar had formed. Gabe was right behind him, but it wasn't until he saw Jace lunge out of the water and race to the far side of the small island that he realized what had drawn him.

A wolf. Lying amid the twisted branches of a long-dead tree, the animal wasn't moving. Was it dead? Gabe couldn't tell, but there was no scent of decay. If there was any life left in the wolf, Jace could heal it. He was so much like his parents, both talented healers with the ability to go inside a creature and heal damage on a cellular level. As Jace's father said, they fixed what was broken.

Jace had tried to teach Gabe. After a few aborted attempts, even Jace had to admit there were some things he couldn't fix—like Gabe's ineptitude as a healer.

Luckily, Gabe had other talents, but as he knelt beside the bloody and lacerated body of the female wolf, Gabe knew he'd give anything to be able to do what his buddy was so good at.

"What the hell happened to her?"

Jace glanced at Gabe and shook his head. "She looks like she's been whipped. The lacerations follow a pattern. See? A crosshatch design all along her shoulders, back and flanks." He focused on the wolf again, running his fingers through the thick clots of blood caught in her fur. "Damn it. Gabe, I left my bag on the bank, and we're gonna need some pictures."

"I've got mine." Gabe slipped his pack off his shoulder and dug through the clothes for his phone.

"Good." Jace let out a disgusted sigh. "We'll have to report this, and the rangers'll need evidence. She's alive, but barely. I can't heal in my wolf form, but I don't want to frighten her, either. This is one wolf who has no reason to trust humans."

Gabe moved to the other side of the wolf so he could get a better shot of the damage. Raw muscle and, in a couple of spots, what looked like her ribs were visible beneath the horrible wounds, but blood was slowly seeping from the deeper cuts. She still lived. He hated to think of any sentient being doing this kind of vicious damage to a living creature. "Could a bear have done this, slashed her back like this?"

Jace shook his head. "A grizzly, maybe, but any bear that tears up another animal this badly is probably going to eat it. Get your pictures and then shift. We'll talk later. I don't want to lose her."

Gabe snapped a few more shots before he stuffed his phone back into the pack and shifted. Lying close to the wolf with his muzzle touching hers, he breathed in her breath, imprinting her scent on his mind as Jace gently spread his fingers over the wolf's shoulders.

• • •

As exhausting as it was to heal this way, Jace knew this was the most sublime act he would ever experience. Connecting on the cellular level and using the telepathy that all Chanku were blessed with, he literally went inside an injured or ill person, rebuilding damaged tissue, removing pathogens causing illness or infection. His father had been the first to experiment with the process, saving the life of his first mate when she'd suffered a serious head injury.

Jace often wondered what would have happened if the pack alpha and Gabe's father, Anton Cheval, hadn't challenged Jace's dad, Adam Wolf, to do what he did best—fix things. And so Adam had gone into Eve's damaged brain and fixed her.

And now Eve was their goddess and Liana, the original—but flawed—goddess, had become Adam's mate—and Jace's mother. Amazing sometimes, how things worked out.

Just as amazing as what he discovered as he left his body and slipped inside the badly injured wolf.

This was going to blow Gabe away. But first Jace had to make sure she survived. Slowly, carefully, he began repairing the torn and bruised flesh, removing the debris left by the dirty river water, healing a wolf who was so much more than he'd expected.

• • •

Gabe lay in the warm gravel, enjoying the late afternoon shadows that helped cool the air. His muzzle rested on the front paws of the wounded wolf. He sensed Jace working inside, saw the horrible wounds slowly closing and beginning to heal, but the wolf hadn't opened her eyes, hadn't shown any sign that she was aware anyone was near.

Her breathing was shallow, her heartbeat rapid. Her eyelids occasionally flickered as if she dreamed. Considering the condition she was in, he had to believe they were nightmares.

He wondered if he and Jace were too late, if the damage was too much for the creature to recover. Sometimes, severe trauma had so badly damaged an animal's will to survive that no matter what Jace did, it wasn't enough.

Gabe rarely asked for favors, but he called on Eve. He didn't expect the goddess to respond in person—unless it was his sister Lily doing the asking—but Gabe had no doubt that Eve was always aware when one of them needed her. He hoped she wouldn't be insulted that he bothered her about a wild wolf, but there was something about this one, something special that called to him.

I think Jace is doing just fine, Gabe. Be patient. Now you should hunt. Jace will need to eat. Healing takes a lot of energy.

Eve? I wasn't sure you'd answer. She's just a wolf.

He heard Eve's soft laughter. *All creatures are important to me, Gabe. Go, now. Jace is almost finished, but he's very weak. So is Romy.*

Romy?

The wolf, Gabe. The wolf is named Romy.

He shook his head and stood. There was no way to communicate with Jace while he was healing, so Gabe took a moment to check the area around them to make sure it was safe to leave Jace and the injured wolf when they were both so vulnerable. All seemed as it should be, so he quietly slipped away and swam to the far side of the river, opposite the side where Jace had dropped his pack. They'd have to go after it later, but for now he focused on the hunt. Once he'd crossed the narrow stretch of water, Gabe lunged up the steep bank into the woods. The forest was wilder on this side, but only a few yards in he glimpsed what looked like a large meadow, an area more likely to support game.

He kept to the thick grasses and brush along the northern edge. With his head low, he hunted by scent rather than sight, keeping the gentle breeze in his face. The scent of game grew stronger. Carefully planting his feet, moving as silently as a wraith, Gabe moved close to a herd of about a dozen pronghorn antelope.

It was easier hunting with the pack, or even with just Jace. Driving game to a partner was more effective than trying to sneak up on one of the fast little animals and then take it down on his own. He knew he couldn't outrun one, but luck was with him. The antelope grazed barely ten feet away, heads down as they fed. He studied the small group and picked out an undersized yearling. Not only did he need to be able to bring it down by himself, he'd have to carry it back to Jace and the injured wolf.

One of the older does raised her head and sniffed. The wind had stilled and his scent wasn't blowing away from them. He didn't have time to plan. Instead, Gabe burst out of the brush and caught the yearling just beneath its jaw. Weight alone snapped the animal's neck, but Gabe crouched over the body as the rest of the herd scattered, blowing from the burst of adrenaline that always came with a kill.

He waited, listening, but the forest was quiet once again. He clamped his jaws around the animal's neck and dragged it back to the river, silently cursing the roots and tangles that got in the way. It would probably be easier if he shifted, but there was a certain code of honor about dealing with a kill as a wolf, not a man.

Gabe shifted. "Fuck honor." He leaned over the small body, grabbed it around the middle, and threw it over his shoulder. Sixty pounds at the most—a burden for his wolf, but easier as a man. Jace needed food now. Gabe hoped the animal's spirit would forgive him.

Once he reached the river, it was easier to shift again and drag the antelope through the current with his strong jaws clamped around the creature's neck. Grunting, he pulled it up on the sandbar near Jace and the wolf.

Romy. Her name is Romy. How come he'd never realized that wild wolves had names?

Jace had shifted back to his wolf and was lying beside his patient. She was still unconscious. Gabe stared at his buddy and decided Jace didn't look much better than the one he'd healed. But when Gabe dropped the small buck in the sand, Jace's nose twitched and his ears tilted forward. Gabe ripped into the belly, tearing through the tough hide, making it easier for Jace to feed.

Then he stepped away.

Jace crept forward on his belly and buried his nose in the warm blood, lapping it slowly. After a moment, he stood and attacked the kill in earnest, growling softly as he fed. Gabe moved closer, waiting silently while his packmate ate his fill. When Jace finally sat back, his belly visibly full, Gabe took his turn.

Jace shifted and sat beside the wolf. Gabe finished eating, and then he shifted as well. "Will she make it?" He ran his fingers over the wolf's coarse black coat. "You did a great job, Jace."

"She's not a wolf."

"What?" Gabe spun around and stared at his friend. "What do you mean?"

"I'm not sure. I'm positive she's Chanku. Could be a Berserker because she's big for a bitch, but I know she's a shifter." He shrugged. "Well, I'm almost sure she is. I felt Eve when I was healing. She doesn't usually show up when I'm working on wolves."

Gabe stared at the sleeping wolf but his mind was reeling. "I asked Eve to help. She spoke to me, said you were doing fine on your own, that

I needed to hunt because you would have to eat when you were done."

"She was right." He grinned at Gabe. "Thank you. But we'll have to get her to shift as soon as she's able. It will help the healing."

"Her name's Romy."

This time it was Jace spinning, staring at Gabe. "How do you know her name?"

Gabe shrugged. "Eve. She said her name's Romy, but she never said she's Chanku. Just that the wolf's name is Romy."

"Well, that's more than we knew when we started." Jace stroked his fingers over her back. She'd been badly beaten; that was obvious. He wondered if the shift had come because of her pain. He'd heard of that happening. Gabe's mother, Keisha, had been assaulted. She'd shifted before she knew she was Chanku. Shifted and killed her attackers.

"I hope Romy killed whoever the bastards were who did this to her."

Gabe nodded. "You're thinking of my mom, aren't you?"

"I am. No one has a right to treat any person or animal with cruelty." He stroked the broad curve of her skull.

The wolf growled.

Shift, Gabe. She's going to be afraid of men. I'm sure of it.

• • •

Romy slipped into consciousness slowly, aware of the scent of men, of long fingers stroking her head. She was still a wolf. She wasn't restrained, though she felt very weak. Without even opening her eyes, she snarled.

The fingers disappeared. She would have laughed, if wolves could laugh. Power. She'd never known such power! Rolling her shoulders, she was aware of pain, but it was muted, as if the deep cuts and slashes from Reverend Ezekiel's whip had already begun to heal. How long ago had she been beaten? She hadn't expected to live, as badly as they'd hurt her. It must have been days ago. And had she really killed her father? Left the good reverend lying in the dirt, bleeding from a deep gash across his chest?

Where was she now? She smelled the river and the clean, sharp scent of cedar and pine, which meant she couldn't be back at the compound. There, all the natural smells were overpowered by the stench of the open garbage pit. Opening her eyes, she gazed across the flat sandbar. This was the same one she'd wanted to reach as she'd struggled against the current. She remembered swimming to it, dragging herself out of the water, but only to rest. She'd not intended to stay long, but she'd hidden beside a twisted tree trunk turned silver from sun and weather.

The river flowed slowly and the sun was still fairly high in the sky. Had she been here overnight? Carefully, she planted her front paws in the gravel and struggled to her feet. Standing unsteadily, she swayed with weakness, her vision foggy and her muzzle almost touching the ground.

Where was the man who'd been touching her? She thought she smelled wolves, not men, though she plainly recalled the sense of someone stroking fingers through her fur. Fur . . . she really was a wolf. A very hungry wolf.

The scent of fresh game was strong. Not a smell she would have appreciated as a woman, but it called out to the wolf. Blinking slowly, she drew in a few deep breaths, searching for the source of what had to be fresh meat. Her attention wavered and she stared at the river for a few seconds, watching the water flowing by. She'd escaped by swimming upstream in the river that ran by the compound. That much she could remember, but how long had she been here? She knew she couldn't have gotten far enough away. They could still find her, but she was too weak to go anywhere right now.

The coppery smell of fresh blood hit her scent receptors again, and her mouth filled with saliva. Turning her head, she saw it, not three feet away. A freshly killed pronghorn antelope, its belly torn open, one haunch partially devoured.

She'd never eaten raw meat before. Never imagined burying her nose in the still-warm flesh of a freshly killed animal, but she was starving, and no one was trying to stop her.

Moving stiffly, she sniffed the dead creature and then tore a thick piece of muscle and hide from the haunch. Gulping down great hunks of warm flesh, she felt her strength returning.

And with it, her confidence. Nothing could stop her. Not now.

• • •

Jace watched the she-wolf eat, gorging herself on Gabe's fresh kill. Healing would have used up whatever energy reserves she might have had, but it shouldn't take long for her to regain at least some of her strength. She was badly hurt, though, and he'd not taken the time to heal everything, not when they had no idea if someone was trying to find her.

He'd decided to wait to approach her. Let her eat and get her bearings first. Gabe had crossed the river to retrieve Jace's pack, but he waited on the bank for Jace's signal that it was okay to return. They didn't want to frighten her. Jace alone might be okay, but two males could be overwhelming.

She seemed to have her hunger under control. Jace watched as she carefully licked the blood from her muzzle before dipping her face into the river for a quick drink of water. Once she was done, she sat on the bank and studied the far shore.

Jace sat up. He'd been hidden behind a small shrub, but she'd not really been looking for anyone, either. He watched her for a moment before using his telepathy to connect. *Who are you? Who hurt you? I want to help.*

She spun around, almost toppling as she turned to face him on shaky legs. *Who are you?*

He remained sitting on his haunches, trying to appear as nonthreatening as he could. Just another wolf. *My name is Jace. I'm like you, Romy. A shapeshifter. I am Chanku. I healed your wounds as much as I could. If you can shift, that will heal them further.*

Did you leave the meat?

No. That was Gabe. My friend. He's behind me, on the bank. We didn't want to frighten you.

She seemed to relax as she gazed across the river to where Gabe sat on the bank with Jace's pack looped around his neck. He looked more like a large service dog than a vicious wolf. Jace might have laughed under other circumstances.

He can come back. I'm not afraid. How do you know my name?

Eve told Gabe.

Eve? Who is Eve?

Eve is our goddess.

And she speaks to you? In words in your head, the way you're speaking to me?

Sometimes. Only when it's really important.

She cocked her head to one side, and he wondered if he caught what he said, that she was obviously important. At least important enough for their goddess to intervene. While the wolf seemed to think about that for a moment, Jace let Gabe know he could come across, but he concentrated on Romy. After a moment, she stood and walked closer to him. Sniffed his shoulder, his flank, the side of his face. He wondered if she was trying to commit his scent to memory or if she was merely curious about her wolven abilities. Jace wasn't sure, but he had a feeling she'd never shifted before.

Then Romy answered his unspoken question.

She must be the one who showed me how to shift. I was dying. She saved me, but I think I killed a man when I escaped. Maybe two. The others will be hunting for me.

Where were you? How far from here?

I don't know. It's a fenced compound not far from the river. The home of the Glorious Salvation in Truth. They're a religious order led by Reverend Ezekiel. He's a follower of Aldo Xenakis, the one who believes all shapeshifters should be relegated to animal status, their rights as humans taken away.

Aldo is dead. His son, Sebastian, killed him. Sebastian Xenakis is one of us.

She raised her head and stared at him. *When?*

Not long. About six weeks or so. Are you so cut off from the world that you wouldn't have heard?

The men might know. The women aren't allowed news of the world. We're prisoners there, subject to the whims and decrees of Reverend Ezekiel and the men who follow him. You said Aldo's son is one of us. Please, tell me again. What are we?

Before Jace could answer, Gabe trotted across the sandbar, shrugged the waterproof bag over his head and shifted, standing tall and entirely naked beside the two wolves. The female's hackles rose along her back and she snarled. Gabe merely smiled at her, but he was digging his pants out of the bag. "I hear someone coming. Sounds like a group moving through the woods along that side of the river."

He pointed to the bank he'd just been standing on. "I shifted so I can chat with them, but you two need to hide." He looped the pack over Jace's head and then went back to dressing, shoving his arms into the sleeves of his shirt. "Hurry. I don't want them to see you." He frowned then, glancing at Romy. "Are you strong enough to swim to the bank? It's almost shallow enough on this side to walk."

I can make it. They'll not catch me. Not ever again.

She stepped into the slow current and started across. Jace glanced once more at Gabe, and then followed Romy. A great blue heron took flight near the opposite bank as if something had disturbed its roosting place. Jace moved faster, herding Romy through the shallows and using his chest to help push her up the steep bank.

They slipped into the brush just as a group of at least half a dozen men broke through on the far side of the river. Jace caught the glint of sunlight off rifle barrels as he moved deeper into the thick undergrowth with the dark wolf.

3

"**H**ey! You. Out on the sandbar."

Gabe raised his head as if he'd not heard them coming. "Yeah?"

"We're huntin' a wolf. Big dark one. You seen it?"

"It's illegal to hunt wolves. They're protected." He turned and folded his arms across his chest. Bastards. Looked like a bunch of assholes as far as he was concerned. Waving their rifles around. A couple of them even had big, heavy-duty compound bows.

"This one killed two men. It's gone rogue. Either that or it could be rabid."

He decided it was time to look interested. He shouted back, "When did that happen? Where?"

"About four hours ago. Maybe a mile downstream, west of here."

Gabe shook his head. "That might be what I saw." He kicked at the remains of the antelope, drawing their attention to the bloody body. He and Jace and Romy had eaten most of it, but there was enough of the carcass left to show it was a recent kill. "I saw something eating this antelope. Thought it was a big dog. Might have been a wolf. Black all over."

"Yeah. That's the one. Where'd it go?"

"Hell if I know. It saw me and jumped into the river. Swam east, against the current, which was weird. Appeared to be injured. Looked like it got out of the water up near that snag." He pointed to an area about a quarter mile to the east where a huge pine lay half in, half out of the river. It would take them at least an hour to get that far through the thick growth close to the water. They didn't look smart enough to figure out the river was low enough that they could probably wade the distance.

"Thanks, brother. C'mon."

Muttering, "I'm no brother of yours, jerk," Gabe watched the men as they disappeared back into the brush. He heard them barging through the undergrowth, cursing and making enough noise to scare away any game within a mile, but he waited for a few minutes until the sounds faded and all was still, until he was sure they were gone. Then he waded through the shallow water to the bank where Romy and Jace had fled.

He found them hiding in a thick copse of scrub willows. Squatting down in front of Romy, he studied her amber eyes for a moment. "You okay? Are you in any pain?"

I'm sore, and not very strong, but it's manageable. Are they gone?

"Yeah. I sent them upstream. I imagine they'll be heading back to the compound eventually, when they can't find any sign of you. But while they're headed east, I think we need to go west, get past the compound and keep going. The forest gets deeper and there are a lot better places to hide."

Besides, Jace added, *that's where we're headed. I hope you'll come with us, Romy, but we have a job to do and only another month or so to finish. You're welcome to travel with us. We can teach you more about being a wolf, about who and what you are.*

"We promise not to ask you to do anything you don't want to do," Gabe added. "From the look of those idiots, I have a feeling your life hasn't been your own for a long time."

The she-wolf rested her muzzle on her front paws and sighed. *No . . . not for twenty-six years.*

Jace turned and stared at her. *How old are you?*

Twenty-six.

• • •

She started to say that she really didn't have a choice, whether to go with them or not, but then she realized that yes, she did. She could strike out on her own, as she'd first intended, or she could take advantage of their kindness. For whatever reason, she trusted them. Or at least her wolf trusted them.

Romy wasn't certain what she'd think when she was in her human form.

Can you shift, Romy?

Jace gazed at her out of amber eyes so much like her own. Exactly like Gabe's. It was disconcerting, to say the least, this sense of companionship. The feeling she was very much like these two men. She'd never felt anything like this before.

It's your wolf. It recognizes the need for a pack. Recognizes us as po-

20

tential packmates. Wolves don't do well alone. Jace raised his head. *You'll need to learn to shield your thoughts. Right now you're broadcasting, and that's how we're aware of your concerns. Gabe and I will never hurt you. We've taken responsibility for your safety. You are . . .*

No one is responsible for me, except for me! She stared at Jace, then looked directly into Gabe's eyes, recognizing her act for what it was to the men—a direct challenge.

Except, why was Gabe grinning at her?

"Your wolf is in charge right now, Romy. We're Chanku—shapeshifters—but still pack animals by nature, no matter what form we take. The pack has a strict hierarchy. It's not one we consciously accept. It just is. Another thing about the Chanku—the packs are matriarchal. The females are in charge, so when Jace said we're taking responsibility for your safety, he means that as long as you're with us, we will protect you. Even if that means protecting you from our baser needs."

Base? If wolves could laugh, Gabe, I'd be crowing right now. Jace stood. *Romy, there's a lot you need to know about the Chanku, including Gabe's reference to "baser needs."*

She raised her head and stared at the tent at the front of Gabe's loose pants.

Exactly, Jace said, and she was certain she heard laughter in his mental voice, but it was difficult not to look at Gabe. He was absolutely beautiful—tall and broad-shouldered with thick, dark hair. She wished he'd let her get a better look at him naked, but he'd started tugging his clothes on so quickly, she'd only caught a brief view of his muscular thighs and what looked like an absolutely perfect butt. He hadn't given her even a glimpse of what was now tenting his pants. She'd never been interested in those parts before. Why now?

Jace's voice popped into her head. It was still weird, talking this way, but it was getting easier the more they did it.

Come with us, he said, *at least until we get beyond the compound. And Romy, if you don't want us eavesdropping on your private thoughts, you'll have to shield them. Think of closing a window, one of those old-fashioned types that you pull down to close or push up to open. Sometimes, just the act of hypothetically shutting the window will shut your thoughts away. Gabe doesn't need to know how much you admire his ass.*

Oh. How embarrassing! She did exactly as he suggested. Pulled the heavy window closed, and then she thought as clearly as she could, *What would you say if I told you I wanted both of you to leave me here?*

Neither of them reacted. They merely watched and waited while she ran a few other random thoughts through her head. Then she opened the window in her mind. *Did you hear that? Did you hear what I asked you?*

21

Gabe shook his head. "Nope. Must have worked. You coming with us?"

In answer, Romy lurched awkwardly to her feet. She'd grown stiff, hiding here in the brush. Her back and flanks hurt.

"If you shift, even for a moment, your wounds will heal better. They won't go away entirely, but any major damage that Jace repaired will settle in a lot better. They won't hurt as much."

I don't know if I can, but I'll try. She thought of what the voice in her head—was it really a goddess speaking?—had shown her. Recalled the explicit images. The shift was so natural, so easy, that Romy wondered why she'd not been able to figure it out before.

Gabe reached out a hand to steady her as she straightened and stood upright. She couldn't help but notice the way he looked at her, the way his body reacted to her. The tent below his waist grew even more pronounced. She should have been frightened, at the very least, embarrassed. Romy felt nothing beyond the subtle relief of pain, just as they'd said would happen.

Then Jace shifted. She'd not seen him in human form yet, but he was even more impressive than Gabe. The muscles across his lean chest and roping over his shoulders and down his long arms were sharply defined. He was a bit taller, though lean compared to Gabe's more muscular build. Jace had dark blonde hair streaked with gold and the face of an angel—the kind she imagined standing guard over the gates of heaven with a flaming sword grasped in his hands. She knew she was staring but it was impossible to look away.

His gaze was fixed on her just as intently. It took a moment for Romy to figure out what it was she was feeling—an almost visceral sense of lust, and it was radiating off of Gabe and Jace in equal measure. If any of the men at the compound had stood this close, pumping out pheromones the way these two were, she would have done her best to get away, far enough that they wouldn't think about her. She'd let them know she wanted nothing to do with them.

Now, though, with Jace and Gabe, she fought a powerful desire to rub against both men like a cat in heat. But why? She'd never experienced sexual need. No matter what her father had done to her—and he'd done things that she'd known were not normal between a man and a woman, much less between a father and his daughter—she'd never felt desire. Never wanted his touch. Not any man's touch.

Now, though, she couldn't deny the dull ache in her womb or the dampness between her legs. The unexpected fluid bathing her pubic hair and moistening the soft skin of her inner thighs had her blushing with embarrassment.

And it only got worse when she realized she was staring at the erection jutting out between Jace's legs. It was huge—not covered up with pants like Gabe's—and many times bigger than her father's had been. She thought it was beautiful, flushed a dark bronze, standing tall against his flat belly. Dark veins circled over its girth, and it looked hard as steel, though the broad head was smooth, almost soft-looking, and the wrinkled skin covering his balls was drawn up tight between his legs. She licked her lips and fought a powerful need to drop to her knees between his bare feet and take his entire erection in her mouth. She wondered at his taste, if his flavor was unique to Jace and only Jace. Licking her lips, she realized how close she was to kneeling before him.

It was something her father always wanted her to do for him, but she'd refused. He'd been able to force her to do just about anything else, but never that. She fought him over it so strongly that he'd eventually given up.

Jace cleared his throat, and his voice sounded deeper than she remembered. "Turn around, Romy."

She jerked her head up and stared at him. Images flashed through her mind, images of the two of them, of Gabe joining them, of the two men having sex with each other while she watched, then of both of them taking her from the front and the back, the images so powerful she clenched the muscles between her legs in a futile attempt to stop the flow of moisture.

It took her a moment to realize it wasn't all her—she was picking up on images, either Jace's or Gabe's, and that realization sparked her arousal even higher. She knew that men lying together was supposed to be a sin, but she'd long ago decided that whatever the reverend said was wrong was probably perfectly normal and right. And the women talked among themselves. A lot. They might be idiots, but most of them actually liked the sex. Some of them were sister-wives and shared a man. None of them had ever admitted to sharing two men.

For some reason, Romy found that a lot more appealing than sharing a man with another woman, but how had her mind wandered in *that* direction? She stared at Jace and, with those visuals filling her mind, asked, "Why? What are you going to do?"

Jace took a deep breath and let it out slowly, but his gaze seemed to burn wherever he looked. "I want to see how bad the lacerations are. I may have to do some more healing." He touched her shoulder and she shivered, but she slowly turned around. Gabe gasped and fumbled in his pack for something. Jace sighed, and she heard him softly whisper, "Holy shit. If you hadn't killed the bastard already, I'd want to do it for you. You getting pictures, Gabe?"

"Yeah. Damn. Goddess, Jace. They were definitely trying to kill her.

Romy, this looks like hell. Are you sure you're okay to do any traveling?"

Shaking her head, she said, "I don't hurt that badly. Not now. Even if I did, we'd have to go." She glanced toward the river. "I'll be okay. I don't want those men to catch me. Catch us."

"You're right, Romy. We need to get a move on. Gabe, take the clothes off. We can move faster as wolves, and it's easier to hide. Hurry."

Gabe had packed his cell phone with the pictures and was already stripping off the loose shirt and pants. He shoved them into his pack and looped it over his neck. When he shifted, it was still there, only now it fit snugly around the wolf's neck. Jace checked his bag, put it over his head and shifted at the same time as Romy. Together, the three of them put their heads down and followed a barely visible game trail through the thick undergrowth.

· · ·

She was strong. He'd give her that. Romy kept pace with Gabe, following close on his left flank as if she'd run as a wolf all her life. Jace stayed behind her, forcing himself to concentrate on the sounds of the forest, the scents of anything but the bitch he followed. She was absolutely beautiful, her scent an aphrodisiac like nothing he'd ever experienced, and he knew that if he didn't have her under him soon, he'd go mad. It was that simple.

The deep wounds across her back didn't seem to slow her down a bit, but he knew she'd be tiring if they kept up this pace. They were at least fifteen miles west of the compound and he was beginning to feel a bit safer. They'd maintained a pretty decent rate of speed, though, and it was time to think about finding a place to rest for the night.

Gabe slowed their pace and came to a halt beneath a huge cedar. *Aren't we close to that lodge that Stefan bought a few years ago? The one with the rental cabins?*

Jace sniffed the air and glanced at the ridgeline of a low range of mountains not far to the north of them. *We are. It's near a lake at the base of those mountains. Let's check it out, see if they've got an empty cabin. I'd rather have a bed than a spot under a bush. We need a clean place to rest where Romy won't risk infection.*

Are we far enough from the compound? I really don't want them to catch me.

I think we're safe, Romy. Jace glanced at Gabe and then focused on the female. *No matter where we stay, you'll have Gabe and me standing guard. We'll do our best to keep you safe.*

Gabe shifted, reached into his bag and dug out his cell phone. He placed a call, and after a couple of brief comments he stuck the phone in his pack. "They've got one cabin, the one Stefan and Xandi save for their use, and they'll hold it for us. The manager said he wants to clear it with Stef, but there won't be a problem. It's a little over a mile, Romy, but I doubt your reverend will think to look for you there."

He adjusted the bag around his neck and shifted. Jace fell in behind Romy, and they trotted along the trail, slower now that their destination was close. He wondered what Romy's reaction would be when she shifted again and finally had a chance to relax, when the powerful stirrings of her libido would ultimately affect her. There was no doubt in his mind she was Chanku, and if he'd doubted it, Eve's obvious intervention was all the proof they needed. But he was certain Romy knew nothing about her Chanku heritage. About the strength of her arousal after a shift.

He hoped she wouldn't deny her body's needs, though as badly as she'd been hurt, her libido might not be enough to overcome the pain. If the healing had worked, though . . . No matter. It could prove to be interesting. Or not. It all depended on Romy. No matter what he and Gabe might want, it came down to her choice. Her decision. And so far, she hadn't seemed nearly as charmed with either of them as they'd been with her.

• • •

It was only a mile, but each step was agony. Romy wasn't sure she could go another foot, much less a mile more through the thick brush, but with Gabe leading at a slower pace and Jace's constant presence behind her, she wasn't about to give up.

For the first hour or so of their journey, she'd been so enthralled by this first opportunity to appreciate the senses of her wolf that she'd been able to ignore the pain. Now, though, while the novelty of racing along a hidden trail on four feet hadn't yet worn off, the pure joy she'd felt in this new body was beginning to wane.

She hurt. Each cut from the whip left its own slash of pain, each step she took exacerbated what was already enough to knock the breath from her lungs. She'd not been able to close her mind and go away, not the way she'd done when her father raped her or even when the reverend had beaten her. Not while she ran. Not with the scent of two beautiful males filling her nostrils.

It had only taken a short time to realize she was so attracted to both Gabe and Jace that she couldn't step away from arousal, couldn't block out the pain without blocking out the two males. She wasn't willing to do that, though there was no way she wanted sex with either of them. Not hurting like she did, and certainly not with her twisted sexual history. Two decades of incestuous rape had definitely done a number on her.

She wouldn't have known it was rape if not for the other women. Enough new women had come into the group over the years to bring outside knowledge with them. The men never knew how they talked among themselves, but the women loved to talk. Of course, they all knew about Romy's father, and they said it was wrong, but the fact that Reverend Ezekiel approved had created quite an argument among them. Some said the reverend spoke with God's voice, and if he said it was right, it must be.

Like it was ever okay to rape a six-year-old? Even Romy knew that must be wrong, no matter who condoned it. The reverend's approval didn't make it right—it merely made him complicit in what had to be a terrible crime by any society's standards.

You doing all right, Romy? Jace's voice dragged her out of her thoughts. *We're almost there.*

I'm hurting, but I'll make it. Even speaking with her mind was difficult. She wondered if she'd reinjured herself.

You're bleeding again. Once we get into the cabin, I'll help you get cleaned up and do another healing. The fact we've had to run so far so soon after the healing this afternoon has reopened some of your wounds. He continued running in silence for a dozen or more paces. Then he added, *I'm glad you killed the bastard. He had it coming.*

She didn't answer, but the ones hunting her had said she'd killed two men. That meant both her father and the good reverend were dead. The fact she was the one who had killed them gave her the strength to keep up the steady pace. There was a great deal of satisfaction in knowing she'd finally avenged her mother's death. Romy ran now with a sense of purpose. A sense of accomplishment.

But the pain was increasing, and she was relieved they didn't have far to go. The sun had set at least an hour earlier, and the glow from lights in some of the cabins filtered through the trees. The three wolves stopped within the dark shadows of the forest. Gabe shifted, dressed, and walked out into the clearing, past a picnic area and up a flight of steps into what looked like an office.

Romy and Jace lay in the dry leaves, tongues lolling, panting softly, waiting patiently. As a woman, Romy had never been particularly patient, but she'd discovered subtle differences in her wolf's personality. This creature could wait without growing totally frustrated by the lack of action. Of course, maybe the bleeding gashes on her back had something to do with that.

A few minutes later, Gabe stepped outside with an older man. They talked for a minute, then the man pointed toward a single cabin set off by itself, shook Gabe's hand, and went back inside.

Gabe glanced their way. *I'll go open the door,* he said. *Meet me there. Jace, I told him you're with me, but I didn't mention Romy. He knows we're friends of the owner and that we're Chanku. I told him not to tell anyone there were Chanku staying here, that we liked to keep that quiet. He seemed to understand, said he liked working for Stefan, didn't have any problems with shifters. In case anyone comes looking, I don't want to risk him giving her away. Romy? Try and stay out of sight until the door is open.*

Keeping to the shadows, she and Jace trotted around the edge of the woods to the cabin. It was set off by itself, the front turned toward the forest and not the other cabins, which made it much more private than the others. Gabe left the lights off and held the door open for them.

They took the three steps up to the deck and then went through the door. Romy sniffed the air and padded around the single large room. It was sparsely decorated with a grouping of chairs by a front window and two queen-sized beds against the back wall. A small kitchenette with a sink, a refrigerator, and a microwave was tucked into a corner. A doorway on the opposite end of the room opened to a dressing area with a mirror, vanity, and a bathroom.

Gabe went straight to the refrigerator. "I called Stef. He said we'd find this place stocked. He wasn't kidding. He and Xandi stay here when they travel. It's a good place to stop on the way to San Francisco when they choose to drive." He held up a cold beer. "Jace? You want one?"

Jace shifted. "Later, maybe." He knelt beside Romy. She held very still as he inspected her back with gentle fingers, and then sat back on his heels. He was semi-erect, but he treated his own nudity as if it were perfectly normal. Romy had to force herself not to stare. She'd never cared about men, and sex with her father always had disgusted her, but Jace?

He was fascinating.

Even more than Gabe, which made no sense. Both men were gorgeous. Both so kind she wasn't sure why she should be drawn so powerfully to one and not the other. Nor did she understand why she was growing aroused. She was never aroused! That part of her hadn't ever developed.

At least that's what she'd always thought.

Jace traced the edge of her right ear with his fingertips, drawing her gaze to his dark amber eyes. "I want you to shift so I can get a better look at your wounds without all the hair in the way. It looks like a bunch of the deeper slashes have reopened. I know they've got to be horribly painful. Damn, Romy, why didn't you say something? We wouldn't have pushed you so hard. You're tough, girl. Really tough."

His soft words had to be the nicest compliment Romy'd ever gotten. She'd felt like such a baby, limping along behind Gabe, but Jace thought she was tough. He ran his fingers along her blood-encrusted coat.

"I hate what that bastard did to you. It makes me wish I could kill him all over again."

With that thought in mind, Romy shifted. Before she even thought to be embarrassed, Jace had taken her hand and led her to the closest bed. "Lie on your stomach, okay."

"I don't want to get blood all over the bed."

He laughed. "Actually, it's all over the floor. When you shifted, the blood on your coat fell away."

"I'll get it." Gabe was already wringing out a towel in the kitchen sink.

Romy stared at the rusty stain on the wood floor. Her blood. A lot of it, but the visual seemed to pulse in time with the pain in her back. She couldn't really focus on anything. It was all she could do to remain up-right.

Jace put a hand under her elbow. "Hang on," he whispered.

She nodded.

"Is there another towel, Gabe? A large dry one? I'll lay it across her bed in case the bleeding doesn't stop right away."

Gabe brought the towel. Romy heard him cursing under his breath. At first she wondered if he was mad at her about something—she was always getting in trouble at the compound—but then she realized he'd just gotten a good look at her back.

She was glad she couldn't see it, though she'd have to look at some point. Just not now. Jace spread the big towel over the bedspread before helping Romy lie down on her stomach on the soft terry cloth. He was so gentle, so nonthreatening that she felt no embarrassment at all over being naked in front of him. Not with Gabe, either. That was something she was going to have to think about. So many things, so much she'd never done. Didn't know.

She wanted to stretch her arms over her head, but it hurt too much, so she lay on her belly with her face turned away from Jace, both arms at her sides. Not a very pretty picture, she figured, but Jace was so gentle, his voice so filled with empathy, that she didn't care. He stretched out beside her and pressed his fingertips to her back and shoulder. The pads of his fingers were rough, but his touch was so gentle she felt tears gathering. Not from pain. No, from the mere pleasure of being stroked in such a caring way. Then she felt something warm slip inside, and she knew that Jace was working his magic.

Lying there, so close beside a man she desired, both of them naked and connected on a level she'd never imagined, Romy drifted into fantasy, imagining lying with Jace in the act of love, the two of them intertwined, his thick cock filling her.

At least she'd remembered to put up her mental barriers before she turned her mind free to dream. The sense of him healing her injuries was soothing, the soft touch of his fingers against her torn back an amazing comfort. She drifted with her dreams, and then she merely dreamed, sleeping as Jace worked his magic.

4

This was a totally new experience, to be inside a woman, healing one he was sexually attracted to. Romy fascinated him. Physically, she was nothing like any of the women he'd known among the Chanku. Most of them were tall and lean, some almost whipcord thin. Not Romy. Her appearance and body type were totally unique—and uniquely feminine. Her shoulders were broad, her breasts and hips full and round, yet her waist was narrow and her belly flat with defined muscles. She was easily six feet tall, with large hands and muscular arms; her overall form was one of physical strength. Her features reminded him of photos he'd seen of their pack alpha Anton Cheval's Romanian mother, with her dark amber eyes, long, thick curls of sable hair, and her sensual mouth with full lips and a strong jaw.

There was some resemblance as well to Daciana Lupei, who was mated to both Matt and Chris, also known as the Deacon. Daci was a Gypsy, and her mother had been Romanian. Was that where Romy had gotten her name? Had her mother wanted to emphasize her daughter's heritage, the fact she was a shapeshifter? So many questions, and yet Jace felt no pressure to find the answers. They would come, all in good time. When Romy was healthy again. Healthy and safe.

It wasn't merely her appearance that fascinated him. She'd been raised in an isolated compound, surrounded by members of a religious cult led by one man who was likely deranged. How could she be as intelligent, as aware of things as she was? Her mind fascinated him as much as her body drew him. Somehow, Romy had learned enough to know that the lessons she'd been taught were wrong. It had to have been her mother. No one else she'd mentioned seemed capable of raising such an amazing young woman.

One who was mentally strong and physically as close to perfect as Jace could possibly imagine. As he once again repaired the horrible damage to her back, his mind was caught in the vision of her mouth, imagining those full lips encircling his engorged cock. Even though he was inside Romy in spirit, having essentially left his physical body behind, he was certain he must be erect right now.

Immediately he focused on the healing, not on what he desired at some point in the future. He didn't want to frighten her. She'd been through enough today. She'd been hurt enough. The last thing he'd ever want to do was add to her pain.

• • •

Almost three hours later, a little after midnight, Jace carefully pulled away from Romy and then lay beside her, exhausted but filled with a sense of completion. Hunger gnawed at him, but he'd repaired all the damage from her horrific beating. At least this time he wasn't going to force her to run for miles after healing her. No matter what she thought she was capable of, he fully intended to make her lie here in this bed until every single laceration was entirely closed, until there was no risk of her wounds reopening.

He wasn't sure if he'd prevented scarring, not with the extent of the damage. He'd never seen injuries like hers. She should have died. Some of the lacerations went entirely through muscle, exposing ribs along both sides of her back. He had no idea where she'd found the strength today to cover so many miles. They'd maintained a grueling pace, figuring she'd let them know if she needed to rest, but she'd kept up.

Kept up when she had to have been in agony. The healing he'd done earlier had merely been a quick fix, holding the skin together to keep her from bleeding, repairing the worst of the damage to muscles and tendons.

Tonight, exhausted and in pain, she'd fallen asleep while he worked, and her trust in him was an unexpected honor. He lay there, staring at her. She'd turned her head while his consciousness had been inside her with his inert body lying next to hers on the bed. He'd been looking at her tousled hair when he began, but now her lips were mere inches from his.

As tired and hungry as he was, Jace wanted her. Wanted to taste her, to feel that long, strong body of hers pressed against him, but there was no way in hell he'd disturb Romy tonight. Not tonight, and probably not for a few more nights.

But he had no doubt they'd make love. Not just sex. Not with this woman. No, he had a feeling that when they finally got together, it was going to matter way too much to think of any joining as mere sex.

Just thinking about loving Romy had him hard and wanting, but there was a simple solution to that. One that wouldn't disturb her. First he crawled out of bed and made a quick detour into the kitchen. He dug around in the freezer, found a pack of ground beef and stuck it in the microwave. When it was thawed but still raw, he choked the meat down, but at least it satisfied his body's need for protein.

He headed into the bathroom and found new toothbrushes and toothpaste in the medicine cabinet. He brushed his teeth and reached for a washcloth, when he decided a shower would probably help him relax. A shower and Gabe.

His buddy was asleep in the second bed, but he'd left room for Jace to crawl in beside him, and knowing Gabe, he'd be more than ready for whatever Jace wanted. That was half the fun of doing the annual count, checking on wolf populations the way they'd done for years. The fact it was just Jace and Gabe, together without any other partners.

They were as close as brothers, closer, even, than Gabe and his twin brother, Mac, who tended to be more serious, more introspective than Gabe, who found joy in everything he did. Growing up in the pack compound in Montana, Jace and Gabe had always gravitated toward one another. Jace's parents, Adam and Liana Wolf, were the pack healers, while Gabe's were the undisputed ruling alpha team. All the children had been raised together. Jace and Gabe had been the best of friends since they were toddlers, and lovers since they were barely into their teens. They'd shared girlfriends and boyfriends, and yet they'd always come back to each other every summer when they followed the wolf packs.

This was the first time they'd ever picked up a stray.

Jace stepped into the glass enclosure and raised his face to the hot water. He had a feeling Romy was going to prove to be so much more than merely a stray.

$$\bullet \bullet \bullet$$

Ten minutes later, Jace was crawling into bed beside Gabe. His buddy moved over and made room for him, then rolled to his side and rested one hand on Jace's shoulder.

"You okay? That took a long time."

"Yeah. Goddess, Gabe, she's a mess. I had to repair muscle tissue, a couple of tendons that were slashed. Thank goodness none were severed, but the damage is horrible. I'm amazed she's alive."

"I'm amazed she kept up with us." Gabe's fingers rubbed the taut muscles along the base of Jace's skull. "We didn't make any allowances for her injuries. I honestly didn't even think about it after you healed her this afternoon. I figured she must be okay. We ran hard, but she never complained. Never asked us to slow down."

Jace thought of the way they'd run for hours, with Romy keeping up that fast pace over rough ground without a single whimper or complaint, even when they backtracked to throw off anyone who might be following them. "I think it was more important to her to get as far away from the compound as she could than to give in to the pain. She really shouldn't have survived that beating."

"She said someone—just a voice—helped her. I wonder if Eve kept her alive?"

"I don't know. I hope so. She heard a voice, and you did connect with Eve." He bit back a moan of pure pleasure. "Damn, Gabe. That feels so good."

"I can make you feel better."

Jace chuckled. "I know you can, but I'm exhausted."

"I'll do all the work."

Jace opened one eye and stared at his buddy. "You don't honestly think I'm going to turn you down, do you?"

Gabe just grinned. "Roll over. I'll rub out your back. Your muscles are tied in knots."

Jace flopped over on his belly while Gabe straddled his thighs. He knew exactly where this was going to lead. Sighing, smiling, he let himself sink into a massage that Gabe would be turning into the most exquisite foreplay known to man.

It really couldn't get much better.

Well, yes, it could. He turned his head so that he was staring at Romy while Gabe started in on his shoulders. Staring and dreaming what it would be like when she accepted both of them into her bed, into her body.

• • •

Something dragged Romy out of an absolutely beautiful dream. She'd been lying with Jace while he kissed her. Sweet, tender kisses along her shoulder, her throat, even the sensitive skin behind her ear.

Then the kisses ended, replaced by a rhythmic squeak that had to be bedsprings. Fear brought a whimper to her throat and her heart stuttered in her chest. No. It couldn't be him. Her father was dead, right? She was alone in her bed. Terrified, Romy slowly opened her eyes.

There was a low light on over the vanity that threw little more than shadows into the sleeping area, but she could make out dark figures on the bed next to hers. Finally she understood the source of the sound of bed-springs. Two men. Together. So beautiful; she thought it must be like watching a dance, though dance had been forbidden in the compound.

Still, the new women had spoken longingly of the beauty, the way two people, usually a man and a woman, of course, would seem to float across the floor, so perfectly in sync, one with the other. Jace and Gabe were like that. So perfect, so intent on one another that Romy doubted they even saw her. Probably had forgotten she was in the room.

Jace was on his back, his knees drawn up close against his chest, his hands grasping Gabe's broad shoulders. Gabe half knelt, half lay between Jace's legs, thrusting slowly, his muscular thighs and taut buttocks clench-ing and releasing. He'd braced one hand on Jace's knee, and the other was wrapped around Jace's erection, his fingers barely able to encircle his girth.

Gabe thrust forward and stroked up, pulled back and stroked down. Jace had laced his fingers around the spooled headboard and his back was arched, his lips pulled tight in a rictus of pleasure.

Gabe's mouth was twisted in much the same way, and Romy knew they must hover at the edge of the pleasure so many of the women had talked about.

An edge only a few were lucky enough to cross.

The men at the compound didn't concern themselves with their women's pleasure, so the women were very careful about discussing the particulars. Romy only knew that when it happened, it was supposed to be wonderful, and when the men didn't help their women find that pleasure, then the women would wait until the men went to sleep and take care of themselves.

They did it, even knowing if they were caught they'd be punished.

They'd never told her how, and she had no idea what it might feel like, but watching Jace and Gabe she knew it must be wonderful. Romy wanted so badly to be with the two of them, but they'd obviously done this with each other for a long time, because they seemed so comfortable with one another. They didn't really need her.

Gabe leaned close and kissed Jace full on the mouth, and she tried to imagine what that kiss would feel like. She ran her fingers over her lips, surprised when they tingled under her touch. Then Gabe sat back on his heels and dragged Jace closer, pushed Jace's legs back tighter against his chest and began thrusting much harder. As their rhythm picked up, Romy's fingers somehow ended up between her legs, and she stroked her-self.

She'd never touched herself before—the punishment was severe if any woman was caught pleasuring herself. Reverend Ezekiel said it was a terrible sin, and more than one woman had been strapped in the stocks, where the reverend had used a riding crop between their legs.

But those men said the reverend was dead, and this felt so good that Romy couldn't believe she'd never tried it before. So good it would have been worth the punishment. Jace let out a long, low groan and Romy's attention returned to the men. Gabe's fist was sliding up and down his friend's penis and thick streams of white fluid poured from the top. Gabe suddenly drove hard against Jace and cursed. Jace laughed and held his arms up. Gabe slowly toppled into his embrace and lay there, the two of them laughing softly, whispering words that Romy wished she could hear.

To be part of something like that, to feel that connection . . . what would it be like?

She sighed and drew her fingers away from between her legs. She was getting wet down there, something her father had said meant she was a slut. She wasn't. She knew that much. The only one who had ever had relations with her had been her father, and each time he took her to his bed he made her pray for forgiveness. It was all her fault, he'd said. Her fault for looking so much like her mother.

He had no idea what a wonderful compliment that was. She missed her mother so much. Missed her every day, especially now, when she finally knew how to become the wolf. She hoped her mother knew. She had to know. Romy wondered if the voice she'd heard, the voice that had told her how to shift . . . could that voice in any way be connected with her mom?

She'd probably never know, but it was nice to think that maybe, just maybe, her mother was looking out for her. Still watching out for her and keeping her safe.

Romy wanted to roll over and sleep on her back, but she was afraid to move too much. She didn't want to hurt herself again. There was no pain now. Not after Jace had spent such a long time repairing all the damage. She shouldn't have run so hard today, but she'd had to get away. She was never going back.

Never.

She heard the guys get up, the two of them whispering as they walked toward the bathroom. Then she heard the shower running and imagined both of them together under the spray, maybe washing one another. Sighing, she shifted her position and tried to get comfortable, but she'd never been able to sleep on her stomach. It made her feel too vulnerable.

Especially since her father had forced her to share his bed. She never knew when he might want her, but it was especially bad when she slept on her belly. Then he did things to her that hurt even more than the other.

"Romy? I heard you moving around. Are you okay?"

"Gabe?"

"Yeah. Jace is just getting out of the shower. I'm sorry if we woke you. Are you in any pain?"

"No. I just can't get comfortable, sleeping on my stomach. I don't know what my back looks like. Do you think I can roll over?"

"Let me check."

She felt Gabe gently lift the sheet away from her back, but he let out a gust of air and a soft curse that told her she probably looked pretty bad.

"I'll ask Jace. He'll know better than I do."

She waited a few minutes until Jace knelt beside the bed. "How are you doing?"

His face was only inches from hers. He was absolutely gorgeous, so much so that she thought he was much too pretty to be a man. She swallowed back a sigh and said, "A lot better. Can I roll over? I don't want to undo any of the work you did." She tried to smile but she was really uncomfortable and so tired. And unsettled. Her body was trying to tell her something but she didn't know what. She didn't have to pee and she wasn't thirsty, but she needed something.

"Let's give it a try. I'll help."

"Okay." She slowly shifted her hips and let Jace do most of the lifting, but he got her to her back and she didn't feel bad at all. Except she still needed.

Just . . . needed. But what?

Jace gently brushed her hair back from her face and smiled. She could lose herself in his smile. In his kindness. He was so kind, when men were never nice unless they wanted something. Except all he'd wanted was to help her. But how could he help when she didn't really know what was wrong?

His grin grew wider. "You're not blocking, sweetie, and you do need something. It's the libido thing. It's part of being Chanku. A big part. When you shift, your sex drive ramps up really high. We all come out of a shift highly aroused. You just need to release that pent-up energy."

"Is that what you and Gabe were doing?"

He grinned at her. "I thought I caught you watching. Yeah. We fuck every night, since we spend most of each day as wolves. It's easier to check the pack populations from our animal form, and those shifts really do a job on us. Turns us into a couple of horny bastards. Will you let me take care of you? I promise not to hurt you."

She swallowed. "Have sex?" She wasn't all that sure it would help. She'd never once felt relaxed after sex with her father, but Jace was shaking his head.

"No. Well, not really. I don't want to risk reopening any of the patches

I did today. Why don't you close your eyes and relax. Spread your legs a little, and I'll help you." He glanced at his partner. "Gabe, too."

Then Jace turned away before she had time to wrap her mind around his absurd offer, and said, "Gabe? We need to help Romy relax. She's really keyed up from the shift but I don't want to risk sex with her because we might open up the wounds. However, I think if we're careful we can get her off without any damage."

He chuckled, a soft sound that would have made Romy smile, except she was still afraid of what they might do. But she wasn't afraid of Jace and Gabe. Not after they'd saved her. She was sure she could trust them. Almost.

Jace was still stroking her hair. It was mesmerizing, the soft pressure of his palm against her forehead. Then his fingers stilled and he glanced at her, but he was still talking to Gabe. "Today was Romy's first shift. Combine that with the pain, the fear, and the stress she's been under, and I can't even imagine the level of her arousal."

This time he laughed out loud and grinned at her. "Well, actually I can, when you broadcast like that. Sweetheart, that's not going to help you sleep, and you need your rest if you're going to heal."

It all made so much sense the way he said it. Romy lay back and closed her eyes. She wasn't sure she wanted to watch what they were going to do, but just knowing they planned to do something had her skin shivering in reaction to Jace's gentle touch, to the warmth of his breath across her rib cage.

Then the bed dipped between her legs and beside her at the same time. Her eyes flashed open. Gabe knelt beside her right shoulder and Jace was kneeling between her legs. "Just relax," he said. "Close your eyes. We won't hurt you. We're going to help you get some sleep."

Gabe's hands threading through her thick hair wasn't what she expected, but his long fingers massaging her temples and moving in gentle circles across her scalp felt better than anything she'd experienced in her entire life. Ever. She moaned, and heard Gabe's soft laughter.

"I knew you'd like this," he said. "I don't think there's a woman alive who doesn't want to have her scalp massaged. Relax. I'm just going to keep doing this until you turn into a puddle of warm goo."

"I think I'm already there."

Gabe chuckled. "You're not even close. Give Jace a few minutes. Between the two of us, you haven't got a prayer of staying awake."

Smiling, she relaxed into Gabe's thorough massage, but then she felt Jace move between her legs and she fought her muscles' involuntary reflex to tense. He lifted her hips, holding her so gently that none of her injuries complained a bit. Romy wanted to open her eyes and see what he was doing, but Gabe's touch had her so relaxed she decided she really didn't need to see anything at all.

Jace nuzzled her inner thighs. He hadn't shaved tonight and his shadowed beard was rough against her sensitive skin, but not at all uncomfortable. The gentle abrasion sent shivers of awareness across her belly and she felt a taut clenching in her middle. It should have been unpleasant, all the shivery, tickly feelings he was causing, but it wasn't. She wanted more, wanted to know what and why he was doing this to her. It certainly wasn't relaxing her.

Not a bit.

But she wasn't about to complain, not about sensations that were not only totally new but absolutely wonderful. He kissed her inner thighs—both of them—and then higher, licking at the crease between her thigh and her groin, putting his mouth where no man had ever tasted her before. She should make him stop, really. She should, except Gabe's hands were working such wonderful magic that she didn't want to do anything that might interfere with his massage.

Right. No way could she sell that one, not even to herself.

Jace was working his own kind of magic and it had nothing to do with healing. Or did it? These two males, with all their gentleness and caring, were showing her a side of men she'd never dreamed existed. A kind and loving side, and it fascinated her even as it terrified her. Trust wasn't easy. She'd never had a reason to trust anyone except her mother, and she'd definitely never trusted a man.

How could she possibly trust these men? She hardly knew them.

No. That was wrong. She knew them better than anyone she'd ever met. Understood them, because she was one of them. A shapeshifter. Already she knew shapeshifters didn't bow to a vengeful god. Instead, they actually communicated with a kind and loving goddess.

One who spoke to them directly. Who protected them. Who'd protected her.

"Ah!" she gasped, arching her hips. What felt like the soft sweep of a warm tongue over those ultrasensitive places between her legs left her panting. Panting and wondering, except she knew. Impossible, but Jace was using his tongue on her! She tried to hold back her sounds but another whimper escaped.

Romy was almost certain she felt him smile against her sex, but then his tongue was sweeping over her labia and circling her clitoris, and she didn't even try to control her cries. She did, however, try to hold on to her sanity. Allowing a man to sweep her away was dangerous. But this didn't feel dangerous at all. It felt loving. Good and kind. And she was so damned twisted up inside. She didn't believe the things the reverend had taught. They were lies. She'd do best to remember her mother's teachings, because at least her mother had Romy's best interests at heart.

Romy knew the names of all her parts. She knew those places that Jace was licking and touching—her labia and her clitoris and even into her vagina—but that was only because her mother had taught her so long ago. Reverend Ezekiel had said that naming those parts of the body gave them the power to sin, that women had no right to their bodies because they were created to be the helpmate of the man who claimed them. And that meant serving, in whatever capacity they were needed.

Yet Jace and Gabe said that among the Chanku the women were in charge. It was a matriarchal society, which meant Romy was no man's servant. Although, with what Jace and Gabe were doing to her now, she probably wouldn't complain if they wanted her to serve them in much the same way.

And then something changed between her legs and it wasn't Jace anymore. It was his wolf—and this time she opened her eyes, wide, and saw him. Dark gray in the dark room, he might have been pure fantasy, but she was all too aware of the weight of his heavy paws against her thighs and the sharp bite of his toenails, of the coarse gray coat brushing her calves and the cold wet nose nudging between her legs.

But she didn't try to get away. She wasn't stupid, and she wanted to know more. Romy spread her thighs to accommodate the huge beast and cried out when his long tongue snaked over her hip and then down again. It swept between her legs, the rough texture of his abrasive tongue leaving damp shivers wherever he licked. She cried out and arched against his muzzle, her body taking over where her mind refused to go.

Jace licked her again and then his tongue slipped inside her vagina, delving deep and curling up against the sensitive inner walls. Gabe was still rubbing her head, his fingers massaging across her scalp and down over the taut muscles of her neck and shoulders. He'd moved and she hadn't even noticed, but now he was behind her, his legs spread wide so that her head rested against his belly. She felt his erection along the side of her throat, stretching almost to her shoulder, and the soft cushion of his testicles beneath her neck.

Jace was licking deeper, harder, and Romy's tension rose. How was this possibly going to help her sleep? His tongue speared deep and then curled back along her inner walls, and her cries seemed to echo in the room. Beyond whimpers now, she cursed, words she knew she shouldn't say, but they felt right and so she said them again, louder.

"Fuck me, Jace. Dear Goddess, fuck me. Now."

Instead, he used his tongue and his teeth, slipping deep inside and then circling her clit until she couldn't stand it anymore, until all the rules she'd grown up with, all the fears and the baggage of her mother's death and her father's incestuous cruelty dissolved like shadows opened to sunlight. She turned herself free, gave in to the sensation of Gabe's loving touch, of Jace's wolf, and screamed as her body flew.

Over the precipice, off that highest peak, the one she'd wondered for so many years if she'd ever climb. She'd finally found her way, but she hadn't called on her father's god. No, she'd called on Jace and Gabe's goddess. Put herself in the Goddess Eve's hands—and in Jace's and Gabe's hands as well.

And in doing so, she'd found the release only love could give her.

Love from two guys she'd met only hours ago, after a lifetime of wondering if she would ever know love. If she'd ever feel cared for. Needed.

"Thank you," she whispered as exhaustion claimed her.

She wondered if they heard, if they knew she thanked them. All of them. Jace. Gabe.

And Eve.

5

Romy awoke to the smell of coffee brewing in an otherwise empty cabin. She sensed voices in her head, soft sounds that must have been Jace and Gabe. They weren't really blocking her, merely trying not to wake her. She sat up. They were close. Maybe on the front deck, possibly already having a cup. She loved coffee but she'd rarely been allowed any at the compound. It was reserved for the men.

She wasn't at the compound anymore.

Smiling, inhaling air that actually tasted free, she quietly arose and went into the bathroom. She was still naked, as she'd been since she'd met Jace and Gabe, but it was different in her wolf form. Now, as a woman standing almost as tall as those two very tall men, she worried over what she could wear.

Then, when she turned on the bathroom light and looked in the mirror, she worried about what she was going to do with hair almost to her waist, tangled beyond redemption. She ran her fingers through the mess, snagging on the thick curls. Then she looked closer at what generally hung in corkscrews unless she bound it. The waves were looser this morning. The texture not as coarse.

She turned, for the first time taking a chance to check out the damage on her back, but she kept her eyes closed for a moment. It didn't hurt right now, and she was afraid that once she saw what the reverend had done with his vicious bullwhip she'd feel the pain of her beating all over again.

She took a deep breath, opened her eyes, and gasped. Not because of the pain or the horror of her wounds but because of what she didn't see or feel. Yes, she was badly marked, with red lines in an almost perfect herringbone pattern from her shoulders to the tops of her thighs, but that's all they were. Lines. No open wounds, no deep lacerations or seeping sores.

What Jace had accomplished was beyond magic. It was a miracle. She stretched her shoulders, slowly raised her arms over her head, then bent at the waist. She twisted to the left, then the right. There was a tightness, some pulling beneath the skin as if he'd had to knit pieces together where skin or muscle had actually been lost, but she felt no true pain.

She'd been so lucky they found her. No. That wasn't it. It couldn't be. The fact Jace and Gabe were the ones who found her was so much more than mere luck. The Goddess Eve must have been involved. Somehow, their meeting was fated, but why? She stared at her reflection for a moment longer, wondering. She might have asked Eve, but somehow that felt presumptuous. Maybe another time?

Sighing, she shook her head and gazed about the small room, realized what she was thinking and burst out laughing. This probably wasn't the right place to be asking a goddess for answers to important questions, even if it was a very nice bathroom.

Still giggling, Romy used the toilet, amazed by all the conveniences in what was supposed to be a rustic cabin. Then she stared at the shower. Her mother had taught her to read and write, and she'd used the faucets and toilets and such in some of the more modern cabins, but the one she'd lived in with her father lacked indoor plumbing and electricity.

This shower was different than the ones she'd seen, with only one handle instead of two. But there was an *H* on the left and a *C* on the right. She turned it one way and then the other. Nothing. Then she pulled the handle toward her and turned it to the left. Cold water came out of the overhead sprayer, but after a few seconds it turned warm. She twisted the lever more to the left and the water grew warmer.

She could do this! Maybe she wasn't as stupid as her father'd always said. Bypassing the dry towels on a shelf near the shower, she went straight to a damp one on the towel rack that carried Jace's scent and held it to her nose. After a couple of deep breaths she hung it over the shower door, but not until she'd buried her nose in it again. Since her first shift she'd noticed her senses were sharper, her hearing, even as a human, seemed better, and her nose had definitely improved.

The fact she recognized Jace's scent on the towel was a definite plus.

She stepped beneath the spray and let the hot water spill over her shoulders and soak into her hair. She'd expected that her back would at least feel sensitive to the heat and the force of the water but it didn't hurt a bit. She found a bottle of shampoo and scrubbed her hair, though Gabe had told her that any dirt she might have collected would come off when she shifted. He said it was really handy when they didn't have a shower or a creek nearby.

Personally, she really loved the shower. Wherever she ended up, it was going to have indoor plumbing. Her father had been such a sanctimonious fool. How could hauling water and using an outhouse bring anyone closer to God?

She pushed thoughts of the man out of her head and reached for a bottle of conditioner. Such luxury, after a lifetime of coarse, homemade soaps and washing her hair in a bucket of cold water, of using homemade apple cider vinegar to work out the tangles. She left the sweet-smelling conditioner in her hair for a few minutes and just enjoyed the soothing spray across her back and shoulders. Then she rinsed her hair as thoroughly as she could, scrubbed the rest of herself to feel clean, shut off the water, and stepped out of the shower stall.

There was a plain white robe hanging from the back of the door, but her hair was soaked and it would take forever to dry it. What if she shifted?

"Only one way to find out." She looked at herself in the mirror as she called on her wolf, but it happened so quickly she didn't see the actual shift. Besides, as a wolf she was too short to see in the mirror over the sink. Curious now, she rose up on her hind legs and planted her big paws firmly on the counter.

A beautiful wolf, black all over except for sparkling amber eyes and very white teeth stared back at her. She felt almost dizzy with the reality of her new life. She really was a wolf. A beautiful wolf, even larger than her mother had been, with sharp teeth and what must be a dark pink tongue. Colors were different to her wolf, but colors or not, there was power in this form. Power she'd never known in her life.

She shifted back to her human self, but once again it was too fast to see. She really did need to ask the guys how that worked. She felt nothing, sensed nothing beyond the change in senses from human to wolf, from wolf to human. The human thought in a different way, without the input of smells and tastes on the air, without the subtle addition of sounds her wolven ears could hear. Tall again, she looked in the mirror. Her body and hair were dry, but the weirdest thing was that even the tangles had mostly disappeared.

In fact, the corkscrew curls were more like loose waves than actual curls. Frowning, she lifted a long section of her hair and stared at the changed texture. It had definitely softened. Curious, she ran her fingers through the dark thatch covering her pubes, and even those coarse, crinkly hairs felt softer.

Jace and Gabe would know what was going on.

So many questions she wanted to ask. She hoped they had answers because a lot of this was going to drive her nuts if should couldn't find out. That was something that had always bothered her at the compound—the lack of curiosity most of the women had. No more. Now if she wanted answers she knew she could ask Jace and Gabe.

She slipped into the robe and belted it around her waist. It was obviously designed for much shorter women, and the hem hit just below her thighs. That was enough reason for punishment at the compound, but her new reality told her that it was probably more than acceptable here. Satisfied, she stepped out of the bathroom and went in search of the guys.

"I thought I heard you." Standing in the small kitchen area, bare-chested and bare of foot, wearing only his soft black knit pants, Jace grinned at her and held up a fresh cup of coffee. "Do you take anything in it?"

"No. Thank you." She took the steaming cup from his hand and realized she was grinning like an idiot. "I looked at my back. What you did . . . Jace! It's healed. I mean, I can see where the whip cut me, but there's nothing open, no pain. My skin feels tight, and I know you had to have somehow put things together where there must have been tissue missing. I know how hard he hit me, but it doesn't hurt me anymore."

"May I see?"

Nodding, she set her cup on the counter, unbelted the robe and turned her back. She lowered the robe to just above her buttocks, holding it over her breasts in the front, though why she should feel any shyness around a man who'd licked between her legs really made no sense. No sense at all.

So why was she still grinning?

• • •

Jace ran his fingers lightly over Romy's back when what he really wanted to do was kiss each mark and nuzzle behind her ear. Maybe run his tongue along the perfect line of her throat and . . . no. He really couldn't go there. Not yet. Not until she was more comfortable with him. No matter what they'd done last night, he was starting fresh today.

It had come to him during the night that he didn't want to fuck this woman. What he really wanted to do was court her and make love to her. He'd never courted a woman in his life, but then he'd never before met the one he wanted to keep.

He wanted Romy.

"Grab your coffee and come on out on the deck. Gabe picked up some stuff for breakfast in the main lodge. Food's still warm."

She followed him outside. Gabe was dressed exactly like Jace, which meant he was just as naked, wearing nothing but his soft knit pants.

"Good morning, Gabe."

"Good morning to you, too." He stood and pulled her into a light hug, kissing her cheek. Then he winked at Jace. *You owe me for that one, bro. You know I'd like to do a whole lot more.*

Any man with blood in his veins would want to do more. Just don't. Jace grabbed a chair and stuck it between his and Gabe's. Closer to his. Gabe laughed out loud.

"What's so funny?" Romy took the chair when Jace offered it.

Jace sat beside her and grabbed a tray filled with bacon and scrambled eggs, some cheese and warm tortillas. "We call it male posturing," he said, but he winked at Romy and hoped she had a clue what he was talking about. She'd led a terribly protected existence in so many ways, and yet she'd lived through hell for most of her life. Now probably wasn't the time to tell her how much he wanted her. How he could barely keep his hands to himself when he was around her. So he changed the subject. "Have you ever made a breakfast burrito?"

She shook her head. He shot a grin her way and piled bacon and scrambled eggs and some shredded cheddar onto the flour tortilla, then wrapped it up. "I'm going to stick it in the microwave—have you used one?"

Once again she shook her head.

"Then come with me. This invention has saved the lives of countless unmated men over the years. Busy women, too, for that matter."

He wrapped the burrito in a paper towel and put it in the microwave, gave it about fifteen seconds and then took it out, almost too hot to hold. Romy carefully took it from him, wide-eyed at how hot it was.

She stared at the tiny microwave for a moment and shook her head. "We didn't have these at the compound, but I remember some of the women talking about them, how much they missed modern conveniences. Now I see why."

He really wanted to ask her about those other women, what could possibly make them want to live in a compound where they were nothing more than slaves, but that would have to wait for a later time.

Romy followed him back to the front porch. He'd already eaten two burritos and figured that would hold him for now. It was more fun watching Romy eat, especially when she sighed her pleasure after the first bite.

She glanced briefly at Gabe but focused her attention on Jace. "Tell me about the Chanku. I want to know everything about what my mother was. What I am."

"There's a lot to tell." Jace shot a quick glance at Gabe. "But I'll start at the beginning, which was long before there were any humans on Earth. Our ancestors were refugees from a dying planet who landed on Earth long before modern species of anything had evolved."

"We're aliens?" She stopped with the burrito halfway to her mouth. "From another planet?"

"Our ancestors were." Gabe rolled his eyes. "You have to admit, it does explain why Jace is so . . . uhm . . ."

"I'm talking here, Cheval." Jace shook his head. "Okay. Back to the history lesson. Over time they scattered across the planet, but what they didn't realize is that a certain grass the original settlers brought from their home world and planted in an area in the shadow of the Himalaya Mountains where that first ship landed was the necessary element that gave them the ability to shapeshift."

"I know about the grass. Mama called it magic grass. It grows near the compound."

Jace nodded. "That's the stuff, except the descendants of the first Chanku had forgotten about the grasses. They ate them because they lived where the grass had become plentiful, but when they emigrated to new areas they didn't think to take seeds with them. They'd forgotten that the nutrients in the grasses were important to their body's development as shifters.

"Without the grasses, ensuing generations lost their ability to change shape, and over time their descendants forgot all about the grasses. The race as shapeshifters essentially died out, but the genes are carried in the female line, and those genes remain dominant no matter how many generations pass without shifting. The ability to shift was rediscovered in our parents' time, and one major pack is rebuilding. Gabe and I are part of that pack, though there are still undiscovered Chanku all over the world. You, obviously, are one of them."

"But how could my mother know about the grasses? How did she learn to shift?"

Jace shook his head. "I honestly don't know. We're wondering if Eve somehow got involved. She's told us she doesn't recognize when people carry the Chanku gene unless they've already made the shift, but if your mother was already eating the grasses . . ."

"But how would she know to eat them?" Romy wiped her hands on the paper towel. She'd finished her burrito while Jace was talking but didn't even seem to realize she'd eaten.

"Did you like it?" He nodded at the wadded-up paper towel in her hands.

She glanced down and blushed. "I guess I was hungrier than I realized."

"That's good. It tells me you're healing well without any infection. As far as the grasses—if you have the Chanku genes, you're drawn to the grasses. It's as if our bodies recognize the nutrients we need to be complete, but the plants weren't common here in this part of the world until after our existence became public knowledge. Shapeshifters lived in secret until 2013, when we got outed, quite literally, on the national news. One of our packmates shifted in order to prevent a terrorist from blowing up a room filled with kids. Unfortunately, he did it in front of cameras on the national news."

Gabe laughed. "It was definitely big news. Before that, shapeshifters were nothing more than myth and legend, and then suddenly the human population realized we lived among them."

Jace nodded. "They're still getting used to that whole idea. Anyway, once the secret was out, Chanku started scattering the seed. The grass adapts readily and fills a good ecological niche without any of the drawbacks of many introduced plant species. Those who have the Chanku genes are often drawn to them."

"Like my mother was." Romy's eyes were filled with a sense of understanding, as if so many mysteries of her life finally made sense. "I was, too. I always wondered why I loved eating it and the other kids thought I was nuts. It wasn't real plentiful. I used to watch for the first shoots in spring. One of the best patches grew near my mother's grave."

Jace nodded, thinking of a little girl growing up without her mother. At the same time knowing how proud Romy's mother would be of the woman she'd become. "We've had a few people come to us who've actually ingested enough of the grasses that they've shifted on their own, or they've had just enough to be having vivid dreams of running in the forest, hunting game on four legs or doing other wolflike things, and they wonder if they might be Chanku. Often they are."

"Sometimes they're just nuts. Really nuts." Gabe laughed. "It's like the stories of being abducted by aliens. Some folks need to believe they have special powers and they're convinced they're Chanku."

"I knew from the time I saw my mother shift and she told me about the magic grasses." Romy's eyes filled with tears. She used the paper towel to wipe them away. "I didn't know what we were called, though, and I only saw her shift once. That was the day the reverend shot and killed her, but she'd given me her diary to read and told me never to let anyone see it. That was my only link to my mother and to my wolf."

"But you'd never shifted until yesterday?" Jace couldn't keep from touching her. He gently gripped her leg, just above the knee. Even with the cotton robe between his palm and Romy's skin he felt the connection, as if a link were trying to form.

She shook her head. "No. It wasn't easy to get the grasses and I'd often go weeks between finding any. I wasn't allowed out of the compound because I'd threatened to escape. I tried a few times but they always caught me."

"What happened when they caught you?" Gabe's soft question made Romy shiver. Jace felt it. Softly, rhythmically, he stroked her leg.

Romy looked down at her hands, where she was carefully, almost methodically, shredding the paper towel. "I was beaten, but never as badly as yesterday. Yesterday they meant to kill me. I don't know what stopped them."

"You didn't shift during the beating?"

Again she shook her head, but she stared at the torn paper in her hands. Then at Jace's hand, where he slowly stroked her leg. "No. Not until they took me down off the whipping frame. They'd put me on a blanket to use like a stretcher, said that if I didn't die they'd turn me over to the young men as their whore. That's when I asked for help. With my mind." She raised her head this time and looked directly into Jace's eyes.

"I said, 'Please help me.' And a beautiful voice told me to shift. When I said I didn't know how, she gave me images that were perfectly clear, though even now I know I couldn't describe them. But it was just so easy, exactly the way she said it would be. I don't know how, but I knew what to do with fangs I'd never used before. I slashed the chest of the reverend and tore out my father's throat, and then I ran. I didn't feel at all guilty, even though I'm sure I killed my father. I'm surprised the reverend died. I didn't think it was a killing wound."

Jace nodded and took both of Romy's hands in his. "That was definitely Eve who helped you. I'm certain of it. And if those guys were wrong, if the reverend is still alive, if he comes after you, he won't be alive for long. You have us now, Romy. Gabe and I will do whatever we can to keep you safe."

Her dark brows came together in a frown, and slowly she shook her head. "But why? You don't owe me anything. Why would you risk your safety for someone you don't really know?"

Jace couldn't help himself. He wrapped his fingers more tightly around both her hands and held them against his chest. "I know you, Romy. I spent hours inside your body yesterday, healing you. I made love to you last night. I'm sitting beside you this morning trying to figure out how I can possibly keep a woman as brave, as strong and as wonderful as you are in my life. I would risk everything, including my own life, to keep you safe, because I don't want to lose you. Not ever."

There was absolute silence and he figured he'd probably scared the crap out of Romy, but he couldn't help himself. He grinned. Damn it all, he'd never been known for his patience.

"So there you have it." This time he laughed, but he couldn't bring himself to look at her face. Didn't want to risk seeing denial written all over her expression. He gave her hands a comforting squeeze, thankful when she didn't pull free of his grasp. "Now, don't do anything stupid or I could end up dead, okay?"

Gabe folded over, laughing himself silly. "Damn, Jace. You've always had such smooth moves, but that's a new one." He put an arm around Romy, who looked as confused as a woman possibly could. "Point being, Romy, you do matter to us. Your safety matters to us. Be careful, be alert. You just have to meet us partway and trust us to do whatever we have to do to keep you safe."

• • •

Standing in front of the small sink in the kitchen area, Romy played over what Gabe had said so easily. *You matter to us.* She hadn't mattered to anyone since her mother's death. Her mother's murder, because that's exactly what it was. She'd needed a few minutes alone, so she'd offered to clean up their dishes from breakfast, and now this simple chore allowed her mind to spin in so many directions, searching for answers and still finding only questions.

How could she matter to those two wonderful men? Gabe, who teased her as if she were a beloved sister, never saying cruel or hurtful things, and Jace, who looked at her as if she were someone special? Someone worth loving. She rinsed their coffee cups and the few utensils they'd used and put them away. She was still wearing nothing but a robe, but until she shifted, it was all she had to cover herself. Those were things she understood. The dishes needed to be washed. At some point, she needed clothing. But how did she understand Gabe and Jace?

She glanced out the window. They'd pulled their chairs close together and were talking seriously about something. She wasn't sure but suspected they were discussing her. She'd definitely screwed up their work schedule—Jace said they still had over a month's worth of their survey to complete. Their goal was to be home by the middle of September, before school started. Romy hadn't been at all surprised to learn that Jace was a teacher and worked with the pack's children. As caring and compassionate as he was, she imagined he was wonderful with kids, but it was already August and their schedule meant a lot of travel if they were going to finish the loop through Oregon and up into Washington, then across Idaho to Montana and the pack's home.

Her home, now. That's what Jace said. He'd even contacted Gabe's dad to let him know about her. To tell Mr. Cheval, their pack alpha, they'd be bringing home a new member of the pack. She still couldn't quite believe that, the fact that no one seemed to question her right to belong.

49

She wiped out the sink and walked back outside. Jace smiled at her and gestured toward the chair next to him.

She sat. "You're sure it's okay? I don't want to interrupt."

"No interruption." He leaned over and kissed her cheek. She'd not expected that.

"We were talking about you, anyway." Gabe grinned at her. "Do you mind if we use this cabin as our command center for the next couple of days? Jace and I can check on the pack that was in the area last time we were here and you'll have more time to heal before we do any serious traveling."

She wasn't used to being consulted about anyone's plans. It was nice. Better than nice. It felt spectacular. "I don't want to hold up your schedule. If you'd rather not stay, I'm sure I can keep up." She glanced from Gabe to Jace and couldn't look away.

What was it about this man? The fact he'd healed her? That he'd taken away her pain, or was it something else? Something deeper. She wasn't used to being so confused. Certainly not about a man.

Jace smiled, shaking his head. "No need. You're almost entirely healed now, but there's no reason to push things. And honestly? I like the idea of a bed at night. And a shower in the morning."

"And getting laid." Gabe flipped him off and Jace laughed.

"Well, there is that." He grinned at Romy. "Pardon our rude behavior. We've been around each other a little too much. I'm hoping you'll be a civilizing influence."

"Me?" Romy pointed at herself and kept a serious look on her face. It wasn't easy, but neither was joining in when they teased. She wanted to. Wanted to be part of everything they did. Shaking her head slowly, she said, "Honestly? I don't think I'm up to the job. In fact, I think both of you are impossible."

Jace chuckled. Gabe rolled his eyes. "She catches on quick, doesn't she? We need to work on our cover a little better." Then the two men looked at each other and laughed.

"How can you say that, Romy?" Jace held his right hand over his heart. "You hardly know us. We're good, solid, upstanding characters."

Glancing away, she muttered, "You're definitely characters." Sighing, she added, "I know enough." She tried to look prim and proper, but it was impossible wearing nothing but a soft cotton robe with her hair in wild disarray about her face. Why was it that merely sitting close to Gabe and Jace—especially Jace—made her feel sexy?

Exactly like the wanton her father had always accused her of being.

Gabe grinned. "Sorry, sweetheart. You're not nearly wanton enough for us."

Jace cupped her cheek in his hand before she could look away. She leaned into his touch and fought a strong impulse to turn her head and kiss his palm, even as she knew she was probably blushing beet red. "I'd like that," he said. Then he chuckled. "And don't worry. That shade of scarlet is very becoming."

She groaned. "I know. Windows. Down."

"Yeah." He was laughing outright now. "Unless you want us to hear every sexy thought you have in that amazing mind of yours. You'll get used to it. Eventually blocking will be second nature."

"Until it is, I think I'll just go hide in a corner, okay?"

What she really wanted to do was bury her burning face in her hands until she didn't feel like such an idiot, but then Jace leaned close and kissed her. It was so unexpected, the soft warmth of his mouth on hers, the smile she felt against her lips. Before she could react and kiss him back, he'd pulled away.

He stared at her, his big warm hands cupping her face, and she almost sighed aloud when he spoke. "Which reminds me. It's not commonly known that Chanku are telepathic. We try not to make it obvious when we're mindspeaking around those who aren't like us."

"I'll remember." She glanced down at her hands, remembered seeing them as paws. She really wanted to shift and run, but the guys had a job to do.

Jace wrapped her hands in his. "You'll get your chance. You have a whole lifetime ahead of you for running. For now, though, I want you to go in and rest. Give yourself time to heal so that when we leave here I don't have to worry about you. Gabe and I need to check on the local wolf pack, make sure everything is okay. Wolves are protected nationwide, and there's no hunting of any kind allowed here on what is essentially Chanku property, but poachers still sneak into the area. We used to chip the wolves, keep track of them that way, but the bad guys learned to hack the codes and they used the signals to find the animals. The wild wolves here recognize our wolves and know we're here to help."

He stood and pulled Romy to her feet and led her inside. "C'mon."

"Stay inside," Gabe added. "Don't let anyone see you here. This is a housekeeping cabin. No maid service, so don't let anyone in—there's no reason for anyone to check the place. Lock up as soon as we go."

She nodded. "How far away will you be? Will I still be able to contact you? With telepathy . . . you know, mindspeaking?"

"It's hard to say." Jace shot a glance at Gabe. "Gabe and I are good for a few miles, but that's a stretch. Gabe's dad could easily touch us here in Oregon while he's in Montana. Of course, Anton Cheval is scary powerful. We've never tested to see how far away we can go with you." He brushed his fingers through her hair. "Of course, that's mostly because I hate the idea of being away from you." He reached into his pocket and pulled out his cell phone. "Do you know how to use one of these?"

She shook her head. She'd never even seen one. Not until Jace's and Gabe's.

"They're fairly simple." He quickly tapped the screen and handed it to her. "If you tap the icon of the dopey-looking poodle, Gabe's phone will ring."

"Hey? Who you calling dopey?"

Jace appeared to ignore him. Romy grinned and tapped the poodle. She liked the fact it was wearing a pink bow. Gabe's phone made a sound like a blue jay squawking. He answered it. "Jace's ringtone," he said.

She wasn't quite sure what he meant. The jay?

"Hold it up to your ear."

Romy did, and Gabe's voice was perfectly clear. Of course, he was only standing a few feet away. Still . . . "This is amazing." She grinned at Jace. "Does yours sound the same when Gabe calls you?"

Jace laughed when Gabe dialed his number. A yappy little dog barked. "Does that answer your question?" Gabe faked a swing at him. Jace ducked. "Okay. I'm leaving my phone with you. Any problem, anything at all, call us. Even if you just get lonely. We'll try not to go too far, but it depends on where the pack is."

"I'll be fine. There's enough in the refrigerator to snack on, and I promise to stay inside."

"And away from any open windows." Jace wasn't teasing now.

She yawned. "No open windows. Now, though, I think I'm going to take that nap you said I need."

She turned to leave, but Jace stopped her with a light touch on her shoulder. When she turned he pulled her close, wrapped his arms around her waist and kissed her. His lips were soft and warm and moved across her mouth like satin. Her entire body grew warm and liquid, a pulse throbbed deep in her womb, but then he was backing away, smiling at her.

"I'm going to worry about you the whole time we're gone. Lock this place up tight, okay?" He leaned over and kissed the tip of her nose. And then he turned, and with Gabe following close behind, left the cabin.

Romy stood there like an idiot, off balance from his kiss. The door closed quietly. She shook herself, rubbed her hands up and down her arms, then walked across the room and slid the dead bolt into place.

Good girl. Now get some sleep. We'll be back as soon as we can.

Be careful.

Smiling, she turned away from the locked door, paused long enough to close all the curtains, and then crawled into bed.

6

They hiked into the forest bare-chested, wearing nothing but their loose travel pants and sandals, prepared for a shift. Once they were far enough into the tall trees and low-growing brush that the cabins were no longer visible, Jace stopped.

"This is far enough. I don't want to be gone too long. Besides . . ." He was agitated for whatever reason. Unsettled, but why?

Gabe raised his head and stared at Jace. "You feel it too, don't you? Something's not right."

"Something is very wrong. I want my wolf's nose about now."

"Then shift."

Jace nodded and stripped off his pants and sandals. He'd left his pack at the cabin, so he shoved his clothing into the crotch of an oak.

Gabe had brought his pack in order to carry his phone. At least they had a way to contact Romy if they had to. Or if she needed them.

Gabe looped his pack around his neck and shifted at the same time as Jace. His dark brown fur shimmered with golden highlights as he stepped into a sunbeam and raised his nose to the air. *Do you smell it?*

I do. Fresh blood. Wolf, not human.

This way. Gabe took off at a run with Jace following close behind. They had gone barely a hundred yards before Gabe veered off the trail. His nose had always been better than any of the others' in their group. Today it led him to a dark gray wolf lying beneath a fallen tree.

A carbon arrow—the kind hunters used with a compound bow—protruded from the animal's side. The young male was alive, barely conscious, but panting and obviously in pain. His eyes rolled in fear, but his snarl was more of a whimper when Jace reached his side and shifted.

"Shit. It's buried between his ribs, Gabe. He's blowing bloody bubbles. I bet the damned thing's punctured his lung."

Gabe shifted and sat beside Jace. "Can you save him?"

"I don't know. The blood's fresh and the wound isn't too old. Keep an eye out for whoever might have shot him. I'm going in."

He placed his hands on the wolf's shoulder and felt the animal's body tremble, absorbing the creature's sensations and emotions. The wolf was in excruciating pain and absolutely terrified, hurt by men and now more men were beside him. Gabe shifted and crept around to the wolf's head, taking a submissive posture, whining softly.

He showed no threat to the one that was wounded. The animal seemed to understand. The local pack had grown familiar with Gabe and Jace over the years they'd been studying the wild wolves, and whether this one had known them or not, he at least seemed to understand that they meant no harm. Jace watched him a moment, until he was comfortable that the animal wasn't as afraid as he'd been.

It took Jace mere seconds to dissolve his thoughts into something that was a form of energy he'd never been able to describe. While his body sat motionless beside the wounded animal, it was little more than an empty vessel when his mind took him inside the creature's body. But the part of him that was doing the healing was more than mere thought. He became physical energy with the ability to affect nerves and deaden pain, to move individual cells, to heal wounds by physically repairing the damaged tissues. He couldn't replace missing blood, but he could close torn blood vessels and push foreign objects like bullets and arrows out through damaged flesh, repairing the injuries as he went.

The arrow was barbed and ugly, but the wound had been torn open enough that he was able to carefully work the barbed head back out without causing more damage, moving it between unbroken ribs, closing the tear in the wolf's lung and sealing the torn veins and arteries.

Time lost meaning as he worked, but it was the closest he knew he would ever come to creating art—that was how he saw each injury he'd healed since his parents had first taught him how to do this miraculous thing. In rebuilding bodies that might not have otherwise had the strength to heal, he was painting a new reality for each creature—Chanku or wild thing—he healed. It was a gift from the goddess, this ability he'd inherited from his mother and father, and he'd never, ever taken it for granted.

Once the arrow was out and the wolf's damaged lung was repaired, Jace began repairing torn muscle and skin. This was a repetitive, time-consuming process, but not nearly as difficult or intricate as the lung, and it allowed him time to think of Romy, of the way he'd gone inside her body as a healer, and how he wanted now to go inside her as a man, to make love to her as a woman needed to be loved. But would she ever be ready? She'd allowed him to love her last night, but he'd only used his hands and his mouth. After what she'd been through, would she ever be able to accept a man in her bed without thinking of a lifetime of incestuous rape?

He wasn't sure how it had happened so fast, but Jace knew Romy was special. Knew she was meant for him, and he hoped she could one day feel the same way about him. He sensed her interest. Knew she looked at him differently than she did Gabe.

But was it enough?

Jace felt Gabe's hand stroking his shoulders and realized he must have closed up the last of the deep wound. The wolf was breathing evenly now, and Jace was the one trembling. Healing took everything he had. It didn't matter. He'd give whatever he could if it meant saving a life. Blinking, he slowly returned to his body. The wolf was alive, but very weak.

The bloodied arrow lay on the ground beside him. The hand stroking his shoulders was gone, and now Gabe's wolf stared at him out of dark amber eyes.

Shift. I brought you something to eat.

Blinking slowly, Jace turned to the scent of game. A freshly killed cottontail lay next to him. He shifted and ate most of the rabbit. Then he gently nudged a piece of it with his nose, moving it close to the injured wolf. Without opening his eyes, the wolf sniffed and then licked at the bloodied haunch.

Gabe moved away and shifted. "I'm going to get some water. He's probably dehydrated. I know you are." He emptied out his pack and left his clothes and phone beside Jace. Then he took off through the woods toward the sound of running water. A few minutes later he returned with the pack half filled with water. Still lying down, Jace lapped up enough water to help rehydrate his exhausted body, and then Gabe held it for the wolf.

The animal sniffed and then slowly struggled to his feet. Shaking, he stood still for a moment as if testing his strength, then stuck his nose into the pack and drank. After drinking almost all of the water, he lay back down again, panting.

Jace shifted. The wolf blinked, and then sniffed his hand and turned his head away.

"Ungrateful bastard, don't you think?" Gabe grinned at Jace and set the pack to one side. "We're taking him with us, right?"

"Well, we can't leave him here. He's too weak to defend himself or hunt for food, and I have no idea where his pack is."

"Do you think he'd let me carry him? We're not that far from the cabin. I called Romy and said we might be bringing an injured wolf back with us. She said she'd figure out some sort of bed on the floor for him."

Jace stared at Gabe. He'd been so deep into the healing he'd not even heard Gabe make the call. "How'd she sound? Was she afraid? How long have we been gone?"

Gabe shook his head. "A lot longer than we'd planned. You've been working on your buddy there for almost five hours."

Five hours? No wonder he was so exhausted. They needed to get back to Romy. "I'll see if I can communicate with him." Jace shifted again and looked into the wolf's eyes. There was intelligence there, though of a feral kind, unable to reason beyond basic needs. He sent him visuals of Gabe lifting him, of carrying him to safety and food. And then he said they needed to find the ones who had hurt him.

That seemed to get the animal's attention. *I think he might let you pick him up, Gabe. Want to give it a try?*

Gabe had pulled on his pants and sandals and he slipped his pack over Jace's head. Then he carefully slid his hands beneath the wolf's body. The animal growled and bared his teeth, but Jace calmed him with a few soft mental commands. Sometimes he wondered how it was he knew what to do or say, but he'd always been able to work with wounded creatures, whether Chanku, human or animal.

The wolf relaxed and Gabe carefully lifted him and stood. He grunted, adjusted the animal's weight, and started walking back toward the lodge. Jace grabbed the bloody arrow in his teeth and carried it, staying within the wolf's view, trotting alongside Gabe.

When they got to the tree where he'd left his clothes, he shifted and dressed, and the two men walked out of the forest together. Gabe carried the injured wolf, while Jace hung on to the arrow. It had an interesting insignia on the shaft, something he'd never seen before, and it was evidence should they decide to report the wounded wolf.

Romy? Are you awake? Can you unlock the door for us?

I'm glad you're back. I was getting worried. I'll get the door.

Jace saw the curtain pull to one side and then the door opened. Romy stayed behind it, out of sight, and he sensed her nervousness. Was she afraid of the wolf?

"No," she said.

He grinned at her, acknowledging she'd picked the thought out of his mind, but her attention was all on the wolf. "Not of the wolf, poor thing. Will he be okay?" She had thrown a towel over a couple of pillows on the floor, and Gabe set the wolf down in the soft bed. After he was settled, Romy knelt beside the animal. "I found some steaks in the freezer and took out a couple to thaw. I wasn't sure what else we could feed him."

"I'm sorry we were gone so long." Jace studied Romy. She seemed perfectly relaxed, more at ease than she'd been since they'd found her. "It took me a lot longer than I realized to repair all the damage."

"What happened to him?" She sat back on her heels, raised her head, and focused on Jace. He liked that about her, the way she gave whomever was speaking her undivided attention.

"He was shot, but whoever did it used a compound bow." He showed her the bloody arrow. "The barbed point caused a lot of damage and it pierced his lung. Took me longer than most healings." He chuckled. "Except maybe yours. Hopefully I won't have to do this guy twice."

"Let me see that."

Romy reached for the arrow. She didn't seem at all concerned about the blood. Instead, she wiped it away with the tip of her finger and stared at the insignia. "This is the arrow? You took this out of him?"

"Yeah. What is it?"

"The symbol, the tilted cross with that yellow slash through it . . ."

"Looks like a lightning bolt to me." Gabe leaned over Romy's shoulder and stared at the arrow.

"It's a shaft of sunlight. It's supposed to represent God's salvation. This is the emblem for the Glorious Salvation in Truth, the cult I grew up in. The one I just escaped from." She raised her head and stared at Jace. "They're hunting me. Some of the men at the compound hunt with bows and arrows. I don't know how skilled they are, but sometimes they bring in fresh game."

"Shit." Jace glanced at the wolf, sleeping peacefully now that he was in a comfortable, safe place. "He's dark. Not black, but unusually dark for a wild wolf. You're black, but if they only got a quick look at you . . ."

"I attacked and escaped in less than a minute. Where did you find him?"

"Not all that far from here."

Gabe walked back from the kitchen area. He'd grabbed a damp cloth and was cleaning the wolf's blood off his chest and arms. "We can't know how far from here he was when he was shot. He could have traveled for miles before the loss of blood brought him down. I wish there was a way to ask him."

"I know. Gabe? Do you remember that ranger's name, the one we talked to about the traps we found a couple years ago? You went to college with his son."

"Yeah, Howie Salazar's dad. John, I think. I've got his number. Should I call him?"

"Definitely. We need to report this, and he was pretty cool. But Romy, if he comes out, you'll need to hide. I don't want anyone to know you're with us. Especially now."

• • •

The ranger arrived within the hour. Romy hid in the bathroom, listening. He was courteous and sympathetic and definitely interested in the marked arrow. Sitting on the floor with her back against the door, Romy paid close attention to their conversation.

"Do you think he's going to make it?"

She pictured the ranger looking down at the sleeping wolf and she wanted to say that of course he was going to make it. Jace had healed him. Just like he'd healed her.

"I hope so." Jace's voice. It was so soft and deep, almost melodic. She'd bet he was great in the classroom with his kids. She loved listening to him.

"He's lost a lot of blood, but I was able to repair the damage to his lung. That was the worst of it. Now we just have to worry about infection, but the wound was surprisingly clean. I removed what little debris I could find."

"Amazing how you folks can do that. When I think of the injured animals I've found, with no recourse but to put them down, I wish I could heal them. It's frustrating."

"Not all of us can do what Jace does." Gabe usually teased Jace, but Romy was sure she picked up a bit of envy now in what he said. Envy and maybe even hero worship. "He's got a talent that only a few of us share. Unfortunately, I'm not one of them."

"Yeah," Jace said, "but you've got one hell of a nose. Gabe's the one who found the wolf. Scented his blood and took us right to him."

"Days like this, I regret I'm merely human." The ranger's sense of awe was obvious—and she knew it was welcome by the guys. They'd told her how often they had to deal with resentment from the human population, and Romy sensed their appreciation of this man's easy acceptance of their abilities. After a few moments of silence when Romy figured the ranger was probably going over his notes, she heard the sound of the men moving around. "I think I have everything I need. Your pictures with the arrow still in him and the shaft with his blood on it are all that I'll need to file a report. Did you know that the repercussions for hunting wolves in this county are felony charges and some really lengthy prison terms? The fact this occurred on privately owned property that's an established preserve makes the penalties even higher. The shooter could go away for a very long time."

"All the more incentive for us to catch the bastards."

Romy grinned. Gabe sounded particularly bloodthirsty.

But Jace? Jace sounded sad. She knew he must be looking at the wolf, thinking of the pain the animal was in. He was like that—a man who worried about things.

That's not it at all, Romy. I'm sad because of you. Because I'm worrying about you. I want this over. I want to know you're safe. Actually? I just want you.

Oh. There really wasn't any answer to what wasn't really a question. No, it sounded more to Romy as if Jace might be making a vow. She decided she liked that. A lot.

It seemed to take forever before the ranger finally left.

· · ·

Jace opened the door and stood there, feeling sort of awkward after essentially spilling his guts to Romy. She must think he was such a jerk, but damn. Romy was everything he wanted, and she was in danger.

Gabe stepped up behind him before he could make an even bigger ass of himself. "I'm going back out, Jace. I want you to stay here."

He spun around before he even had a chance to say a word to Romy. "What? What do you mean you're going back out?"

"I'll recognize the scent of the guys who were after Romy. I want to go out as a wolf and sniff around, see if they were hunting here or elsewhere. I don't intend to go far, but I want to check things out. We can't leave Romy alone, and we can't leave the wolf alone with her—it doesn't know her and we have no idea how dangerous it could be. I'll stay in touch, but I need to do this."

And you need time alone with Romy. Please, Jace. Don't fight me on this.

He shouldn't have had to think about it for more than a second, but he did. And all he could see was Gabe's generous nature and love for him. It was a humbling experience.

Thanks, Gabe. I owe you.

Gabe gave him a cheesy grin. *You owe me big-time. But it's okay. You'd do the same for me. I hope.* He leaned over and gave Romy a quick kiss before she could even react. "I'm going out for a bit, Romy. Keep an eye on this guy for me, will you?"

"Yeah. Sure." Obviously confused, she shot a quick glance at Jace.

"Be careful, Gabe. Keep a link open and stay in touch."

"I will."

Gabe left the two of them, stopped to check on the sleeping wolf, and then with a quick salute was out the door.

Jace was alone with Romy for the first time.

"C'mon," he said, holding out a hand to her. "Our patient is feeling better."

"Oh. Okay."

She stood, still dressed in that silly robe, and he wondered how they were going to get clothes for her. And she'd need a pack to carry, one like he and Gabe had that could drape around a wolf's neck as well as a human's. But that wasn't important. Not now. He took her hand and led her into the main part of the cabin. The wolf was awake now. He lay on the soft bed Romy had made but his head was up, his eyes more alert.

He growled when they got close, but Jace went down on his knees and turned his throat, showing a submissive posture that the wolf seemed to recognize. Instead of aggression, it whimpered. Romy went down on her knees, but somehow she knew to put her hand out and allow the wolf to sniff. He must have recognized that she was female because he stared at her without any sign of aggressive behavior.

She backed away and went into the kitchen. A minute later she returned with a bowl of water and another of thawed steak, cut into small pieces and warmed in the microwave. She set both bowls in front of the wolf and backed away.

It stood on shaky legs, drank half the bowl of water and then attacked the meat. Within minutes the bowl was empty. The wolf stood there a moment longer, wobbling on weak legs. Jace slowly scooped him up in his arms and headed toward the front door. Romy held it open, but he noticed that she was careful to remain out of sight.

It only took a couple of minutes for the wolf to do its business in the shadows beside the cabin, out of sight of the lodge. Then it waited patiently while Jace leaned over and scooped him up in his arms. "Don't get too used to this service, big guy."

The wolf turned his head and stared at Jace, almost as if he understood what Jace was talking about. "It's okay. You'll be able to run free before much longer, but for now, I guess you might as well enjoy the ride."

He was smiling when he carried the animal back inside and settled him on the bed of pillows. Romy waited near the kitchen, and neither she nor Jace said a word. The wolf whimpered and then sighed. And then, as if holding his head up took too much effort, he rested his muzzle on his front paws and closed his eyes. Romy quietly took away the empty food dish but left the water. She carried the bowl into the kitchen and set it in the sink, and then she walked toward the beds at the back of the room.

Jace frowned. What was she up to now?

Romy paused by the bed. "You've been saying how much you want me. I don't really know how I feel about you, though I know that I'm attracted. But I'm still afraid. I don't like being afraid. I've spent my entire life, ever since my mother died, afraid of what men can do to me. Last night, you showed me that it's not all horrible." She laughed, but it was a harsh sound and there was no humor in it. "Definitely not horrible." This time there was more warmth in her smile. "I'm not ready for two of you, but that's why Gabe left, isn't it?"

Jace stood. It took a lot to leave him absolutely speechless, but Romy's words had succeeded. She was right on all counts, so he wasn't going to disagree. Like dealing with the wild wolf, he showed her his submissive side. His hands hung loosely against his thighs and he smiled gently, looking as nonthreatening as he could. "You're right. It is part of the reason why Gabe left. But whatever happens between you and me? It's up to you, Romy. We don't have to do anything at all. Not now, not ever, unless you want to. It's your decision. It will always be up to you. I will never force you. Neither will Gabe. Whatever you want. Whenever. It's your call."

She stood so straight and proud, and she looked him in the eye without fear. This woman was the epitome of a Chanku bitch, a strong woman willing to fight her own demons. He could barely imagine what those demons were, but she'd been through hell from the time she was a little kid. She had witnessed her mother's murder. Been raped and abused by her father for two decades, and yet she stood here, tall and strong and proud.

He thought of the other women in the pack, so many of whom had survived terrible things and come out of a personal hell stronger and more determined than ever. It was an old saying and probably a cliché, but he couldn't help but think that the strongest steel was forged from the hottest fires.

Romy was the finest steel he'd ever seen. And he wanted her. Wanted her with a need unlike anything he'd known. Wanted to love her, to hold her, to protect her.

But not until she was ready. Not until she had good reason to trust him.

• • •

Romy sat in the middle of her bed, legs crossed, robe tucked close for modesty and her hands folded in her lap. Silently she watched as Jace merely stood beside the bed and smiled at her. She knew she looked calm and perfectly relaxed, but she'd slammed those windows to her thoughts down as tight as she could and locked them for extra insurance.

Calm on the outside, but inside she was shaking so hard it was all she could do to draw one breath after another. What would he do? Did he want sex with her now? She knew they were going to do it, but when he did, would he hurt her? He was a gentle man, so maybe it wouldn't be too bad, but how could she know for sure? She'd had a lot of sex, always with her father, a man who was supposed to love her and protect her, and it had always hurt. Had always made her feel horrible afterward. Like she was dirty. She didn't ever want to feel that way again, and even though Jace said it was her decision, when had she ever been able to trust a man?

Any man.

It seemed to take him forever to stop looking at her, to take the step that brought him even closer to the bed. Her body grew tense with each fraction of a second that passed, until she felt like a spring overly wound, as if she'd fly to pieces the minute he touched her. She braced herself, drew on everything she had not to come apart. He was a good man. He wouldn't hurt her. He'd promised.

Instead of sitting on Romy's bed, Jace turned to the one he shared with Gabe and sat there. Not on her bed, but on his and Gabe's. He just sat on the edge with his bare feet on the floor and his hands planted on the mattress on either side of his hips. He'd kicked off his sandals and his chest was bare, but he still wore his black knit pants. The beds were about four feet apart, but she was in the middle of hers and he was on the closest edge of his.

Even if she stretched her arms she couldn't reach him.

He couldn't reach her.

She let out a deep breath, one she hadn't realized she was holding. Jace smiled at her, and she actually smiled back.

"I bet you still have tons of questions," he said. "I've been thinking about everything you've gone through in just two days and a night, and it's hard to imagine what it must be like for you, starting out the day as a normal human, having some bastard try and kill you and then turning into a raging wolf and running away." He chuckled softly. "You're amazing, Romy. I think most people would be screaming in pure fear at so many changes, but you're handling all of it with so much style and grace. And bravery. You're really brave."

7

Style. Grace. Bravery. She'd never heard those words applied to her. Not once.

She must have been shaking her head in denial, because Jace said, very softly, "Hear me out, Romy. Let me tell you more about who you are. What you can be."

She raised her head and focused on Jace, on his beautiful amber eyes and gentle smile. He was always so direct, just as he was now. He met her gaze, still smiling, still as relaxed as if this was perfectly normal, for an unmarried man and woman to be sitting alone on a couple of beds, one dressed only in a skimpy cotton robe, the other bare-chested and so very male he made her mouth water and her breath quicken.

As relaxed as if it were perfectly okay.

And in his world, maybe it was.

Her world, now. She needed to stop thinking like a human woman. Like a victim. Somehow, she had to let go of her life in a repressive, murderous cult that was the only life she'd ever known. How was she going to learn? Could she leave that awful life behind and actually be what she was now, a shapeshifting Chanku, a female in a matriarchal society—a society where her voice might be heard, her desires known—when her entire life had been ruled by men?

How could she learn to be free after a lifetime in Reverend Ezekiel's prison? She glanced away from Jace, lowered her gaze and stared at her clenched fingers. Her knuckles were white from the nervous strength of her grasp. She consciously relaxed her fingers, still staring at them, so filled with questions she had no idea where to begin.

"Questions, Romy. Your mind has to be filled with them. I bet it's hard for you to ask, hard even to know what to ask, but if you'd lower your shields so I can tell what you're thinking, it would be easier for me. For you, too. C'mon."

His voice was wheedling now, urging her with smiles and laughter to lower the shields she'd only just learned to raise, but it was so hard. So hard to expose herself that way, even though she knew he was right.

"I know you have questions. Maybe I could answer them for you."

She raised her head, nodded, and, step by step, unlocked the latches and raised the windows in her mind.

Jace's grin had her smiling in return. "Good. That's better. I teach the history of our kind to the kids, so I should be able to answer anything you want to know."

"Why isn't my hair as curly as it was?" And wasn't that a stupid question to blurt out, but it seemed to represent a lot more than the way her hair curled. So much more.

"You would ask that one. Why did I expect that?" He laughed. "That's such a girly question."

"Well?" She raised one eyebrow. Everyone at the compound had always made fun of her eyebrows, as dark and arched as a raven's wing, but if Jace could laugh, she could relax, right? It couldn't be that hard. Shouldn't be.

Shaking his head, Jace shrugged those broad shoulders. "That's one we really don't know, and obviously it's not something that happens to those of us who are born Chanku with our bodies already capable of shifting at a very young age, but the older women in the pack, the ones who lived as humans before finally learning about their Chanku genetics, had the same questions. It seems to have something to do with the shift. Keisha Cheval, Gabe's mom, is African American, and before she shifted she often wore her hair in cornrows. She said it was nappy, whatever that means, but with each shift it grew smoother and straighter. We think it has something to do with our hair becoming more like that of the wolf. All of us have really thick, relatively straight hair, including the women who were born human and didn't turn until later in life. Daci Lupei, one of our packmates, is Romanian. Her hair was really curly with corkscrew curls that went everywhere just like yours, according to her guys. She still wears it long, but now it falls in perfect waves past her waist. When yours straightens out, I bet it's longer than Daci's."

He was grinning broadly, and it was impossible not to meet that smile with one of her own. Romy got the feeling he was speaking in the same cadence he used in the classroom, but she loved listening to him.

He stood, leaned toward her and reached for a long strand of her hair. He looked at it for a moment and then wrapped the curls around his fingers. "Your hair is absolutely gorgeous. I've always loved long hair on women, and a lot of our men wear theirs long as well, even when the human population styles are short. It's all a personal thing. We don't have any rules about how we're supposed to dress or what style works best for the pack. We're all the same species, but we're each different, with our own desires and wants. I like that. The fact we're free to be the people we're meant to be, not to have to conform to someone else's idea of what is right or wrong."

He shot her a sideways glance and laughed. "I'm rambling, aren't I?" Then he sat back on the edge of the bed across from her and folded his hands in his lap. After a second or two, he looked down at his lap and twisted his fingers together, took a deep breath and glanced her way again.

Is he nervous? He was! Jace was just as nervous as she was, him sitting here on his bed, Romy on hers, just the two of them. With Gabe around, the pressure was off, but now it felt as if something had to happen, as if there might be a schedule they had to adhere to, but that wasn't the way things were. There was no schedule. It was just Romy and Jace, learning to be friends.

Everything had been so intense—her near death and first shift, her escape and then Jace and Gabe finding her, healing her. Last night. Oh . . . last night. She knew her face must be fiery red, but she couldn't think about last night without her breasts tingling and pleasure pulsing rhythmically through her womb.

For whatever reason, Jace's long, somewhat convoluted answer made her relax like nothing else could. "I think," she said, still working her way through years of living in what was essentially a dysfunctional commune, "that this is what I need to be doing right now. Sitting here, talking to you, getting to know more about you and about my Chanku heritage. It still doesn't feel real, the fact I can shift, that I can speak to others with my mind and not my mouth. They say that knowledge is power, right? I want to know more."

"More? I can do that." And he did. Sitting there on the bed across from her, he told her how one man, Stefan Aragat, had been trapped in the middle of a shift when he had no idea he was a shapeshifter; how the love of one woman, Alexandria Olanet—and of Anton Cheval, a famous magician Stefan had blamed for his curse—not only taught him what love really was but helped resurrect the entire Chanku race from oblivion.

He told her about Gabe's sister, Lily Cheval, and her amazing trip as a little girl—a journey that took her onto the astral plane and into the world of the Chanku race's ancient ancestors. Men who had waited millennia for just such a child to appear, one with the intelligence and bravery to carry on the history of a people once on the verge of extinction.

He explained what they understood of the mechanics of shifting, how it actually occurs within another dimension, utilizing a time shift that affects only the individual and the immediate space and time they occupy. That it's gradual in that dimension, but time is folded back upon itself so that it's instantaneous for the shifter and those around him.

Romy knew it was going to take a long time for that to make any sense at all, but did it really matter that she understood it? Not really. Not as long as she could do it.

They talked about life before the world knew the Chanku existed, and the many changes in the years since—most of it good, some not. But as Jace told Romy about her heritage, so many things began to make sense. Jace, though, was the one to nail the most important fact, at least in Romy's mind.

"You said that sex with your father always felt wrong, that life in the commune felt wrong, even when you were a little girl. Do you have any idea why?"

Romy shook her head. "When I was a teenager, one of the women asked me if my father was finally leaving me alone. When I said I didn't know what she meant, she said they all knew he was having sex with me and wondered if it had finally stopped. It hadn't, and I told them that he said it was my duty, but I didn't think that could be possible, that even though our God was a vengeful god, I didn't understand any god creating subjects for the purpose of being hurt. The older I got and the more my body developed, the more things my father wanted me to do with him. And more often. One of the women asked me if I knew I was sinning, and I had to tell her that while I knew it couldn't be right, one of the things we women were taught was that the man of the house was always right, no matter his demands. And I said that Reverend Ezekiel knew it was happening and was still friends with my dad. Their questions convinced me that my feelings about what my life was like were correct. That what my father made me do was wrong. Only I blamed myself. It was my sin, not my father's. I thought that way for the longest time."

"What about the commune? The way it was run, the things you were taught?"

That was easy. "Everything always felt wrong to me, but I'd had my mother's diary, and she was not at all sympathetic to the reverend."

"I think it's something more." Jace got up and stepped across the short space between the beds. He shot her a quick grin as he sat down on the edge. Without commenting at all on his change in position, he said, "Chanku have an innate sense of honor, of integrity. Even though we live and play by our own rules and those rules are constantly evolving, our honor, our inner perception of right and wrong, never wavers. I think it was your Chanku sense of morality that wouldn't let you accept that kind of life."

"Then I was definitely the only Chanku in the group, because everyone else followed everything the reverend said. If they were told to shun a member, they did. If someone was to be beaten, they lined up and watched, but no one intervened. If a woman was told to service the young men, she went to them and her husband didn't say a word. Reverend Ezekiel said he was God's prophet, and his orders came from the Lord. I think he's a manipulative bastard, but when I tried to tell the other women that they should stand up for themselves, they took me to the reverend to be punished."

"Were you?"

"Always," she said, remembering the pain, the sense that it was worth it to try and convince the others that they were being used and manipulated.

"Why did they stay? What could possibly make the women remain in such a horrible place?"

She glanced down at their clasped hands and wondered how any man like Jace could possibly understand. He was strong. He not only had his family to lean on, he had an entire pack. A community that was the antithesis of the Glorious Salvation in Truth. "All of the women, my mother included, had been living on the streets. Some were prostitutes, all of them homeless. The more handsome of the young men go out into the cities and recruit them. They tell them they'll have plenty to eat and a place to sleep, a chance for a normal life with children and a husband. At first, they're treated like queens. It's like seduction. That's what my mother called it. By the time I was born, she was trapped—she had no idea how to escape with a baby.

"In her diary, she said that when I was about a year old, she discovered the grass growing inside the compound. It was pretty and she chewed on a stem while working in the fields. She thought it was some kind of mind-altering drug because it made her dream so vividly, and she figured at that point that if she couldn't physically escape, she could at least escape mentally. She began eating it, escaping in dreams of running as a wolf, of changing into a wolf and escaping, but she never could figure out if it was real or a hallucination."

"The dreams are pretty amazing, from what I've heard."

Romy glanced at Jace, sitting so close beside her, and nodded. "I had them. I've had them for years, but I guess Mom was giving me the grasses in my food. Enough to dream, but not enough to shift. We didn't know."

"We have pills with the components of the grasses at pack headquarters, though now that you've made the shift you won't need the nutrients as much. The grass grows around here. Gabe and I noticed it just outside the cabin, so if you feel a craving for it, it's available. Your body will tell you what it needs."

Romy stared at him, at the strong line of his jaw, the straight nose and brows so much darker than his sun-bleached hair, and realized she knew exactly what her body needed.

But she was still afraid. Afraid of somehow destroying this fragile bond she'd felt growing between them. Of failing Jace in some way. What did she know of normal relations between a man and a woman? Between shapeshifters, since it was obvious the Chanku had a totally different view of the sexual act. Jace had said that if she had any questions, he'd do his best to answer them. Except, she had to ask.

He shook his head and lifted her chin with a single finger. "No, you don't." He kissed her nose and chuckled softly. "Your shields are down, your windows unlatched and open."

When she blushed and tried to look away, he gently held her in place. "That's a good thing right now, Romy, because this is one I can answer. The only way we're different from humans is that we don't view the sex act as something to manipulate or punish. Sex is, for us, the most basic of human needs. Our bodies need it to maintain balance, because our libido is so strong, so much a defining force in our existence that it can overrule common sense. That's why a lot of women who are Chanku but don't know it end up in the sex-trade business. They love sex, they need it, but have no idea why it's such a powerful force. Men often use that to their advantage."

"I wonder if that's how my mother got sucked into the cult? Because her body needed sex? She wrote about going to the young men when they needed a woman, and she said it wasn't awful because it gave her some variety. By then she really hated my father. More than she loved me, I guess, because she was willing to leave without me."

Romy had never before said that. Never admitted it, but it had to be true. Her mother had hated her father more than she loved her daughter. She'd given her diary to Romy that morning and turned to leave. If she hadn't been shot, she probably wouldn't have come back.

"Or she might have been planning to get help and then come back for you, sweetie."

Jace nuzzled her hair. He moved closer, wrapped one arm around her and held her against him. She sighed, pressing her face against his warm chest and felt his heart beating. It was racing, thumping away almost as fast as hers. His skin was smooth, the muscles beneath hard as iron, yet he was so very much alive. She sighed and then slowly inhaled, breathing in his scent, absorbing the sense of him.

"I'll never know," she said. "I still miss her, no matter what she did. It had to have been hell, living with my father. He was a very cruel man. I think he enjoyed inflicting pain, and I often saw him hit my mother."

"Did he hit you?"

She nodded. There was no point in going over the ugly details. The way he'd hit her for any little transgression. The way he'd used sex to punish her. Of course that was the reason she was so convoluted about her body's sexual needs now—because of the way he'd conditioned her to behave. But the longer she let his lessons rule her life, the longer she allowed him to stay in charge. The man was dead. He couldn't hurt her anymore, but by denying herself what she wanted—and she truly wanted Jace—she was still letting her father control her life.

She sat back, far enough that she could look into Jace's eyes. "Were you listening?"

His grin was actually sheepish, and she thought that must be a difficult expression for a wolf. Except he was also a very handsome, extremely male, man.

"I was," he said. "And you're right. At some point, you'll make decisions based on your own needs and wants, not as a reaction to your father's horrible treatment. It's never going to be easy, but I love the way you work yourself through your questions, the way you weigh the reasons for your own behavior. Considering the fact you were raised in such a restrictive environment, I'm amazed that you have the insight into your problems and can tie them to your father's behavior. How do you do it? How do you see things with your own free spirit and not through the lessons you were raised with?"

"I don't know. It had to have been my mother's teaching. There were things we talked about that were never mentioned in front of my father. Politics and religion and the way the world worked. What other countries were like. She used to tease me and say I was an old soul, that I shouldn't understand what she was talking about, but I did. There was no real schooling for children in the compound. Girls are usually paired with a man by the time they're fourteen or fifteen. There's just no way out. Few of the escape attempts are successful. I wasn't married off because my father refused to give me up. Not until a new woman came to the compound and he was more interested in her than in me." She laughed. "I was too much trouble. I used to fight him. He tied me to the bed for sex when I got really bad. Sometimes he beat me first, other times when it was over, if I hadn't pleased him."

It really wasn't that big a deal. That was just the way she'd lived. She'd known it had to be wrong, but there was no way out, not when everyone she knew had accepted her father's behavior as his God-given right. But she really had fought him, and she was proud of that.

• • •

This was so damned hard. Every moment, listening to Romy, he had to struggle for control, and it wasn't an easy battle. The anger he felt, such a deep, visceral fury over the way she'd been treated, had him totally twisted inside. Her childhood—her entire life to date—had been horrible, her rescue a miracle. The fact he and Gabe had been the ones to find her must have been Eve's doing. No one else could have helped Romy. Very few among the Chanku would have been able to heal her. Now, with every word she spoke, his need for her grew.

As much as he wanted her, needed her, he knew she couldn't possibly be ready. Not yet, with so many issues clouding her mind. He glanced at her, and she was grinning at him. Smiling as if nothing at all was wrong. Then she laughed.

He frowned. "What?"

"Windows. Open." She leaned close and kissed him. "Jace, I'm seeing your thoughts. They're as clear to me as if you were speaking them aloud, but you're missing the important part. As long as I deny what my body and heart want—which is you—I'm letting my father run my life. He's dead. I killed him. You can't imagine the sense of power that gives me, the fact that I was stronger, faster, more capable, and because of that, he can't control me anymore. I want you, Jace. I want to know what sex between two normal adults is supposed to feel like. What my father did was perverted and wrong. I know that. I have always known that. You won't be anything like him. I know it here."

She pressed her hand over her heart. "I know it because I know you. In just the short time since we've met, I know you better than any man ever. And I want you to make love to me." She sighed. "Really, it will be my first time. No man has ever made love to me, not completely, though last night with you and Gabe came pretty close. You're the only ones who've ever made me feel."

He cupped her face in his hands and stared at her for a long moment. She was not a traditional beauty. Her eyebrows were heavy and dark, her eyes widely spaced with a unique quality that made it feel as if she looked into a man's soul. Maybe she did. Jace didn't know, but he could easily imagine a lifetime trying to figure her out. Her wide mouth and full, sensual lips fascinated him. He imagined kissing her, just losing himself in the contours of her mouth, the firm line of her lips, the curious sweep of her tongue. Her taste.

Goddess, how he wanted to taste her.

"Then do it." She covered his hands with hers and then ran her fingers along his arms to his shoulders. He felt her touch as if she stroked him inside—an electric current flowing from her fingertips into his bloodstream—and the sensation locked him into more sensation, into the rush of blood in his veins, the thunderous pounding of his beating heart.

The thunder—every bit as loud and as fast—of Romy's heart beating in time with his. Mesmerized by her touch, he closed his eyes and reached for more, for the inner sense of her. He had to know what she was seeing, feeling.

Wanting.

But he found more. A link as strong and true as any he'd ever established with Gabe. He saw himself through Romy's eyes, felt the sleek length of his arms beneath her fingertips, the texture of his hair when her fingers finally settled at the base of his skull where they tangled in thick strands curling around the back of his neck.

Her growing arousal spiked his. Jace pulled her close, pressed his lips to hers, tangled tongues with a woman whose hunger was every bit as voracious as his own. She moaned into his mouth and wrapped her arms around his shoulders, stroked his back with fingertips and nails until he had to have her, needed to touch her, to taste.

To know her in every way possible.

Her loose robe gaped wide, and he palmed her breast with his right hand, cupping the full weight, locking her turgid nipple between his thumb and forefinger. She gasped, then softly whimpered and shared the sensation, a streak of fire from nipple to clitoris, sharp and almost painful in its intensity.

Her fingers fluttered over his ribs, across his belly, and she slipped them shamelessly beneath the loose waistband, stroking his hips, cupping his buttocks and pulling him against her. They wore so little, and yet anything was too much. Jace shoved her robe off of her shoulders as Romy grabbed the waistband of his pants and tugged them down until they caught on his erection and stopped.

Laughing, he let go of her and slipped off the bed, dropped his pants on the floor, crawled across the mattress, and trapped her against the headboard. "I've got you," he said, leaning over her on hands and knees. She gazed up at him, lips parted, eyes wide and sparkling, and there was no fear. None at all.

Need. Want. Desire. But no fear. The robe was still tied at her waist, but her breasts were bare. Full and firm, the areolas a dark rose against her creamy skin. He caught one nipple between his teeth, gently worrying it until the scent of her arousal filled his nostrils and he knew she was growing wet, her body preparing for him. Panting, she reached for the tie at her waist, but Jace was there first, pulling the belt free and tugging the robe out from under her.

Naked, they paused. The sound of their thundering hearts—both Romy's and his—had become a steady drumbeat calling him. Jace's cock stood high and hard against his belly and his balls had drawn close up between his legs. He hovered on the edge of climax, yet Romy hadn't even touched him.

If she touched him, he'd be lost.

Instead, he kissed her again, and this time he drove his tongue deep, licking inside her mouth, behind her teeth, over her tongue. Tasting her, absorbing her flavors, her scents, the very textures that made her the woman he wanted.

He marked himself with anything he could take, or taste, or touch.

She came up for air, gasping, clutching his shoulders, staring at him wild-eyed with need, and he almost laughed. This was not the gentle lovemaking he'd envisioned. No, this was so much more, so primitive, entirely feral, and yet it suited Jace. Suited Romy as well.

She shoved him back and straddled his legs, and then she stared at him. At his erection arcing over his belly, at the thick white drops of fluid trailing across and down the smooth crown, collecting where his foreskin stretched tightly around his shaft. She reached out, one finger only, swept through the drops and smeared them over the tip.

Fascinated, he watched her. She acted as if she'd never seen a naked man before, but . . .

I haven't, not like this. Nothing beyond the quick glances I've gotten of you and Gabe, and you've been entirely too circumspect around me. She grinned at Jace's bark of laughter, but then she sighed. *I'm glad that not once in all the years he raped me did my father allow me to see him naked. I want no memories of him in my mind. I always thought this part of a man would be ugly, but you're not. You're beautiful.*

But you watched Gabe and me, last night, we . . .

She laughed, but it was a rough, choked-off sound filled with need. *It was dark and I couldn't see you that well. When you both came to my bed, I kept my eyes closed.*

"Why?" And then, still speaking aloud, he asked, "Were you afraid to look at us?"

"Truth?" Her eyes sparkled. "Gabe's massage felt so good I didn't want to open my eyes."

Jace snorted. "You realize that if I tell him that, I'll never hear the end of it."

Then don't tell him. She leaned close and ran her tongue over his leaking slit, and at the same time he connected with her thoughts, tasting himself as Romy tasted him. Feeling the heat and the way his cock felt against her tongue. Inhaling his musky male scent from Romy's perspective. Immersed in her sensations, he found more control than he might have otherwise. Seeing himself through Romy's eyes, sensing through touch and taste and smell gave him the distance he needed to force back the orgasm hovering within a mere touch, a flick of her tongue, the sweep of her fingers.

Scooting back, Romy spread his legs wide enough that she could nestle between them. Using her hands, she stroked his full length, curled her fingers around his testicles and scraped her nails gently across his perineum. More fluid leaked from the tip of his cock, totally beyond his control, but he held on.

Until Romy bent at the waist and, still cupping his balls in her left hand and circling his shaft with her right, wrapped her full lips around the tip of his penis and sucked. Jace clutched the bedding in both hands as she slowly but surely destroyed him. Her mouth was hot and wet, her lips firm yet so soft as they slid over the crown and down along the length of his shaft. He felt the curious tickle of her tongue as she explored the folds of his foreskin stretched tightly behind the broad head, as she licked around the surface of his shaft, and then back over the smooth crown, dipping into the small slit and tasting him.

Cursing softly, he tangled his fingers in Romy's hair and lifted her away. "This isn't the way I want our first time together to be. Not with you doing all the work. It's my turn."

She sat back and stared at him for a moment, and he tried to see but she'd closed her shields again and he had no idea what she was thinking. Obviously, she was a quick study, as far as shielding her thoughts.

"You don't understand." She glanced away and then looked at him so directly that he was certain she would never hide from anyone ever again. "Before I escaped, this was something my father wanted me to do and I refused because it disgusted me. But with you, I want to. It's like I crave your taste. I want to have your scent all over me. I've never felt this way about any man before. Not until you."

Jace brushed her hair back from her face and held it away so he could see her. All of her. The high forehead, the prominent cheekbones, the dark wings of her brows, and he knew.

This wasn't about making love or having sex or anything so simple. This was what love felt like. The soul-deep kind of love that led to forever. He'd heard his parents talk about it, the way it was so deeply rooted within a person that there was no describing it, no dislodging it. He'd never expected to find it for himself, especially here in this little sliver of

Chanku property in southern Oregon. Stunned, he stared at the woman kneeling over him. Thought of spending the rest of his life with her, and realized that, whatever questions he had, Romy was the answer. After a life filled with questions, she was the answer to all of them.

"Romy, I've never felt this way about anyone. Not ever. I want to make love to you. Today and for all the days to come."

Her eyes went wide. Smiling, Jace shook his head. Not cool, to scare her off in the very beginning. "But we'll just start with today and take it one day at a time. Is that okay? Are you ready to see where what we have can go? Will you let me make love to you?" Then he laughed, embarrassed when he admitted, "But if you keep doing what you're doing, I'm going to be totally out of commission, at least for a while."

She grinned, a big, wide smile verging on laughter. "Well, we certainly don't want that, do we?"

"No. Definitely not." He lay beside her, and this time, while the arousal was a deep, burning pleasure thrumming through his veins, Jace was in control. For now.

8

The trail of blood left by the wounded wolf was easier to follow than a Goddess-be-damned freeway. Gabe loped through tall grass and heavy forest, his nostrils filled with the coppery tang of blood and the stench of desperation. The poor beast had covered a lot of ground with an arrow in his lung. He was lucky he hadn't bled out. Too lucky.

Gabe had to wonder if the Goddess Eve had once again involved herself in their current drama. Had she ensured that he and Jace were the ones to find the wolf? Was the animal's attack and injury a warning to them to watch closely for those who might be after Romy?

He'd gone almost four miles before the smell of blood was overlaid with the acrid stench of shock and fear. The shooting had to have happened nearby. He paused and sniffed the air, narrowed down the place where the wolf had been shot.

The grass was trampled, as if the animal had spun around, trying to bite at the arrow. Dark blood spattered the beaten grass and the trunk of a tree. Gabe looked up, his eyes drawn to another arrow buried in the wood. It was too high for his wolf to reach, but he shifted and stretched and the man was able to grab it and pull it free.

It carried the same mark. Proof that men from the Glorious Salvation in Truth had no qualms about hunting Chanku. They'd seen Romy's shift, knew they hunted a sentient creature, and they hadn't cared. They'd shot a wild wolf by mistake. A wolf that could have been Romy or any one of them but had, instead, been a truly innocent creature of the wild.

Gabe stuffed the arrow in his pack with the fletched end sticking out the top. It was too long to go entirely into the bag, but he wanted to show it to Jace. Shifting once again, he sniffed the ground around the tree and then raised his nose to the gentle breeze. No scent of humans.

He began circling the area, going farther with each successive loop, searching for the site where the shooter had waited. It took him five turns before he found the place, a rocky outcropping that would have given a man a panoramic view of this area of the forest and a nearby meadow.

They were slobs, that much he could tell. Paper wrappings and a couple of beer cans. For a religious order, they didn't appear to adhere too closely to commonly held tenets of good behavior. He recognized the scent of at least one man—one who had been with the group hunting Romy near the river yesterday.

This place was only a couple of hundred yards from the river. Within reason if that was the corridor they thought she'd been using for her escape. Nose to the ground, Gabe followed their trail for another hundred or so yards to a service road that followed a power line. They'd come in that way, probably in a four-wheel drive. The road wasn't well-maintained but was still passable. Obviously, as tire tracks in the dust were fresh.

He thought about trying to contact Jace. It was a stretch, but they'd been pushing the distance they could connect telepathically, and their best so far had been a little over five miles. He hadn't gone farther than that. At least he didn't think he had.

His wolf loved to run. Sometimes, when he'd covered ground on four legs, he underestimated the distance. A lot. He'd been gone about four hours now, what with the exploring he'd done around the lodge and the trail he'd followed, but the way Jace and Romy had been dicking around about their feelings for each other, if he tried to connect now he'd probably interrupt Jace right around the time he was finally working up the nerve to make a move on Romy.

That certainly wouldn't earn Gabe any points with his packmate. He decided not to check in. At least not now. Instead, he followed the tire tracks about half a mile until he came to a paved road. Luck was with him. They'd gone through a small creek just before leaving the dirt, and muddy tracks showed them heading west, toward the lodge.

He stood there a moment, sniffing the air and staring at the road. Something didn't feel right, and whatever it was had the stiff hairs along his spine standing on end.

He didn't hear the arrow until it *thunked* into a tree trunk not six inches above his back. Just above it was a large *No Hunting* sign. So much for following the law.

Gabe didn't wait to see exactly where the shooter was, but he got a good enough glimpse of the shaft to spot the symbol. It appeared the Glorious Salvation in Truth was more of a hunting club than he'd realized. He whirled away and raced into the heavy undergrowth as a second arrow whistled by, close enough for him to feel its passing.

He crouched low after quickly circling back and hiding behind a fallen tree about eight feet from the spot where he'd been targeted. Lying low near the tangle of exposed roots, he waited. In less than a minute, he heard the heavy tread of boots and watched as four men crossed the main road. Two of them held heavy compound bows, but only one had an arrow nocked. He held the bow at the ready, his eyes carefully scanning the surrounding forest.

Gabe lay quietly, alert yet confident he was well hidden.

He couldn't tell if the other two men were armed or not—if they had firearms, the guns were small enough to conceal, but the four of them talked quietly, searching the area for the body they obviously expected to find.

After about ten minutes, the big guy with the compound bow shook his head and released the arrow from the firing position. "I was sure I hit him with the second shot. I had the bastard in my sights."

"Him?" The smaller man, one not carrying a bow, turned. Gabe got a whiff of his scent and recognized him as another of the guys who'd been hunting Romy yesterday. "Did you shoot at another male?"

"Yeah. It was a fuckin' wolf. A big male. Of course I shot at it."

The other man shook his head in disgust. "You really are an idiot. I told you when you hit that male yesterday, we're hunting a female. A large black female wolf."

"A wolf's a wolf. I . . ."

"And if someone finds it with one of our arrows sticking out of its dead body, who catches the flack?"

"I coulda tracked it."

"We didn't have the time! Don't you get it? We have to get that wolf, and we have to do it as cleanly and as quietly as—"

"Here it is!"

The other three turned at the shout. The big guy yelled, "You find the wolf?"

"No, you idiot. I found your arrows. One in a tree and one on the ground next to it." He laughed. "Good shot, though. You just about nailed a *No Hunting* sign."

The one with the bow stomped across the small area and grabbed the arrows out of his companion's hand. "Give me those." Gabe watched as he carefully inspected each of the arrows for damage before slipping them back into a quiver attached to the bow.

The smaller guy was shaking his head. "Let's get out of here. Remember what I said. We're not hunting all the wolves. We're hunting one rogue wolf. It's a killer. And it's female. The last thing we need is federal rangers all over our case because you're shooting protected animals. There's no hunting allowed anywhere around here, so our argument's thin enough as it is if we're stopped."

The man was still talking, but they'd moved out of range of Gabe's hearing. He recognized two of the men, but not the ones carrying the bows. They were headed west, toward the lodge. He turned and raced through the woods, back to Romy and Jace.

· · ·

Romy wished she could stop trembling. She wasn't afraid of Jace, wasn't afraid of doing anything with him at all, but tell that to her body. Jace lay on the bed beside her, propped up on one elbow with his long legs stretched out beside her and his erection trapped against her thigh. She was hyperaware of the thickness and length of him, the warmth of his shaft and the blunt tip pressing into her leg, all of it hidden, as if he wanted to keep himself out of her reach. Still, he kept twining her hair around his fingers, and he looked at her. That was it—he merely watched her. It felt to Romy as if he could see inside her, as if he touched her with a gaze as smooth as silk, as hot as fire.

He'd said he wasn't going to rush her, and he hadn't.

She wished he would. She wanted him to take the decision out of her hands and just shove his erect penis in her. Once he did that, she was positive she'd be fine. She knew what that felt like and she'd been dealing with it for years, but this time she wasn't going to go away in her head, not the way she always had with her father. Her body was hungry—that was the only way she could describe this feeling, this *wanting* that seemed to grow stronger by the second. If he put it in her, the hunger would go away. She was positive.

She wanted Jace to make love to her, and she wanted not to be afraid, but how? It seemed that twenty years of conditioning wasn't all that easy to undo. She'd been trying. Goddess, how she'd tried. She wondered if Eve might think this was important enough to help her get past what had to be unreasonable fears.

Well, maybe not so unreasonable. Though she'd never really seen her father naked, she was positive his erection wasn't anywhere near the size of Jace's. Would that thing really fit?

"Are you through now?"

"What?" She jerked her head around. Almost bumped noses with Jace, and his eyes were only inches from hers. "Through doing what?"

"Through trying to talk yourself into having sex? Just for your information, we don't need to start with me shoving anything inside you."

"Oh. Oh, damn. I'm sorry, Jace. It sounds so awful when you say it like that, but that's exactly what I was thinking, isn't it?" She glanced away and sighed. "I'm trying not to be afraid. Honest, I am, but . . ." She shook her head. He must think she was an absolute idiot. "Windows are open again, huh?"

He smiled and she felt like a fool. Her shields went up immediately.

"Don't. Please?" Jace touched her cheek with his fingertips. "I want to know what you're thinking. Then I can adjust, make this good for you. I think that once we make love, which, believe me, is not what your father did to you, you're going to understand just how wonderful it can be. Give me a chance, okay?"

She nodded. What other option did she have? She was going to get past this. Put her past in the past. She was no longer Romy Sarika, victim, and she refused to be a victim ever again. She was Romy Sarika, Chanku shapeshifter, and she fully intended to embrace this new life. A life that was, quite literally, a gift from her mother.

And Jace was the key.

"Sarika, eh? I didn't know your last name."

"It was my mother's name. She and my father never married, so she gave me her name."

"I like it. It fits you." His gaze rested on her for a long, slow moment. Then he said, "I'm going to touch you. Just one finger, a simple touch. Okay?"

She nodded, realized she was holding her breath, and let it out.

His fingertip circled the nipple on her left breast. Just his fingertip, but she felt it between her legs. She sucked her breath back in and closed her eyes. It was too much sensation, but so much easier when she wasn't looking at him. She arched her back, pressed her breast closer.

Jace chuckled. "Okay, but I want you to watch. I want to know you're with me, and if I do anything, anything at all that makes you uncomfortable, I want you to tell me. Got it?"

She nodded. Opened her eyes. He was still right there. Watching her.

He licked his finger and touched the tip of her nipple. Air brushed over the dampness and made her nipple pucker even tighter. Fascinated, she watched him repeat with her other nipple, but when he lowered his head and ran his tongue over that same tip, she moaned.

Sucking lightly, he gently worried the peak between his teeth and then released her, wrapped his lips around the entire areola, licking circles around her nipple. That whimper had to be hers, but Romy didn't remember making the sound. First one breast, then the other, back and forth with

79

tiny licks and nips and then full-mouthed suction, and she felt everything between her legs. One hand rested on her belly and she wanted him to touch her down there where all of her nerves seemed to be firing at once, but he didn't move his hand.

Back and forth, one breast and then the other. She was biting back screams of frustration, but he kept up the same slow assault on her senses, dismantling her inhibitions one lick at a time. And always looking into her eyes. Watching her, measuring her reactions, she was sure.

With just the slightest of moves, he kissed her belly, trailing his lips and tongue over the smooth skin between her navel and her pubes. Her nipples reacted to cool air across damp tips, but her skin rippled beneath his mouth, shivering with sensations she'd never experienced.

He parted her knees with his right hand and knelt between her legs. Instead of touching her, though, he wrapped his fist around the base of his huge erection and stroked up, then down. She watched, mesmerized.

"I call it my cock. Sounds much friendlier than penis, don't you think?" He grinned when she nodded. Who was she to disagree? He wanted to call it whatever, she was fine with that. What she really wanted was to touch it again. To taste him, to explore all those male parts she was just beginning to know.

She sat up, scooted back against the headboard and watched him. He knelt between her widespread legs, stroking his full length, and she wanted to taste him so badly her mouth actually watered. She licked her lips, gnawed on the lower one, and stared at his big hand moving so slowly up, then down. Then up again.

He cupped his testicles in his left hand, moving in a steady rhythm with practiced ease, and she knew this was something he did without any sense of guilt. It was just a part of who he was, this absolute comfort with his own body.

She wanted that same comfort with hers. She raised her chin and realized he was watching her, concentrating on her lower lip and the way she worried it with her teeth. For some reason he seemed fascinated by her mouth, and she wondered what he was thinking. And then she realized how easy it would be to know.

She'd left her own shields down, but she hadn't been listening to Jace's thoughts. Now she reached for him and caught an entire medley of curses as he fought to control his rising arousal. And she'd been right—he was focused on her mouth, but that was because he remembered how it had felt when she licked him, when she'd wrapped her lips around his cock, sucking and licking.

She swept her tongue around her lips, first the top and then the bottom one, and felt Jace's arousal spike. Shifting her legs around, she rose up on her knees, mimicking his stance. She ran her hand over her belly, teased the thick curls covering her mound and then swept both hands up her sides to pinch her own nipples.

Jace's eyes narrowed. A thick bubble of white fluid appeared once more at that small slit on his glans. Romy focused on that, watched it grow into a thick smear running over the tip, one he caught up in the palm of his hand. His eyes were focused on her—on her breasts, on the dark hair between her legs, and she realized his arousal was growing not so much from the way he stroked himself but from the things Romy was doing.

Pinching her right nipple with her left hand, she dragged the fingers of her right hand back along her belly until she reached her pubic hair, but this time she sat back on her heels, spreading her knees wide.

And then she did what had always been forbidden.

She touched herself. Slipping her fingers between her labia, Romy stroked the fluid gathering there. She used it to slide her fingertips over her clitoris, her entire body now hypersensitive to Jace's hot gaze. His hands went still. He clutched himself, one hand wrapped around his cock, the other holding his balls, but his entire focus was on Romy as she slowly stroked herself, pinching her nipple, sliding her fingers over her clitoris while Jace practically quivered, so close and yet not nearly close enough.

He stared at her, his look growing more intense by the moment. Finally, his voice hoarse and his breath coming in short gasps, he said, "I tried, Romy. Honest. I really tried to let you take the lead, but you're cheating." And then he was on her, wrapping his arms around her, pulling her tightly against him. His mouth found hers, slipped to her jaw, her shoulder, her throat. He lay back and pulled Romy on top of him, and there was no fear in her. Only need. Arousal sharp as a spear driving her as she knelt over him, spreading her knees to either side of his thighs, reaching for his long, thick cock and brushing it through the moisture between her legs.

It was so simple, really, to take him inside, to slowly lower herself over the thick, hot length of him, taking him in slow, steady increments. She'd never realized a woman could do this from the top, but she loved the sense of control he gave her. She couldn't move any faster—he was huge compared to her father, and then she stopped that thought. She was never going to think of that man again. He was dead. Dead to her, dead to the world, and the only man she wanted in her mind and her heart was slowly, carefully filling the most intimate part of her body. Her inner muscles flexed and contracted around his heavy shaft, stretching to the point of pain but not beyond, and it was Jace closing his eyes, Jace whose lips stretched tightly across his teeth in a grimace of what might have been pain but Romy knew was arousal.

She opened her thoughts wide, searched for him, found him in her mind, his mental voice once again a soft litany of curses as she slowly took him deeper—as deep as she could. At the same moment her labia kissed his groin, the broad head of his cock rocked lightly against the mouth of her womb. All of her internal muscles clenched.

His mental cursing became a shout.

Grinning, she wriggled her hips just enough to settle him fully inside, and then she paused, not moving at all.

He blinked and stared up at her. His big hands clasped her thighs and he took a few deep breaths. After a moment he returned her smile. "So," he said. "Now that you've got me, what do you intend to do with me?"

She arched one eyebrow. "Whatever I want. I have you at my mercy, Jace Wolf. And I think I like this."

"Oh, Goddess, Romy. I love it." He panted a couple of harsh breaths. "But if you don't start moving, I'm going to."

She laughed, and it was a sound that set her free. She'd never in her life imagined laughing during sex, but this was Jace. This was what she wanted as much as he did, and she rose, slowly slipping away from him and then going back down at the same pace, up and down, slow and steady, but it wasn't enough. Not nearly enough. Leaning forward, she planted her hands on his shoulders and began rising and falling, faster and faster, angling her body so that the upper ridge of his cock hit her clitoris whether she was going up or down.

The soft sucking sound of his cock slipping from her sheath sent shivers along her spine. The scent of arousal, both Jace's and hers, drove her higher. She'd never imagined the many faces of physical desire, the way sensations on so many levels seemed to twist and grow, to come together and expand, filling her heart, her body, her very soul with so many feelings, so many impressions. Filling her with Jace.

She was so close, so very close when Jace reached up with both hands and pinched her nipples. The sharp bite of pain, the hard thrust of his hips and the feral cry that burst from his mouth sent her flying. He grabbed her hips, holding her against him as he rolled her over to her back. He took over, thrusting deep and hard inside her, prolonging her climax, taking her up again and over the top, and then once again until she was sobbing, her body shuddering with the strength of her release, with the sense of Jace in her mind and his warmth and love filling her heart.

• • •

Jace lay beside Romy, trembling like a leaf. He'd never felt anything like this before, never experienced sex on more levels than the mere pleasure of the act itself, the release of tension, the physical joining with good friends, with packmates. There was no way to describe what had just happened, no way to explain the way he felt right now, as if something missing all his life had suddenly been found, as if he'd finally met his other half, without ever having realized that half was missing.

As if all the parts of his life had suddenly clicked into place. Solid. Whole. Complete.

He turned and caught her staring at him, her dark eyes wide, lips parted in what could only be wonder. "You, too?"

She smiled, but her eyes sparkled with unshed tears. "I had no idea."

"Me, either." He leaned close and kissed her and felt his cock beginning to rise. She held her arms out and he rolled over, settling himself atop her with her thighs beneath his, their groins and bellies touching. He supported his weight on his elbows and stared into those dark amber eyes and saw answers where before there had been only questions.

He was hard again, so quickly ready that he wasn't certain if Romy was.

"I am. Make love to me again, Jace. This time I want to watch you. I want to see you."

She welcomed him once again, taking him easily inside this time. He thrust slowly, gently, and she lifted her hips to him, clutching his shoulders with her strong hands, never taking her eyes from his. And when they both flew, once again they were together, and somehow Jace knew he'd find a way to claim this woman. Claim her as his mate for all time.

• • •

Romy had just stepped out of the shower when Jace handed her a towel and grinned. He already had his black pants on and a cold beer in his hand. "Gabe should be here in about five minutes. I've taken the wolf out and he's back on his mat sleeping. He's recovering really well and we should be able to set him free tomorrow. I'll meet you on the deck." He leaned close and kissed her so thoroughly, she was ready to take him back to bed, but then he ended the kiss and said, "We should look as calm and relaxed as possible, or Gabe's going to tease the hell out of us."

She kissed him and loved the surprise on his face, that she'd instigated this one. Almost as much as she loved his taste, the way his lips felt against hers. "I don't care. He can tease all he wants. I'm tough. I can take it."

"Goddess, I sure hope so." He cupped her face in his palms, kissed her again and then pulled back. "I need to go. Now. Or Gabe's going to catch us doing more than merely looking like we've had an afternoon of sex. He'll catch us in the middle of it." With a sexy grin that promised more of what they'd been doing all day, Jace left her to dry off.

It took her a moment to get her bearings. She'd never imagined the kinds of sensations Jace could provoke with nothing more than a kiss. Sighing, she took one look at her tangled hair and shifted. When she shifted back a moment later her curls were looser, her hair and body completely dry. She fluffed it with one hand. And yes, she figured she could get used to this shifting stuff really easily.

There was nothing to put on but that short little robe, so she wrapped it around herself and met Jace on the front deck. He'd poured a glass of white wine for her and had a cold beer waiting for Gabe.

A minute later, Gabe walked out of the woods and crossed the small meadow to the cabin. He wasn't smiling. The first thing he did was set another arrow on the table, an exact duplicate of the first one they'd taken from the injured wolf. Then he took the beer Jace handed him, popped the lid and took a long swallow.

Jace picked up the arrow. "Where'd this come from?"

Gabe set his beer down. "I found it about four miles east of here. Where the wolf was shot."

"Okay," Jace said. "So why are you so pissed off? What else did you find?"

"The ones who shot him."

Jace paused with the beer halfway to his lips. "How do you know they're the same idiots?"

"Because they almost shot me. Missed by a couple of inches. I left that arrow in the tree and the one that lifted the fur on my back lying in the dirt. It seemed like the better part of valor to get the hell out of their line of sight."

"Crap, Gabe. I didn't think you were going to do anything stupid! What were you . . ."

"Not on purpose, believe me. But I got a good look at all of them." Gabe took a deep breath, then told them how he'd first followed the wolf's blood trail, and then the tracks of the hunters' vehicle. "I was just looking them over when an arrow missed me by a couple of inches and skewered a tree trunk just above my back. Same emblem. Second arrow parted the fur on my back. I took off, and then circled back and waited."

"Shit."

"They don't seem to care that there are *No Hunting* signs posted all over the place. In fact, the first arrow hit a few inches below a big sign. I wanted to get a good look at them. There were four guys—two big bruisers with compound bows, two smaller guys. One of them appeared to be in charge, and he was pissed that the shooter had aimed at a male wolf. Said they were hunting a rogue female."

Jace glanced at Romy. "That would be you."

She nodded. The members from the compound were getting much too close.

"We need to get the ranger again. This is proof, and you're an eye witness. Hell, you could have been a body."

Gabe let out a long sigh. "I agree. I'll call John. I can positively ID the shooter in a lineup, and visual and scent testimony by any known Chanku stands up in court."

"There are a couple of guys I recall. Big and not too bright." Romy was trying to remember which members of the cult were the best bowmen, but the one she'd kicked between the legs was a little guy. He might have been one of the other two men Gabe saw. If anyone, she imagined he was probably holding a grudge.

"We definitely need to get the ranger involved." Jace reached over for Romy's hand and held on tightly. "We've got to stop them."

Gabe leaned back in his chair, a move that Romy thought might let him see the rest of the resort. She knew she was right when he glanced toward the lodge, held a finger to his lips and tapped Romy's knee with his other hand, grabbing her attention. *Romy? Go inside. Quickly. Stay away from the windows.*

She didn't question him. Instead, she slipped through the open door and quietly shut it behind her. Only then did she ask, *What do you sense?*

The four guys I was talking about. They're in an open Jeep that just pulled up in front of the lodge. They're the same ones who shot the wolf and tried to shoot me.

Is the Jeep dark green with an emblem on the door? The same stylized cross with what looks like a slash of sunlight through it that's on the arrows?

Yep. That's it. The same four guys. They're all decked out like hunters, even though they're from a rigidly controlled religious cult, and even though there's no hunting allowed anywhere near here. Not on Chanku land, and Stefan Aragat owns a lot of it around here. Nice of them to come here and make it easy on us. Jace? Any reason you might have to go to the lodge? See why they're here, if they actually know Romy's in the area or if it's just our luck this is the only place to stay in either direction for fifty miles.

Jace laughed. *I dunno, Gabe. Considering we happened to find Romy and just happened to rescue a wounded wolf, I'd say our luck's running pretty good right now. Romy, you can't see him, but dear Gabe just flipped me off. Okay, okay! I'm going.* She heard his loud bark of laughter from her spot inside the cabin and couldn't imagine what else Gabe had done that was so funny, but she grinned anyway. They really were funny together.

Then Jace said, *Stay out of sight, Romy. Gabe, they saw you yesterday, though I doubt they'd put you and the wolf they saw today together. But please, both of you, be careful.*

You, too, Jace. They're dangerous men. Romy moved to the back of the cabin, away from the windows, and sat beside the sleeping wolf. He didn't wake, but Jace was right, he was looking healthier already, and though he was a wild animal, he was intelligent enough to recognize they meant him no harm. Sitting close, she gently stroked the thick fur over his shoulders. Touching him calmed her.

Then Gabe's voice slipped into her mind.

Jace is almost at the lodge now. I think I told you that when I registered, I had the manager check with Stefan Aragat, the one who owns this place. I had Stef clear us to use his personal cabin, because I wanted the manager to know we're Chanku, here on pack business. He knows not to say anything to those men.

Is Jace listening to us now?

I doubt it. He's heading toward the hunters. I'm calling the ranger now, Romy. We'll have help here in a very short time.

Romy stayed next to the wolf on the floor with her knees tucked under her chin. She wanted to run, wanted to get as far away as fast as she could, but she knew that was fear talking.

She had two strong men willing and more than able to protect her. For the first time in her life there was no reason to fear anything. Whatever happened, Jace and Gabe would keep her safe.

9

Jace headed toward the hunters, striding along as confidently as if he had business with them. Which he did. No way in hell were any of these jackasses going to harm a hair on Romy's head, and they already owed for the wolf. Not to mention the shots they'd taken at Gabe, proof they were out for blood.

Two of the men had gotten out of the Jeep and had already gone inside, but the other two waited at the vehicle. He wondered which one had shot the wolf, which of them had fired on Gabe. He knew that all of them were hunting Romy.

He focused on the big guy waiting by the Jeep and shared the image with Gabe.

That's him. That's the bastard who said he shot the wolf yesterday. The same guy who took a couple of shots at me today.

Good to know.

As he got closer, Jace got a better look at the driver, a fairly nondescript but big guy, slouched behind the wheel. The second man, the larger of the two and the one Gabe said was guilty of the shootings, leaned against the front bumper. He wore a faded green sweatshirt with the sleeves ripped out, and with his thickly muscled arms folded across his chest he looked more like he should be in an ultimate fighting ring than hanging out at a mountain resort. His ball cap was pulled low over his eyes, but Jace had a feeling the guy wasn't missing a thing.

Jace walked past the Jeep and focused on the two heavy compound hunting bows lashed to the inside of the roll bar that arced over the backseats. Each had a quiver stocked with five or six hunting arrows, each arrow shaft marked with the now familiar insignia.

Jace paused to admire the obviously expensive equipment. "Beautiful stuff," he said. "That's a hybrid cam, right?"

The one leaning against the bumper shoved himself upright and walked around to the back of the Jeep, opposite Jace. "Yeah," he said. "You hunt?"

Jace shook his head. "Not for a long time. This stuff has really improved. What kind of speed can you get with one like this?" He pointed at the bow closest to him, a beautifully built thing that probably cost more than the vehicle it was hanging on.

"Arrows clock in around three hundred and seventy-five feet per second." The man folded his arms over his chest.

Jace raised his eyebrows. "That's over two hundred and fifty miles per hour. Damn."

The guy grinned, showing even, white teeth. "Two hundred and fifty-five point six eight two miles per hour," he drawled.

"You must be hunting bear, then, you need power like that."

"We could. But we're after a wolf."

Jace merely stared at him. "Wolf? Aren't they protected?"

"Not this one. It's a rogue. Killed a guy. Ripped his throat out. Tore up another guy pretty bad. Not sure if he's gonna make it."

"Wow. Hadn't heard about that. Has the animal been sighted?"

The man nodded. "We found a fresh kill. Antelope back up the river. Tracked the wolf, but we lost it a couple miles from here." This time he shook his head. "Can't be too far. We know it's wounded. Shouldn't be too hard to spot. Unusual color for a wolf. Black all over, and big. Real big."

"You think it's dangerous then, eh?" Jace did his best to look concerned. "I'm part of a scientific survey, spending a lot of time in the woods. Good to know there could be a dangerous animal out there. That's the last thing I want to run across."

"You're not kidding. We already know it's a killer. If by chance you see it, let us know, okay? We're hoping to stay here for a couple days, at least until we're sure it's not around. Or we get it."

Jace folded his arms across his chest and stared at the guy, long enough to make the other man uncomfortable. "You know there's no hunting here, no matter the circumstances. A good fifteen square miles is posted and protected. Do you have a depredation permit?"

The big guy straightened and planted one meaty fist on his hip. "It's a killer. And when did this become a no hunting zone? I've hunted here for years."

"Not recently, I imagine. At least not legally. It changed when Aragat Enterprises, a subsidiary of Chanku Global Industries, purchased the resort. That was about six years ago."

"You're shittin' me!" The guy turned to his buddy in the Jeep. "Hey, Bud, did you know the goddamned shapeshifters own this place? No huntin' here."

They both laughed. "Well, I don't think that's gonna be a problem," Bud said. "Hard to stop a man with a compound bow."

Jace shrugged. "Just thought you might want to know." Then he went up the steps and into the lobby, passing the other two men as they left. Whatever had happened, they didn't look happy. Once inside, he nodded to the manager and the man waved him inside a private office.

Jace closed the door. "I'm Jace Wolf, the second guy in Stef Aragat's cabin, staying with Gabe Cheval. Gabe told you about the wolf survey we're doing, right?" When the manager nodded, Jace added, "You didn't tell those two there's Chanku staying here, did you?"

"I figured you might be with Gabe. No, sir. In fact, I was going to walk down to your cabin in a bit and let you know they're here hunting some rogue wolf. I told them there's no hunting, and I didn't rent them a cabin because we're full. This is a fishing lodge, not for hunters, but I got the feeling they don't care. I was planning to call Mr. Aragat, but I wanted to be sure and warn you that if you or your partner shift, be careful. I'd hate to have to tell the boss I let a couple of his packmates get shot."

"Not nearly as much as I would." Jace shook his hand. "Thanks. We're aware of these guys and have notified the local ranger. Hopefully he'll take care of the problem."

"Good to know. John Salazar?" When Jace nodded, he added, "He's a good man. Doesn't take crap off anyone. I'll back off calling the owner then. I'd rather not bother him if you're handling it. Be safe."

• • •

"So that's the deal." Jace had grabbed one of the comfortable chairs in the main room but he'd pulled the window shades, which left the room in shadows. "We sit tight until Salazar shows up."

Gabe nodded. "Works for me. He's over in Grants Pass for a meeting, said he'd be here by six. He's picking up some take-out for us, so we'll get something to eat and figure out how we're going to nail these guys. No shifting until this is dealt with, or at least until he's here. Even though this entire area is clearly marked no hunting, none of us will be safe shifting as long as they're here."

"I can't go out in my human form, either," Romy said. She glanced first at Gabe, but her gaze rested on Jace. "Anyone from the compound would recognize me. I could end up in jail. Remember, I killed a man, maybe two if Ezekiel dies. I really hoped he was already dead."

"Self-defense, Romy. You really don't need to worry about it, even if the law does get involved. If it comes to that, we'll have our pack alpha and the Chanku legal team behind us. Remember, we have graphic, time-stamped photos of your injuries, both as a wolf and as a woman." He took a deep breath, let it out. "I'm sorry the reverend isn't dead. Like I told you, according to those two he's badly injured but expected to live."

The corner of her mouth twitched, almost as if she wanted to smile. "You can't say I didn't try."

"Oh, Romy. Damn." He gazed into those beautiful amber eyes and knew he'd already lost himself forever. It took him a moment to break away from her steady regard. Even then it was almost painful, as if he had to physically wrench himself free. "You did that, sweetheart. The main thing is, you're alive. And c'mon . . . staying inside for a couple more days isn't that bad, is it?" Her shields were up, but he wondered if she was thinking how they'd spent the better part of today. He couldn't stop thinking about it. "I really don't want you running anyway, Romy. I'm worried about you reinjuring your back."

"I'm worried about the local wolves, too." Gabe shrugged. "This pack has been well-documented, and it's pretty stable, but there's danger to them with these idiots running loose, armed and ready to kill something." He nodded at the wolf lying in the corner. "I want this guy to have a pack to return to when this is all over."

Jace stared at Gabe a moment. Gabe was right. And damn it all, but he hated being trapped inside, even with Romy to keep them company. He'd never been comfortable with inaction.

• • •

Salazar joined them at the kitchen table for hamburgers and French fries. This time, the guys didn't try to hide her existence from the ranger. They'd given him her story in a nutshell, and while Romy was sure he had a million questions, he'd accepted her without question and made sure she had plenty to eat.

Romy had never eaten what they called "fast food." She loved it. "I could get used to this," she said, dipping a fry in a bowl of catsup and popping it into her mouth. "I had no idea this kind of food existed."

"So you've spent your entire life in that compound east of here?" Salazar shook his head. "I've heard some strange stories about that place. Is the leader as nuts as they say?"

Romy chewed her French fry and glanced at Jace. He nodded, smiling gently at her. *Only tell him what you're comfortable with.*

If I don't tell him the truth, other young women will have to go through what I did.

It's up to you, Romy. This is your story.

"He's worse," she said. She dipped another French fry in catsup, stirring it around, but now all she could think of was blood. "My father began forcing sex on me when I was six years old, with full approval of Reverend Ezekiel. All the members of the compound knew what was going on but no one stopped him. It was accepted because he said it was God's will. Whatever the reverend says supposedly comes directly from God." She raised her head and stared at the ranger, daring him, but she wasn't quite sure why. "I figured a long time ago that his god must really hate little girls."

"Good Lord. Six?" Salazar stared at Romy, not with the condemnation she'd expected but with so much sympathy she was afraid she'd cry.

She nodded. "The night after my mother died. She was Chanku but she didn't know it for a long time. It explains why she was drawn to certain grasses growing around the compound. One day when my father was beating her, she shifted. I don't believe she'd ever done it before, but she turned into a huge wolf and lunged for him. He ran away, screaming. She knew they'd kill her, and she tried to escape but the reverend shot her. She turned back into Mama when she died, and they threw her body in the garbage pit. A friend of hers and I dragged her out and buried her, but later that night my father said I had to take her place in his bed. And yes, I was six. That happened twenty years ago."

Salazar set his hamburger down and looked at it a moment, as if he'd lost his appetite. He carefully wiped his face with his napkin. "How did you escape? Come to be with these two boys?"

She smiled and glanced at Jace and Gabe. "Boys? Awfully big for boys, aren't they?"

Salazar smiled at her. "I've got a son older than Gabe. They went to Oregon State together." Chuckling, he said, "They'll always be boys to me."

"I like thinking of them as boys. They're not as scary that way."

"Scary?" Gabe glared at her. "How can you say that? Jace, are you scary?"

Jace shook his head. "Not me, but you've been known to . . ."

Romy laughed, but then she thought of the story she was telling. How could she possibly have any laughter left in her? Then she realized that yes, she could laugh. All because of these two boys—boys who were the nicest, bravest men she'd ever known. She focused once again on the ranger. "Yesterday, my father decided to have me beaten to death. It was the twentieth anniversary of my mother's death. I was caught sitting by the spot where I'd helped dig her grave, thinking of her. Wondering if I might be like her, a woman who could become a wolf. My father had found a woman he wanted in his bed, and I had become inconvenient. He denounced me as a sinner, a follower of Satan. They used a bullwhip on me, but I didn't die."

She glanced at Jace, shocked by the tears in his eyes, but his compassion gave her courage. "My father and the reverend decided to turn me over to the young men if I lived. To be their whore. I begged for help, in my mind, and a woman answered. I thought it was my mother, but Gabe said I was hearing their goddess. She told me how to shift. I did. And then I ripped out my father's throat."

Salazar didn't say a word. Jace reached for Romy's hand, and she held on as tightly as she could. He was more than her lifeline. Right now, he was the one holding her up, giving her the courage to tell her story. "I bit the reverend, too, and there was a lot of blood, but Jace found out today that he's still alive. I didn't know for sure. Anyway, I escaped over the fence. Jace and Gabe found me."

Jace picked up the story. "She was smart enough to swim upstream from the compound and was lying unconscious on a sandbar. They'd spent the better part of the afternoon searching downstream, which gave us the time we needed, though we didn't know at the time there was anyone looking for her. When I first saw the wolf, I couldn't believe how badly she was hurt. We thought she was a wild wolf who'd been beaten or maybe mauled by a bear." He glanced at Gabe, who pulled out his phone and showed the photos to the ranger.

"My God." He glanced at Romy. "That's horrible." Turning to Jace, he said, "You were able to repair damage that severe?"

Jace nodded. "It took a couple of tries. At first, I just stopped the bleeding and put some torn areas back together, but we had to get away. There were men hunting her—in fact, they showed up while we were still on the sandbar. Gabe stayed to steer them in the wrong direction while Romy and I crossed the river and hid on the far side. Once Gabe got rid of the search party we headed this way, figuring we could find a place to hole up while Romy healed. We arrived yesterday evening, but a lot of the wounds had reopened and she was bleeding again. I spent a few more hours doing a better job. Romy's still not at full strength, but she's getting better. I'm hoping the scars won't be too bad."

Gabe brought up more photos of her human injuries once she'd shifted, and then how she'd looked this morning. "Anyway," Jace said, "the four men we told you about are in the area, and they're hunting Romy. They shot the guy sleeping in the corner . . ."

"Who looks amazingly improved since I last saw him."

Jace laughed. "He does. I think he's starting to like it here. Romy found some steaks in the freezer and she's been warming the meat to body temperature for him, so at least he's eating well. He understands we're trying to help him, knows we're shifters, and is healing better than I expected. The main issue is blood loss, but the red meat will help him rebuild so we can turn him back out into the wild."

"But that's the problem, John." Gabe stood and leaned over his chair, as if he couldn't sit still with the hunters out there. "We need to deal with the men illegally hunting wolves in a protected area. We can't turn this guy free until we know it's safe. Hell, Jace and I can't do our work, either. Not when we're constantly worried about some idiots who think they're doing God's work by killing wolves." Gabe turned and headed into the kitchen area. "Beer?"

Jace held up his hand and John Salazar checked his watch. "I'm officially off the clock. Yes. I'd love one."

"Wine for you, Romy, or a beer?"

"Wine, please."

Jace and John cleared the table, cleaned up the leftovers and tossed the garbage, and they moved into the small sitting area. Gabe followed them out with a tray loaded with three beers and a glass of white wine. He set it on the small coffee table and then sat across from Romy and Jace, but he turned to John Salazar, who sat on the other side of Romy. "Any ideas for how we handle this without getting ourselves arrested would be much appreciated."

"As Chanku, you have a lot more freedom to deal with problems like this than I do, but I can toss a couple of unofficial ideas your way. First, though . . ." He turned to Romy. "I am so sorry you've been mistreated by the very person who should have protected you, and I am sorry, too, for the loss of your mother. What was her full name? I used to be with the county sheriff's department up in Multnomah County, the one Portland is in, and we had a number of missing persons cases we were never able to solve. Mostly young women, but this was almost thirty years ago. I'm wondering if your mother might have been among the missing."

"Possibly. Her name was Angela Sarika. She was a prostitute working the streets in Portland when Reverend Ezekiel promised her a warm bed and food. He brought her to the compound half starved. It was winter, and the lure of a safe place to stay was all it took. The reverend kept her in his bed for a couple of weeks and then gave her to my father. Within the year, she was more than ready to leave, but she was pregnant with me. Once I was born, she refused to leave her child, but she couldn't get away with me. The walls are guarded night and day, and the punishment for trying to leave is severe."

Salazar was slowly nodding his head. "I wondered if you might be her daughter. I remember your mother. You look so much like the pictures of her that I saw. She'd had a falling-out with her parents and ran away from home. They searched for her for years, but there was nothing. I'm sorry that both of them are gone now because they wanted closure once they gave up ever seeing her again."

"Romy's grandparents?" Jace sat forward in his chair, still gripping Romy's hand. "Her grandmother would have been Chanku. The genes are carried in the mother's line."

"I'm sorry." John focused on Romy. "I understand the Chanku genes pass through the female line, but it would have come from her mother's biological mother. Romy's mother was adopted, her parents quite a bit older when they got her. I don't think they were prepared for the brilliant, headstrong girl they raised—her adoptive mother was a very sad woman who blamed herself for their estrangement."

Salazar's eyes glistened and he glanced away as if to compose himself. Then he took Romy's hand. "I wanted so much to find your mother in the hope that they could reconnect, but both your adoptive grandparents have passed. So many young women disappeared around the same time, we figured there must be a serial killer, that she might have been a victim. Now I wonder how many of the missing women are in that compound. Because it's a religious order, and we had no idea they were doing anything illegal, we've been unable to search it. All the women who disappeared were over eighteen, so we have to assume they're there by choice."

"Many of them are, but the children aren't. They don't know any other life. I am so ignorant of the world, of people. This is the farthest I've ever been from the compound in my life. I can read and write because my mother taught me, and after she was gone I read the books she left behind, but many of the children are illiterate. So are a lot of the mothers. The fathers, not so much. The men can come and go, but the women are essentially prisoners. Still, most of them would choose to stay. They're like sheep. They don't want to have to think."

"So, what made you different?" The ranger grinned at her. "There's nothing sheepish about you."

She glanced at Jace, straightened her shoulders and focused on the ranger. He was a nice man, a good man, and she was shocked that she'd now met three different men who were so unlike any she'd ever known while growing up. Men who treated her with respect. It was an empowering experience. "Jace says it's because I'm Chanku. We're different inside, but I really don't know enough to say how."

Jace squeezed her fingers. "John, how many bank robbers, rapists or thieves have you met who were Chanku?"

"Not a one."

"Exactly. Granted, our population isn't that large, but we are innately different from humans in more ways than just our ability to shift. There's an inborn sense of honor that acts like a full-time conscience. We really can't do bad stuff. It's not in our nature."

"We can kill," Gabe said. Then he shrugged his broad shoulders and laughed. "Just thought I'd throw that in for the sake of the argument."

John laughed. "Well, you are predators. I would imagine killing is part of your natural instinct for self-preservation."

"Very true," Jace said. "We can kill to save our families, our children, even ourselves, but we can't steal or do things that go against our inner code of honor. Our Chanku ethics. Look at our pack alpha, Anton Cheval. I know you've met him. He's a ruthless businessman and he thinks nothing of using whatever he can to come out ahead in a deal, but he will never cheat in a business agreement, never do anything dishonorable to undermine a competitor. He can't."

Gabe laughed. "Well, I think a lot of that is because he knows Mom would kill him."

"There is that." Jace grinned. "Keisha is one scary lady. But he also won't abide anyone within any of his companies breaking rules, breaking the law. Cheating. Ethics are really important to him. To all of us."

He turned his steady gaze on Romy. "Ethics and family. The ones we love. We'll do anything in our power to protect them."

She couldn't have looked away from him if her life depended on it.

It was John Salazar who broke the moment. "So, what are we going to do about the idiots with the compound bows and no ethics?"

Jace turned away from Romy, but the look of determination on his face gave her the confidence to reach for his hand again and hold on. He squeezed her fingers, but his focus appeared to be entirely on the ranger. "We know they're not staying here, but I doubt they've gone far. John, if we could get them to go out into the forest, armed, would you have reason to arrest them?"

"I certainly would. No other reason to go into the woods with a compound bow and hunting arrows unless you're planning to hunt."

"That's sort of what I was thinking." Gabe stood and slipped his shirt off. "Give me a few minutes. Me and my very exceptional nose are going outside. It's dark and there's no wind. Give me an hour, let me see if I can find out where they're camping. Once I find them, we set ourselves near enough to be attractive and do a little wolfly howling at the moon." He pulled his pants off, and Romy gave him a big grin and a raised eyebrow just before he shifted.

"John," Jace said, "do you mind hanging around long enough to give it a shot?"

Salazar slapped his knee and laughed. "Are you kidding? Do you actually think I'd miss this? I'll have to call for backup. I don't want you guys involved in the actual arrest."

"That shouldn't be a problem." He stood and walked over to the door, opened it and let Gabe out. "Be safe, Gabe." The wolf glanced over his shoulder and then trotted across the open area to the forest. Jace closed the door, walked back over to the couch, sat next to Romy and once again held her hand. "We've gotten to know a lot of the sheriff's deputies in the area. They're good people, and they don't like poachers." He glanced at Romy and squeezed her hand tighter. "Or murderers."

. . .

Gabe returned half an hour later, barely visible as he trotted openly across the area in front of the cabin, his dark wolf one more shadow among shadows. Jace let him in. Gabe walked over to the wolf lying in the corner and touched noses with the beast first, and then went straight to Romy, stood up on his hind legs with his big front paws planted on either side of her hips, and licked her across the face.

"Yuck." Shoving him away, she giggled as she wiped the slobber off her mouth. "What was that all about?"

Gabe shifted. Laughing, Jace tossed him a pair of pants and he quickly stepped into them. "Hey, Jace has all but threatened me with bodily injury if I so much as lay a finger on you. I figured that was the only way I'd get a taste."

"Oh?" Turning toward Jace, Romy looked down her nose at him. Jace merely grinned and kissed her full on the mouth.

"You taste like Gabe." He glared at his buddy. "I like it better when she tastes like herself."

Romy leaned over and placed her fingers on John Salazar's knee. "John? You've known them longer than I have. Are they always like this?"

He nodded, very seriously. "I'm sorry, Ms. Sarika, but they've actually been behaving better than usual."

She could tell by the twitch in his lips he was having trouble keeping a straight face. And she loved every minute of this, even knowing there were men not far away who wanted her dead. For now, she was finding out what real life was all about. Not merely fear and servitude. No, it was love and laughter and learning about one another. Sharing a meal, a joke, a look.

She'd missed so much.

"Okay." Gabe grabbed another beer out of the refrigerator and sat on the arm of the chair beside Jace. "They're less than a quarter mile west of here, camped illegally on Aragat property, with an illegal campfire, and they're all drinking. And we're not talking beer." He took a long swallow of his. "How long before you can have deputies here to back you up?"

"I've already called," John said. "They should be here any minute. I told them to meet us at your cabin."

"I think they just arrived." Jace was up and standing at the front door by the time the two pickups pulled into the parking area in front of the cabin. Three men and a woman in uniform got out of the vehicles.

"We're looking for Ranger John Salazar."

"Right here, Ed." John stepped past Jace and greeted the four, quickly filling them in on the plan. "My only question is, how do we do this without making it entrapment?"

The closest deputy merely shrugged. "Wolves howl around here all the time. Heard them last night, not far from the station. Just because they're howling doesn't give anyone a right to shoot them. Especially here. Aragat has this registered as a preserve."

"We're just assuming these guys will take the bait. Gabe, tell us exactly where you plan to be."

It only took a minute, coordinating the GPS on their mobile phones to show the deputies where a small rise near the illegal camp would give them a natural place to howl and the deputies plenty of cover.

Jace turned and wrapped his arms around Romy. "We shouldn't be gone long."

"I'm going."

He shook his head. "It's too dangerous."

"It's my life. Men have been telling me how to live it for too damned long. I'm going, Jace, you can't stop me."

A slow grin spread across his face. "You're right. I can't." He kissed her, just a quick peck on the lips. "Promise me you'll be careful."

She nodded, shocked at how quickly he'd agreed. Shocked and thrilled. She'd really expected a fight. "Of course. I'm not stupid."

He shook his head; his grin spread even wider. "No. You're not in the least bit stupid."

• • •

The knoll rose above the creek bed, a pile of crumbling granite with a twisted tree growing out of one wide crevice in a huge boulder. Three wolves sat at the very top as the full moon rose over the treetops. Romy practically quivered with excitement. This was her first real shift when they weren't fleeing danger. No, they were going right into the middle of it, on purpose. She was loving every minute.

There were two deputies hiding in the brush at the base of the knoll and the other two were in the woods, waiting. John Salazar was manning a video camera fitted for night filming—as he'd said, after a couple of beers he wouldn't be carrying a gun, but he figured that being armed with a camera would make him even more effective.

Jace nudged Romy's shoulder. *Romy? You start. Just look at the moon, tap into your wolf, and make a joyful sound.*

But how? She'd never even imagined doing this. Even her dreams of running as a wolf were mostly that—just running. But howling at the moon?

You'll know.

She raised her head and stared at the moon. The sky was crystal clear, stars twinkling in the darkness beyond moonrise, but she felt the call, felt it and recognized it for what it was. Without actually thinking of what she was doing, she raised her head, opened her mouth, and turned her song free.

The howl seemed to come from somewhere deep inside—not her heart or lungs or even her belly, but deeper, as if she sang the song of her soul. The moment her mournful howl rose over the treetops, Jace and Gabe joined in. The three of them, raising their voices in harmony. It was like nothing she'd ever experienced in her entire life.

In the distance, a series of yips and more howling echoed over the hills as another pack—probably the one Jace and Gabe had come to study—joined Romy's song.

And it was hers, the song she'd wanted to sing all her life. A song of joy, of freedom, of love. Suddenly Jace stopped. *Down, now. They're coming.*

She really didn't want to stop, but Romy wasn't about to do anything stupid. The song ended and the three wolves slipped into the rocks behind the knoll, hiding in the shadows. Romy stood beside Jace. They heard the sheriff's deputy challenge the hunters, but the men didn't stop. Shots echoed, much too close. Someone cursed, someone else grunted in obvious pain.

More cursing and the sound of men fighting. Gabe slipped out of their hiding place with Jace right behind him. *Stay here!*

It was an order. Romy was tired of taking orders from men. She slipped around the tumbled boulders in the opposite direction of her men and found a shadowed, protected area to see what was going on.

One of the deputies had an arrow protruding from his upper back.

Two of the men from the compound were on the ground, handcuffed. She recognized Samuel, the one she'd kicked in the balls, and wanted to cheer. The two larger men, the ones with the compound bows, were missing.

So were Jace and Gabe, and two of the deputies. Romy raced across the open area to John Salazar. He was nursing a badly cut hand, talking on his radio and calling for backup. Romy saw one of the deputies' coats lying on the ground. She quickly shifted and slipped it on to cover herself. Luckily, he was a big man, but it still barely covered her butt.

"John, what happened?"

"One of them must have seen us. They spotted you right off the bat and made a beeline for the knoll, but one of the guys with a bow actually tripped over Ike, the one with the arrow through his shoulder. Shot him point-blank."

"Through?" Romy took a better look. A deputy was with Ike, sitting on the ground beside him, helping to support him while they waited for medical help. She'd thought he was shot in the back, but she was actually looking at the point protruding from his back near his right shoulder blade. The fletched end was sticking out in front.

Romy gasped and covered her mouth.

John patted her shoulder. "Don't worry," he said. "Ike'll be okay, we've got two of these idiots in cuffs, and Gabe and Jace and two of our deputies are on the trail of the other two."

"I want to go after them."

"I know, Romy, but please stay. I'm going to need someone to explain why we have these two bozos cuffed. They have carry permits for their sidearms, and without you here the only thing we can hold them on is trespassing."

"I'll stay." But standing there, gazing in the direction she knew Jace and Gabe had gone, she quietly asked their goddess to keep them safe.

10

They're not even trying to be quiet, Gabe. Do you think it's a trap?

No, but we need to be ready for anything. Gabe paused and raised his nose to the air.

Even Jace could pick up the acrid stench of fear and sweat; the sound of two large bodies crashing through the undergrowth was impossible to miss.

Then all went still. Jace tried to picture the area they were in, knew the forest gave way to a large meadow bound on one side by a rock out-cropping that ran for almost a quarter mile north and south and jutted at least fifty feet in the air. He didn't recall any caves, but there were enough large, tumbled boulders to create plenty of hiding places.

Gabe, we need to split up. You go with one of the deputies, I'll take the other. That way we can communicate. Radios don't work that well here.

Gabe nodded and they both waited. The two deputies who'd come with them, a man and a woman, followed about a dozen paces behind. They were good, moving fast and almost as quietly as the two wolves. Jace glanced over his shoulder. The woman, Deputy Jana something-or-other, quickly caught up. Her voice was low, barely audible when she said, "We think they're headed into the boulders on the other side of the meadow. Ben and I are going to work our way around to the north. If you guys can come in from the south, we should be able to flush them out."

Jace lifted his paw and touched her knee. Then he shifted. She handled suddenly being faced with almost six and a half feet of naked man a lot better than most people. "Let's split up, but you go with me, Ben with Gabe. Gabe and I can communicate telepathically in our wolf form over a short distance, and no, that is not common knowledge and we prefer to keep it that way, but voices carry too easily when you get close to the bluff." It wasn't really a lie, merely an omission of the fact that they could also mindspeak just fine in their human forms.

"I'm good with that. Ben?"

"Agreed."

Gabe slipped into the woods with Ben close behind. Jace shifted, and he and his deputy circled the southern edge of the meadow, keeping to the shadows and moving as quietly as possible. The scent of the two men grew stronger, reeking of fear. Jace paused behind a large cedar and shifted again. Jana stayed low, hiding behind a patch of wild blackberry vines.

"Do you see the big chunk of granite that's sort of square?"

Jana nodded.

"Look at the shadow at the upper left corner."

"I see him."

"Hold on." *Gabe, I see at least one of them. He's on top of that chunk of granite. Looks like he's got night goggles on, but I don't know where his partner is.*

He's on the next boulder over, toward Ben and me. They can't go anywhere. Ben wants to call it in, have the guys come in and arrest them. What do you say?

I'd rather kill them both. End of problem.

Gabe's mental laughter had him smiling, in spite of the situation. *True, but Dad would have a fit. Jana's got seniority. Check with her first.*

"Gabe and Ben can see the other guy. He's hidden from us on the opposite side of the boulder. They can't go anywhere. Ben thinks we should call it in, get reinforcements and arrest them. Personally, I'd like to kill both of them, but Gabe says you guys frown on that."

She shot him a bright grin. "We do, but sometimes . . . Tell them I'll make the call."

She stepped to one side and pulled out her comm unit. Jace connected with Gabe. *Jana's calling it in. We'll just hang back and wait for the rest of the team.*

A sharp yip cut the night, then a staccato burst of gunfire. *Shit, Jace, I'm hit. Arrow in my chest.*

"They shot Gabe." Jace shifted and raced toward the boulder. The bowman was nocking another arrow, not watching his flank. Jace reached the boulder and was on him before he had time to fire. As the man aimed toward the deputy protecting Gabe, Jace went for his throat.

The arrow went wild. Jace heard the satisfying sound of breaking bone, but his weight and the speed of his attack took both Jace and the shooter over the edge of the rock. It was only about twenty feet, but the angle was bad. Jace hit hard. Stunned, he lay there beside the man he'd killed, wondering where the other bowman was.

Then Jana was kneeling beside him and firing into the shadows. The clatter of something falling had her up and running, her pistol grasped in both hands. Slowly Jace struggled to his feet, shook his head and then ran across the meadow to where he knew Gabe lay.

Ben was with him, holding a clean handkerchief over the wolf's bleeding wound. A carbon shaft protruded from the lower left side of Gabe's neck. Jace shifted and ran his fingers through Gabe's thick ruff of hair. There! The point of the arrow pressed against the skin at the back of his shoulder.

"Gabe, you still with me?"

I am so damned pissed.

"Well, you're going to be more pissed, because I need to push this shaft through the rest of the way so I can break off the point. I'd tell you to shift to get rid of it, but it's too damned close to vital areas."

Just do it. Don't tell me about it. Fuck. This hurts.

Hang on, big guy. "Ben? Check on Jana. I think she got the other guy. The one who shot Gabe."

"Okay."

"Ben? When you come back, I'm going to be sitting here like I'm totally spaced. It's because my consciousness won't be in my body. I'll be inside Gabe. I need to close up the wound from the inside. I think it's mostly through skin and some muscle, but I need to make sure an artery didn't get nicked. Keep me as undisturbed as possible. It may take a while."

"Gotcha. I'll be back as soon as I can."

Jace had mentally dismissed the young deputy before the man even left. Now he studied the angle of the shaft to determine how close it might be to major arteries. It passed uncomfortably close to his heart, but Gabe wasn't bleeding too badly, considering the arrow running almost through him, so Jace grabbed the shaft and quickly forced it through the skin on the back of Gabe's neck.

Ignoring the string of curses, Jace snapped the shaft and then carefully pulled it out of Gabe's chest. By the time it was out, Gabe was unconscious and Jana and Ben had returned.

"They're both dead."

Jace nodded. "I need to repair the injury. Please don't let anyone move me. I'm okay; I just won't be connected to my body."

Trusting they'd watch over him, Jace placed his hands on Gabe's neck, closed his eyes, and went inside his closest friend.

• • •

Frustrated enough to take a swing at the man, Romy stared at John Salazar as he carried on a conversation via his comm unit with the woman deputy. He was taking forever and all Romy could do was listen to his affirmative and negative grunts, telling her absolutely nothing.

Jace hadn't been in contact and neither had Gabe. She'd tried reaching them with her mind, but there was nothing and she had no idea what had happened.

Then John clicked off the device and focused on Romy. "Both men are dead, and the coroner is on the way."

"Not Jace? Gabe? Not Gabe. No . . ."

John cupped her shoulders in his big hands, shaking his head. "No. Not your guys. The shooters, the ones they were after. But Gabe's been shot. Jace is working on him, but Jana said he didn't seem to be too concerned. Get some clothes on and come with me. They're not that far from here."

She was crying. They were alive and she was still crying, but Romy started across the field before John grabbed her arm, laughing. "You can't go like that. You need some shoes, pants, and . . ."

"I don't have any." She ripped off the ranger's coat she'd grabbed, leaving John and a couple of other deputies who'd arrived standing here in the lights from the squad cars with their eyes bugged out, but then she shifted, looked at John and growled impatiently.

"Can you find them?"

She yipped. Their scent was clear on the night air now that she'd taken her wolf form. John merely smiled at her. "Then go to them. I have no reason to hold you here."

She spun around and took off, following her nose and, before long, her sensitive hearing as she got closer to Jace and Gabe. Then all she could smell was the overpowering stench of blood and gunpowder. It led her directly to the site.

She raced through the forest and saw Jace on the far side of the meadow. Someone was holding a flashlight—she didn't realize it was the woman deputy until she got closer. Skidding to a halt, Romy stopped beside Jace. The deputy jerked the light, startled, and then held it steady.

"Romy?"

She glanced at the woman and nodded, which probably looked absurd from a wolf, but the deputy didn't even blink.

"Jace said it's not real serious, but it was painful and he wanted to get Gabe put back together. Both the men who were hunting you are dead. I wanted to make sure you knew that."

Romy stared at the woman, wishing she could communicate her thanks, but all she could do was brush the deputy's thigh with a paw and hope she understood. To her surprise, the deputy gently stroked her paw with her free hand.

Romy dipped her head in thanks, but then she focused on Jace. He sat with his legs akimbo, leaning forward, his hands on Gabe's shoulder, and she knew he was inside Gabe, healing him, just as he'd healed her injuries, just as he'd healed the wolf.

Lying beside him, she rested her chin on Jace's knee, and waited.

• • •

Jace was still working on Gabe when Romy remembered the antelope. Jace would need food when he was through, and so would Gabe. She shifted. The deputy smiled at her and shook her head.

"This will be a story the guys at the station just won't believe."

Romy smiled. She was just too damned tired to laugh, but it was funny when she thought about it. "I have to get something for them to eat. Jace will need food when he's done, and fresh meat will help Gabe's healing."

"I'd offer one of the perps but he'd probably give the guys indigestion."

"Food poisoning, more likely, but thanks for the thought. I'll be back as quickly as I can, but I imagine most of the game has been frightened off."

She'd never hunted, and conditions weren't good with all the activity, so she shifted once again and raced back through the woods to the cabin and that well-stocked little refrigerator. She grabbed a couple of steaks, stuck them in the microwave to thaw, cut the meat up and then wrapped it in a plastic bag. The wild wolf was awake and watching her, but he lowered his head and went back to sleep once he figured out the steak wasn't for him.

"Later," she said, carrying the bag to the porch, setting it down, shifting, and then grabbing it up in her teeth. She really needed one of those pouches like the guys had, but for now teeth would work. It took her barely a minute at top speed before she was back at the edge of the meadow. The deputy was still holding the light, but this time there were half a dozen men milling around, photographing the scene and checking on the bodies. Romy ignored them and went straight to Jace's side. She was trying to figure out how to shift in order to get the meat out of the bag without flashing a lot of strange men, when the woman deputy took the bag from her and opened it. "I think Jace is done. He seems to be back in his body, though I can't imagine how he left it."

There was no one close enough to pay attention, so Romy shifted.

"Thank you. I don't really get it either, but look at my back." She turned and the deputy gasped.

"When did that happen? What happened?"

"The man these men follow used a bullwhip on me. That was two days ago. Jace healed me, or I'd be dead by now. He said there was bone showing along my rib cage, and muscles and tendons were badly torn."

The woman stared at her for a moment and Romy felt as if something important passed between them. Then she slowly nodded and said, "Thank you for telling me that. I've been sitting here feeling guilty for shooting the one I got. I don't feel bad at all anymore."

"Please don't." Jace raised his head.

Romy held out the bag of raw steak.

"Thank you." He looked at her and smiled. "Where did you get this?"

"I went back to the cabin. We're going to need to restock the freezer."

He popped one of the cubes of warmed raw meat in his mouth and chewed slowly. "I agree, but I really need this. So does Gabe."

"How is he?"

"He's going to be sore, but I think the repair went well. The arrow missed all the vital areas it could have damaged. His pride, however, has been sorely mangled. This is the first time I've had to heal him." He set some of the steak pieces on a flat piece of bark in front of Gabe.

His nose twitched and his eyes fluttered, and then Gabe lifted his head and grabbed a piece of the meat. In no time he and Jace had finished all of it.

• • •

Gabe insisted on walking back to the cabin—he made it as far as the staging area where John Salazar was speaking to a couple of men who hadn't been here earlier. Salazar glanced up when Jace, Romy, and Gabe, all in their wolf forms, walked into the clearing.

Gabe's legs folded up and he dropped slowly to the ground with a loud groan.

"Gabe? You okay?" John said something to the men and went to check on the wolf.

Romy found the coat she'd worn earlier and snagged it with her teeth, trotted into a shadowed area to shift, and then wrapped herself in the coat. Jace had a blanket tied around his hips and he was kneeling beside Gabe when she returned, but John signaled to her to join him.

With an anxious glance at Gabe, she walked over to John and the two men.

"Romy Sarika, this is Agent Esquivera and his partner, Agent Liu. They're with the FBI, and they've been trying to find out more about the

Glorious Salvation in Truth, and especially Reverend Ezekiel. Would you be willing to speak with them?"

She didn't even have to think about that one. "I would. The two men we were after are dead, but both of them were members of the cult, as well as the two you have in custody. How's your hand, John?"

He had a strip of cloth wrapped around his hand where he'd been cut during the earlier fight. "Okay, but it's sore. I tried to grab one of those arrows by the wrong end."

"Bet you won't do that again." Romy flashed him a grin but then focused on the two agents. "What do you need to know?"

"We're interested in the financing behind the cult, how the reverend made the money that kept the place running. Do you have any idea?"

"I'm not really sure, but you have to realize, I've never lived anywhere else but within the walls of the compound. He could be doing something illegal, but I wouldn't know what it is, if that makes sense. I've never watched TV or seen a movie, I saw my first cell phone yesterday, and while I can tell you what went on there, I don't know what's legal or illegal."

"Why did you stay?"

Agent Liu stared at her as if she were some sort of idiot. And maybe she was. "I didn't know anything else. I was born there. My mother wanted to escape, but she couldn't because the women were guarded and the punishment for attempting to escape was horribly painful. The only education I got was from my mother, who was murdered by the reverend when I was six. A few of the other women who believed in the importance of girls knowing how to read and do figures taught me as well, but there weren't many with that mind-set."

She shrugged, wondering if she'd ever figure it out herself, the reason why she'd stayed. "I think that the income for the day-to-day business comes from the stuff manufactured in one of the sheds. I'm not sure what it is since I was never assigned to that duty, but I know that there was a lot of secrecy involved, and punishment for anyone who asked questions or actually took any of the powder they were making."

"Thank you, Ms. Sarika. We're going to need a warrant to search the compound, and any information you can give us will help."

"About what? The way they brought women in and wouldn't let them go? That can't be legal. Neither can the reverend shooting my mother and then throwing her body in the trash heap. The fact that girls at fourteen or fifteen are married off to older men without any say in the matter? Or maybe the way my father kept me as his bed partner after my mother's death. I was six at the time. And when he didn't want me anymore, I was tied to a frame and beaten with a bullwhip. They intended to kill me." She turned and lowered the coat so that the agents could see the stripes covering her back. "Jace healed me, but he has photos of what I looked like a couple of days ago when this first happened."

She hated the fact her voice was shaking, hated that reciting all the sins of the bastard who'd killed her mother, who had stolen her life, could still make her afraid. She was tired of being afraid. Fed up with the role of victim. No more. Never again.

The agents looked at one another and then back at Romy as if they couldn't believe what they were hearing. "Ms. Sarika, would you be willing to testify in court? Could you describe in detail what you're telling us in front of a judge and jury?"

"Agent Liu, I would love to testify against Reverend Ezekiel. But you want to know what I really wish? That would be to get back the first twenty-six years of my life." She glanced at the three men, but none of them had a response. Then her gaze rested on Gabe and Jace, still in wolf form, resting beside one of the deputies' vehicles.

"Go ahead, Romy," John said. "We know where to find you if we have further questions. As I'm sure we will."

• • •

It felt wonderful to be back in their cabin. Gabe slept, still in his wolf form. Healing, as Romy knew, was an exhausting business, as much for the healer as the one he was working on. She was surprised when Jace suggested sitting out on the front deck, but the two of them wrapped themselves in warm blankets against the night chill and sat beneath the last glow of moonlight before it passed behind the trees.

Romy studied Jace's profile for a moment, curious at her body's almost constant awareness of him. Of her need, which seemed to have grown stronger throughout the day. Finally, she pulled herself away from trying to dissect her arousal. Questioning it wasn't making it go away. If anything, her desire grew. She sighed and smiled into the darkness. "I'm exhausted," she said, "but too wound up to sleep."

"I know. I feel the same way. Plus, I've been putting off contacting Gabe's parents. They know he was injured, but I'm not sure if he had the energy to talk with his dad, other than to let him know he'd be okay. I need to contact him, and a phone call is too impersonal. Would you link with me so Anton can meet you?" Jace laughed. "It might take some of his worry off of Gabe. Give him something else to think about."

Okay. Amazing how easy it was to link with him. Almost as if she'd been doing this for years. *But how do you contact someone so far away?*

I'm not really sure, but all I do is seek him out, and he's always there. Stay with me, okay? Anton? It's Jace.

I've been waiting to hear from you. How's Gabe? And who's with you?

Hello to you, too, Mr. Cheval.

Smart-ass.

Jace laughed and shot a grin at Romy. *Gabe is fine. He's sleeping. The second person in the link is the woman I told you about. Romy Sarika? Meet Anton Cheval, Gabe's father and the pack alpha.*

Romy. It's good to meet you, and I'm glad you're in the link. I tried contacting Gabe but he's not answering. Will you tell me what happened to my son? Because I wouldn't put it past either Jace or Gabe to gloss over a serious injury.

Romy snorted and then bit back a laugh. *You're probably right, sir, but Gabe is fine, just sleeping. I think there was some blood loss, though not much. An arrow went through the loose fold of skin at the lower left side of his neck and came out near his right shoulder. It missed vital areas, according to Jace, and the worst part, as far as Gabe was concerned, was when Jace pushed the barbed tip through the skin on his shoulder so he could break the point off and pull the shaft out. Gabe was alert and flirting earlier, so I don't think he was too bad, but he's sleeping now. Probably why he didn't answer you.*

Gabe could be on his deathbed and still flirting, but if you think he's okay, I'll take your word for it. I know you're both tired, but I'm going to want a full report tomorrow, Jace. Call when you're rested and Gabe's awake so his mother can assure herself he's well.

I will. We're planning to continue with the survey after Gabe takes a day or two to rest. Romy will be going with us, and you'll meet her once we return to the pack.

Good. I look forward to that time. I'll talk to you tomorrow.

And just like that the connection was severed. "He's in Montana?"

"Yep. All the way up past Kalispell, near Glacier National Park."

"He sounded like he was right here."

"I know. Scary, right? I don't know of anything he can't do. Except, maybe, admit when he's wrong, or worried. That business about Gabe's mother needing to know he's well? It's Anton who's worried sick."

"He loves both of you very much. I could feel it in his voice, in the emotion in the link."

Jace nodded as he smiled at her. "Yeah," he said. "He does. Almost as much as we love him."

They sat there beneath the fading moonlight. Romy wondered what that would be like, to live in a pack where the leader loved those under his rule. Where he'd earned the love of his followers. She'd never known anything even remotely close, not at the Glorious Salvation in Truth.

Maybe, just maybe, this would be her chance to learn about love in a real family.

• • •

There was no question of where he would sleep tonight, though he really wasn't planning on sex. As much as he imagined Romy's libido was as fully formed as his own, she had to be exhausted. This had been a pretty traumatic night, though she'd proven herself to be one tough lady when it counted. He was proud of her, of the way she'd handled the FBI questioning, the way she'd offered to testify when needed. She showed all the characteristics of a powerful Chanku bitch. It made him hard just thinking about her turning that power on him.

While Romy showered, Jace took the time to connect with Gabe, who was still sleeping soundly. He wanted to check on the repairs he'd done earlier, and so far it appeared that everything was holding and there was no bleeding, either external or internal. When he pulled himself back into his body, Romy had already gotten into bed. She lay on her side, head propped in her hand, and watched him.

With her hair falling in thick waves over her shoulders and partially covering her breasts, she looked like every man's fantasy. He didn't want to share her with every man, though. Jace had no doubt he wanted her for his very own. Not necessarily as a fantasy.

No, he wanted Romy as his reality.

"Be back in a minute." It was hard to leave her like this, lying there in bed, looking at him as if she wanted him, but he didn't intend to push it. Not tonight. He went in and showered, checked on Gabe again, and then crawled into bed behind Romy. She slowly rolled over until they were nose to nose, and he felt her smile against his lips.

I was afraid you would choose to sleep in Gabe's bed. I'm glad you're here.

Of course I'm here. He kissed her, just a light touch of lips to lips, even though he wanted to lose himself in her taste. Stopping was more difficult than he'd expected. *I hope you realize, when Gabe feels better, he's going to want to sleep wherever we are. We can't leave him alone. Not when he's been hurt. I hope you don't mind including him.*

There was only a slight pause, and then she said, *I think I will look forward to that. But for now it appears you alone will have to do.*

She sighed, quite dramatically. He felt her need envelope him, a warm blanket of pure desire, drawing him closer. Seducing him without intention, merely by being the woman she was. And the most seductive thing about her? She had no idea the effect she had on him.

None at all.

He grinned, and he knew his smile was showing more wolf than man, but he couldn't help it. Not when it appeared Romy wasn't too tired for sex. That smart-alecky comment was all the challenge he needed. She thought he alone would do? Romy was about to find out just how much Jace alone could do.

11

She wasn't sure what had changed, whether it was something in her or in Jace, but suddenly the air felt charged, as if her need or his had become a palpable, physical energy, filling her, surrounding her, making it hard to breathe, harder to think.

She wished she knew more. He'd tried to explain how her libido was now a more powerful part of her actual physiology—a need every bit as strong as hunger, as overwhelming as thirst, as intrinsic to her existence as the necessity of breathing. It was emotional, but physical, too, a change she'd eventually adjust to. He'd said it could be hard to handle in the beginning—but she hadn't expected anything like this. Not her response. Not Jace's.

Was she the reason Jace had that look on his face? As if he could eat her alive, as if there was only the slightest binding of civilization holding him back?

He grinned, and his teeth were white and very straight, so perfect, and yet when he smiled she thought of his wolf's grin, of the sharp canines and the fact he truly was a predator.

Just as she was. Did he feel the same hunger? The same driving need to touch, to taste?

To take?

Curious, she opened her thoughts, threw wide those shields she'd been working so hard to perfect, and he was there, engulfing her in lust, holding her mind, her heart, and most of all her body, in his barely contained desire. Desire focused solely on Romy.

No! Too much. Her shields slammed tight.

Physically backing away, she put distance between them even as she slammed her shields down, closing them tight beneath Jace's powerful wave of desire, a tsunami flooding everything within reach, his needs crashing through and then spiking her own, pushing her beyond any limits she'd ever experienced. Her heart pounded, thudding against her ribs, and for some reason she felt closer now to her wolf, as if that feral creature hovered just out of view.

This was all so new, so terrifying, so horribly raw. She thought she'd experienced arousal and overwhelming desire when they'd made love just this afternoon. That paled in comparison to the glimpse she'd just had of Jace. Of his needs.

Of her own, mirrored in his.

Sucking in a deep lungful of air, then another, slower this time, one deep breath after another, she brought herself under control. Then she glanced at Jace. Afraid to make eye contact, she barely raised her head, hiding her eyes—a veritable window to her feelings—behind her thick lashes.

He looked disappointed that she'd shut him out, but she was afraid. Lust was a new experience, and the firestorm burning in Jace right now terrified her.

Terrified her because she felt the same firestorm building inside. She wasn't ready, couldn't be ready. Not for something so powerful, so out of control. She wanted to know him, to study him long enough to regain her sense of equilibrium.

"What are you afraid of, Romy? Please . . . not me."

He reached for her and she struggled not to flinch from his touch when he wrapped his big hand around hers. Amazingly, his firm grasp on her hand calmed her.

What was she afraid of? Jace wouldn't hurt her. Would never hurt her, and yet her breathing was labored as if she'd run miles, her skin flushed, her body trembling.

"I don't know. It's all so . . ." Helplessly, she raised her head and looked at him. And then she opened her shields once again. He sat there, so patient, so loving, she felt like a fool. Had she imagined everything?

"No, you didn't imagine anything," he said, smiling as he shook his head. "You're no one's fool, Romy. What you saw in me, what you're feeling, the needs you felt burning in my body and yours, those are so new that they have to be scary. Yes, I want you." He laughed, a sharp bark of sound without humor. "Damn but I want you, but I'm not a beast, Romy. Even my wolf has manners." He sighed and gazed down at their linked fingers. "He may want you more than his next meal, but he won't ever force you to do anything against your wishes, and neither will I. Remember that. It's all up to you. Always all up to you."

He cocked his head to one side, and the move was so much like his wolf that she smiled. "What are you thinking?"

"That maybe you're asking too much of yourself. That I'm asking too much of you." He shrugged. "It's Friday night . . . well, probably Saturday morning by now, but you made your first shift Thursday afternoon, right? Your body is still in transition. Your mind, too. You have to stop feeling like a victim, because you're tougher than that. You're a wolf now, Romy. Even when you're sitting here naked, looking like an absolutely breathtaking human woman, you are still a wolf. You have no reason to be afraid, not of me or Gabe or any other man. It's time for you to find out more about who and what you are, and believe me, what you are is one tough bitch."

She laughed. "If anyone had said that to me before, I would have been insulted. Now I see it as the finest compliment anyone has ever given me."

"Good. Now tell me. What is it you want? What does your body want?"

That was easy. "My body wants you, but my mind wants to know you better. To explore who you are. To touch you, and look at you. I feel like I know the man, but I want to know the physical part that carries that man around."

"Makes sense." He sat up, leaned against the headboard, and held his arms wide. "I'm all yours."

Romy looked him over, glad for the moonlight coming through the window, the wide beam bathing Jace in silver light. He truly was a beautiful man, all angles and edges and hard, sweeping muscles, and she wanted to run her hands over him. To delve into the shadows and caress the ridges, to savor each muscle, each tendon, every hard, angular joint.

She took a deep breath, calmed herself as best she could, and moved close. Folding her legs, she sat between his. He was so close that he seemed larger than life, and Jace Wolf, in life, was a very large man. She licked her lips, running the tip of her tongue over her top lip and then clamping down on her bottom lip with her front teeth.

Taking another calming breath, Romy dared to touch him. A simple move, merely reaching for him, running the index finger of her right hand over his collarbone, then spreading her fingers wide and stroking slowly over his firm pectoral muscle. She focused on his flat nipple, tracing the dark areola with her fingertip. Fascinated, she watched as a shiver raced across his skin, amazed when she realized her simple touch had that effect on him.

His nipple tightened. She circled the tiny nub.

Jace groaned. Slowly Romy pinched her fingers together, compressing the very tip, tugging lightly. She'd never done anything like this before. She'd never had the desire to get this close to any man. Never had the opportunity to explore a man she wanted. One she was almost certain she was falling in love with, though that couldn't be possible. Not after only two days.

But what an amazing two days this had been. So many changes, the biggest the fact she was no longer, nor would she ever again be, a victim. She was Chanku. An alpha bitch, and she would never allow herself to be used or mistreated in any way. No longer would she back off from her own wants, her own needs.

She stared at the way her fingers looked against Jace's chest, raised her eyes and gazed into his. And once again, she opened her shields. Without any hesitation at all, she invited him in. His thoughts were steadier now, wrapped tightly enough that the seething lust was under control, but that really didn't change anything.

Didn't change what Romy wanted. What she still needed.

Jace.

Her arousal had been on a slow burn all evening, the sense that she wanted to rub against him, touch him, make love to him, but the tension of Gabe's injury, the FBI agents, even John Salazar's concern for her welfare had all helped Romy keep her need in check.

Not any longer.

She scooted back along his legs to his feet, pulled on his ankles until, laughing softly, he slid away from the headboard, lay on his back, and stayed there. His muscles rippled, as if he were physically restraining himself, but he didn't speak, didn't try and stop her. She knelt beside him and ran her hands over his chest, along his torso, over the jut of his hipbone and down the thick muscles of his thighs. She ignored his cock. It stood there, looking badly in need of attention, but there was more of Jace she wanted to explore. More she needed to touch.

His legs were long and beautifully formed, dusted with dark blonde hair. She ran her fingers their full length, wrapped both hands around his right foot and rubbed for a minute.

"I'll give you an hour to quit that," he said. His voice was gravelly and she wondered if that was desire speaking, if that was how he sounded when he was aroused. She merely flashed him a grin and went on to rub the other foot.

"Turn over."

He rose up on his elbows and raised one eyebrow. "Over?"

"Over."

He shrugged and rolled over on his belly. His back was absolutely beautiful. Not scarred as hers was, but smooth and rippling with muscles.

She stared at his buttocks for a moment, at the firm muscles and the hollows at either side of his cheeks, the way his muscular thighs curved wider than his narrow hips, and the small indentation at the base of his spine. She knelt between his legs, pushing them farther apart, and rubbed both hands from the lower curve of his buttocks all the way to the middle of his back.

A tiny drop of fluid slowly ran down her inner thigh. Touching him like this was making her so damned hot. The air must be redolent with pheromones, both Jace's and hers. She spread her hands wide, trailing her thumbs down the dark crevice of his buttocks, following the line where his butt curved in to meet his thigh.

His balls were right there, flattened between his legs, though his cock must be pointing up and caught beneath his belly. She tugged at his hips and he obediently rose up on his knees. When she reached between his legs and grabbed his cock, he looked over his shoulder, and once again that eyebrow went up.

Stifling a giggle, she flattened her hand on the small of his back and pushed him down, but his engorged cock was now caught just as tightly beneath his belly, pointing back, toward her.

This was what she wanted. Jace at her mercy, and the freedom to do whatever she pleased. And right now, tasting Jace when he couldn't take control pleased her immensely.

• • •

Jace wasn't all that sure what Romy was doing, but whatever it was, she could keep it up all night as far as he was concerned. She'd kept him going on a slow burn, his arousal not peaking so much as simmering, growing hotter all the while, but not enough to make him come. He'd tried getting into her thoughts, but except for a few brief periods where she'd let him in, Romy was keeping herself shielded.

He felt her breath on his ass. Damn. He wanted to look, to see what she was up to now, but he didn't want to do anything that might make her stop. She parted his cheeks with her thumbs, and he fought the natural desire to clench his muscles tight. Her lips left a smacking kiss on his left cheek. Another on the back of his right thigh.

She licked his balls. *Shit.* He almost shot through the roof.

He felt her tongue trace the underside of his cock, licking at the tiny bit of tissue holding his foreskin close under the crown, and with his cock tucked back with his balls on top of the damned thing, he was fully accessible to Romy's inquisitive tongue.

Accessible, and dying, inch by glorious inch.

Uh . . . Romy? How long do you expect this exploration of yours to take?

Long enough to finish.

Finish what?

Whatever.

How could she possibly sound so smug? She'd been terrified just a few minutes ago. Were her shields still up? He hadn't felt any sense of her entering his thoughts, but just maybe . . .

She was open. Open and totally wrapped up in the sense of power and pleasure she had, the fact she had him on his belly, had access to his balls and his cock—except she thought of them as his penis and testicles, and wasn't that going to have to change—and he wasn't trying to make her do anything she didn't want to do.

That thought stunned him. He'd never, not once in his life, been forced to do anything he didn't want to do. Well, clean up his messy room, maybe, when he was a kid, or do the dishes when he'd rather be playing with the guys, but nothing as intimate as sex. Never had he been made to feel uncomfortable. Never had anyone hurt him, and yet that was all Romy had ever known.

She would never, not ever, be forced to do anything against her will again. He swore that, silently but fervently, to the Goddess Eve. Romy was his to protect, his to watch over. And yet, if by some twist or another she decided she wanted another mate than him, he would still protect her. For the rest of her life, and his.

It really does work that way, Jace.

Eve?

Yes . . . I was just checking to see how Romy was doing.

Romy's tongue circled the sensitive crown of his cock. He bit back a terribly unmanly whimper. *Actually, she's doing really well.*

Eve's laughter had him smiling, even as Romy's tongue made him groan.

I can see that.

How does what work? What did you mean?

Ah, I mean that you saved Romy's life. It is now yours to protect. Keep her safe, John Charles Wolf. She is special to me, one who was lost and now has been found. And you, Jace, are special to me as well, because of the love I will always have for your father—and your mother. You are the son I might have had, if things had been different. Be well, Jace.

Before he had time to dwell on Eve's words, she was gone, back to the astral plane or wherever her wherever was. Romy had moved to lie beside him. Her breath was coming in short, sharp gasps and her heart was thundering, the rush of blood in her veins audible to his Chanku hearing. He opened his mind to her, found hers consumed with the pure arousal of a very needy Chanku bitch.

This was such a simple and pleasurable fix. He rolled over her, sliding between her thighs and propping his weight on his elbows and forearms. Threading his fingers in her tangled hair, Jace stared into her beautiful amber eyes. She blinked, as if she'd suddenly realized where she was, who she was with, and then she smiled.

"I need you, Jace. Need you inside me. Make love to me. Fuck me. I don't care, but I really do need you."

"No more than I want you, need you, Romy Sarika." He palmed his erection, pushing it down to meet her warm opening. Bathed in her slick fluids, it was a simple matter to tilt his hips forward, to fill her in one, long, smooth thrust.

She cried out and lifted her hips to meet him. He filled her, sliding through the hot, clenching muscles and touching the small dimple that was the mouth of her cervix. Buried balls deep, he held there a moment, savoring the heat and the wet rippling pleasure as her internal muscles contracted around him. She'd bent her knees to give him better access, now she locked her heels around his back, resting them against his butt.

He began to move, slowly at first, giving her time to adjust to his length and girth, but she lifted to him, pulled her legs back against her chest, giving him total access to her body. And with that access, she opened her thoughts, invited him in. They quickly found a rhythm, but with this new connection he knew it wouldn't last. Knew he wouldn't last.

He saw their lovemaking as Romy felt it—the huge size of him stretching her, the sensation so perfect, verging on pain but embracing pleasure. He was aware of the first tremors of her orgasm, the subtle fluttering in her womb, the sharp spark of sensation from clit to nipples and back to her clit, and that was all it took.

Romy's vaginal muscles contracted, grabbing him so tight he could barely push forward, pull back. She bowed her back and cried out, a sound of terrible pain that frightened him, but he was out of her thoughts and blocked when he tried to return. Her fingernails raked his back, her heels dug into his butt muscles and her body practically convulsed around his. He sensed what this must be, the release of so many years of pain and terror, as if she purged all those horrible memories after the night's awful events.

Her muscles tightened around him in one final orgasmic contraction, and all thoughts fled. Jace's fingers tightened in Romy's hair and his hips surged forward. Once, twice, a third time and his body was gripped by a climax that rattled whatever composure he might have thought he had.

No one had affected him like Romy. No one had ever made him feel this way, want this much, or need so completely. His climax seemed to go on forever, but when it was over, when he was lying replete in Romy's arms, he knew this wasn't an end. It was a beginning.

The most important beginning he'd ever experienced.

• • •

It was still dark when Romy crawled out of bed to use the bathroom. Jace slept soundly and Gabe had returned to his human form and was asleep in the other bed. The wild wolf snored softly from his bed in the corner. When she returned a few minutes later, Gabe had gotten into bed beside Jace. He was already snoring softly.

She thought about sleeping alone in the now empty bed but that didn't appeal to her at all. Instead, Romy crawled into bed on the far side, next to Jace, pressed her face against his warm chest and drifted off to sleep.

A few hours later, a subtle rocking motion awakened her. She was still in bed and Jace and Gabe were beside her, this time with Gabe on the bottom and Jace slowly thrusting in and out of his friend and lover. She watched for a moment, not the least bit shy should they notice her.

Jace had said the evolution from human to Chanku would change her in many ways, some subtle, some not. This was one she considered more subtle, this growing comfort with her own sexuality, with the sexuality of the two men in the same bed beside her.

Gabe's eyes were closed, his hands holding his testicles and slowly stroking his penis while Jace tilted his hips forward, then back, then forward again. Fascinated, she rolled closer and watched as Jace's full length disappeared inside Gabe, stretching that small opening to accommodate a rather large erection. Yet Gabe didn't seem to mind it a bit, if the look of blissful pleasure on his face was any indication.

Romy wanted to be part of this. She wasn't sure how, but Gabe was stroking himself, and she could do that for him. Connect with him that way. Slowly, almost as if she were approaching a wild creature, Romy shifted around until she could lay her head on Gabe's belly.

Jace moved to give her room, and Gabe didn't flinch, not even when she cupped his testicles in her palm and wrapped her fingers around his thick shaft.

He was big—every bit as big as Jace—and at first she thought only to stroke him. Then she looked up, directly into Jace's eyes, and he watched her, as if he wanted her to do more. Slowly she tilted Gabe's erection toward her mouth, licking her lips and then laving the broad, silky crown with her tongue.

Gabe's hips jerked and Jace closed his eyes as if he might be trying really hard not to spill his seed. He didn't seem to mind at all that she might do this for his friend.

No, Romy. I love Gabe, almost as much as I love you. I want to see you take him in your mouth because it will make me think of how your lips and tongue feel on me.

She didn't answer. Not really, though she wrapped her lips around Gabe's erection and sucked him as deeply as she could. He groaned and both his hands fisted in her hair. She let go of his testicles and reached around his thigh, searching for Jace's sac instead. Cupping the warm orbs in her palm, she gently squeezed. He cursed; Gabe's hips jerked and Jace drove into him, deep and hard. He held there, groaning, as Romy gently kneaded his testicles and sucked harder on Gabe's penis.

His ejaculate filled her mouth, a salty-sweet fluid that should have been offensive but wasn't. In fact, it made her want to do the same for Jace, to compare the two men, but for now she'd be happy knowing that Gabe had climaxed and Jace appeared to have done the same.

And she knew she'd helped them both. Licking the last of Gabe's ejaculate off his softening shaft, Romy planted a kiss on the tip and then reached for Jace, pulled him down to her and kissed him as well. "I'm going back to sleep. It's still dark out."

And with that, she rolled away and closed her eyes. At some point, she was aware of Jace snuggling up against her back and Gabe crawling into bed on her other side. He shoved his warm butt against her belly, and she wrapped an arm around his waist. Jace had his arm looped over her back and his hand gently cupped her left breast.

Thinking about all the changes in her life, unwilling to try and make sense of any of them, Romy once again let sleep claim her.

• • •

It was barely seven in the morning when John Salazar knocked on the door to the cabin. Jace had just stepped inside after taking the wolf out for a few minutes. The animal was already stronger, though his massive blood loss meant he wasn't ready to return to the wild, at least not for a few more days. Jace helped settle the wolf and then answered the door.

Romy and Gabe were waking, the two of them curled up together like a couple of puppies. In fact, Gabe shifted to his wolf before Jace opened the door, which would save Romy from any embarrassment. Trying to explain why she was in bed with Gabe might be just a bit much to throw at her or John this early in the morning.

"G'morning, John. Come in." Jace stepped back as John entered with his arms filled with bags and bundles.

He glanced around Jace and shook his head. "Damn. Romy's still asleep. I'm sorry. Guess I just figured you'd be up by now."

"I'm awake." Romy sat up, pulling the sheet up to her chin. Gabe rolled over on his back with all four legs in the air and groaned. "So's Gabe, but I think he's still looking for sympathy."

Gabe grunted and then jumped off the bed and headed for the bathroom. Jace poured a cup of freshly brewed coffee for John and then carried one over to Romy. She smiled when he handed it to her, then closed her eyes, savoring the rich scent. Jace turned away before he gave in to the urge to kiss her. Not now, with John standing so close by in the one-room cabin.

"So what brings you out so early? Didn't you have enough excitement last night?" Jace sat at the kitchen table and John took a chair across from him with his back to Romy.

"Plenty of excitement last night." He laughed. "I'll wait for Gabe and Romy. I want all of you to hear this."

"I'm coming." Romy made a quick run into the bathroom as Gabe exited on two legs, wearing nothing but his drawstring pants. He looked as if he'd dunked his head under the faucet—his hair was wet and slicked back from his face, but at least he looked awake. The wound on his neck was still raw and painful-looking this morning, but the area was clear of infection. Jace didn't think it would leave too bad a scar. He couldn't see the exit wound on his shoulder. Damn. That had been way too close.

Gabe grabbed a cup of coffee and sat between Jace and Salazar.

"Is that Danish I smell?"

"Good nose." John set a bag of warm pastries on the table. "I brought breakfast."

Gabe grabbed something smothered in cream cheese and what looked like pineapple. "Health food. My favorite. Thank you." He took a big bite, closing his eyes with a look of sheer bliss on his face as he chewed.

Romy came out of the bathroom a moment later, wrapped in the terry-cloth robe. They were going to have to get her some clothes, somehow. Jace had no idea where they could shop, but she'd need more than a robe to go with them on the rest of the route.

If they ever got out of here.

John stood when Romy arrived and pulled a chair out for her. "Thank you." She smiled at Jace and Gabe. "Take note, boys. This is how a gentleman behaves."

"I know." Gabe pointed with the remnants of his breakfast roll. "I was just thinking that if Mom were here she'd have my head on a platter." He glared at John. "You're making us look bad."

"You're wounded." John passed the bag of pastries to Romy and then pointed at Jace. "You don't have any excuse."

"You're right." He held up his right hand. "I promise to do better. Now, what's so important that it got you out here at the crack of dawn?"

"We raided the headquarters at the Glorious Salvation in Truth compound early this morning. Very early—around two. Took eighteen women and twenty-seven children under fifteen into protective custody. One of the girls, she's thirteen, I think, is pregnant. Also forty-two men, including Reverend Ezekiel, also known as Franklin Ambrose Smith, were arrested. We're not sure if that's his real name—they were still checking stats and running a DNA ID on him, but Smith has an arrest record going back over thirty years. No convictions, though I think that's going to change. The men were all booked on a variety of charges, including false imprisonment of minors, statutory rape, gun charges, production of illegal substances—that was a meth lab they were running, Romy. Some of the men will probably make bail, but it's been set high enough for the good reverend that he won't be getting out anytime soon. They're doing a search of the grounds for burials of unrecorded deaths, including that garbage pit you mentioned. We have a cadaver dog going out this morning. Romy, would you be willing to go with us and show where your mother is buried? Also, we'd like to get a blood sample for DNA and blood typing."

Salazar focused on Jace and Gabe. "We found the frame that they must have tied Romy to when they beat her. It's covered in blood and bits of flesh, there's blood-soaked dirt beneath it." He turned his attention to Romy. "It's a damned miracle you survived, sweetheart."

"Actually"—she reached out and took both Jace's and Gabe's hands—"it was Jace and Gabe. They're my miracle."

Jace wrapped his fingers around Romy's and hung on. He noticed that Gabe hadn't let go of her either.

"It's a miracle they found you in time, that's for sure. Anyway, we'll need DNA for the court records, to prove the blood is yours, Romy, and a notarized deposition for the hearing when charges will be read. Once we have that, I think you and the boys can go finish out their wolf survey. It's going to be a while before we can get this case ready for prosecution, and we won't need your help until then."

Romy raised her head and gazed at Jace. "Is that okay with you? Will it set you back on your schedule if I go with John now?"

Jace shook his head. "Not a bit, but I'm going with you. Gabe? Can you stay here? I promise to bring you fast food. Lots of it."

Gabe sighed melodramatically as he dug a second Danish out of the bag. "I guess. Me'n the wolf will just hang out. We're good."

John pulled another bag out from under the table. "Romy, I brought some clothes for you. My wife is about your size. I know you don't have anything but that robe, and I thought . . ."

"Thank you." She took the bag from him and dug through the contents. Then she raised her head, grinning, grabbed John by the shoulders, planted a kiss on him and took the bag into the bathroom.

John blinked and stared at Jace. "Well. I guess that wasn't a bad idea after all. My wife made me bring them after I told her about Romy."

Jace took another sip of his cooling coffee. "Smart woman, your wife."

"Yeah, but not as smart as me. I asked her to marry me over thirty years ago and the silly woman agreed. Go figure!"

12

Jace had to show Romy how the door to the truck worked, how to fasten the seat belt, how to adjust the seat, even what button to push to make the windows go up and down, but watching her take her very first ride in a moving vehicle was something he'd never forget.

Another memory, one he didn't want to think about, was Romy explaining that even though there were various vehicles at the compound for the men to use, women weren't allowed to ride in them. Ever.

"What if you had to go to the hospital? Needed a doctor? What then?" he'd asked.

"Reverend Ezekiel prayed over the sick. You got better, or you died. We were never allowed to leave. Not for anything."

The bastard really needed to die.

He shifted his thoughts to earlier this morning, when he'd watched Romy model the very first pair of pants she'd ever worn. "Females of all ages had to wear skirts or dresses," she'd said. "I was always jealous of the boys for wearing pants. They're so much more practical."

Then she'd smoothed her hands down her long, long legs, turned and preened in front of the big mirror in the dressing area, so completely without conceit as she admired her secondhand clothes that it was pure joy to watch her—and a definite turn-on.

Mrs. Salazar had sent a lot of clothes for Romy. She knew she couldn't take much because it would have to fit in the small waterproof bag she now carried—a gift from John that was just like Jace's and Gabe's. Romy still tried on everything, entertaining her male audience as she posed in each outfit.

She'd ended up with a pair of lightweight black pants that clung to her hips and molded the perfect shape of her buttocks, and a bright red halter top that both supported her full breasts and emphasized the narrowness of her waist. John's wife had even sent a pair of black sandals that were a perfect fit, so now she had all she'd need to pass for human when necessary.

Everything was new to her. Jace loved seeing his familiar world through Romy's eyes.

And now this. Romy's wide-eyed amazement at how fast they traveled.

"I didn't realize you'd never been in a vehicle before, Romy." John glanced her way as he turned off the main road toward the compound. "Hope my driving hasn't made you nervous."

"You're kidding, right? This is amazing. Sometimes I feel as if I've been dropped off from another planet. I have so much to learn. Things all of you just take for granted. I read everything I could find at the compound but there wasn't all that much. One of the women had some books she called romances. She had to hide them from the men. They were interesting, but it was hard to imagine the places where the characters lived, the way the women were so free to do things. I kept telling myself that someday I'd do those things, travel to those places." Then she softly added, "Fall in love."

She stared at her hands. Jace sat behind her in the backseat, but he leaned forward and cupped his hands over her shoulders. "You'll get to do everything, Romy. I promise you that. Everything you want to try, to know, to do; you should have the chance to experience it."

She nodded, but she didn't look at him. Her shields were up, her thoughts guarded. But Jace meant exactly what he'd said. He wanted to be the one to help her learn about life, to experience at least some of what she'd missed.

Most of all, he wanted to be the one she loved.

He looked up as they drove through the open gates of the compound. This was the place where Romy had lived her entire life. Where her mother had been murdered. Where she'd killed her father. He wondered what she was thinking.

"It's so strange," she said. "I've never seen the gates open before."

• • •

The morning passed quickly. She'd given her deposition, told the ones asking her everything she knew about the Glorious Salvation in Truth and Reverend Ezekiel.

The bastard.

The men from the FBI and a couple of detectives from the local sheriff's department had questions for her, and a woman from social services had asked her what she knew about the various women and children they'd taken into protective custody. She told them what she could, but it wasn't much beyond first names. She only knew a few of the surnames. Friendships among the women were discouraged. A woman was supposed to devote herself to her children and husband, to cleave to her man, to need only him.

Romy'd only had her father, a man she hated.

No one said anything to her about the fact she'd killed him, and she didn't bring it up. Everyone was very nice and she never felt pressured by any of the lawmen and women who were doing the investigation. The one thing she'd worried most about—showing them where her mother's grave was—hadn't affected her the way she'd expected. Instead of a resurgence of grief she'd felt a vast sense of completion, of closure, as if she'd become the woman her mother had always wanted her to be.

The thing that had taken her most by surprise was the bloodstained frame where they'd beaten her. It was still standing, still covered in blood, the ground beneath it stained a rusty brown. Jace was holding her hand when they walked past it. She'd stopped, physically unable to move past it, and merely stared at the ugly thing while the horror of that terrible beating filled her mind.

Jace turned and wrapped his arms around her, holding her close. *You're stronger than they can ever hope to be, Romy. You're the strongest woman I've ever known.*

That was all it took to give her the strength to move forward, both literally and figuratively, but she didn't let go of Jace's hand the entire time they were at the compound.

Romy only made one detour. She asked permission to go into the cabin where she'd been raised, and she knew Jace was curious about her wanting to see it, but she went straight to the tiny cubby where she'd kept her few items of clothing, dug down into the bottom of the box and found her mother's diary.

She held it for a moment, loath to let it go, but then she handed it to the female FBI agent who'd walked inside with her. "This was my mother's, her record of her years here. I want it back someday, but it might be useful to you. It might give you more insight into what things were like here. I don't think people truly believe me when I tell them, but maybe the words of a woman long dead, murdered by the good reverend, will paint a better picture."

The agent stared at the small ragged diary in Romy's hand. Then she took out a plastic bag and carefully slipped the diary inside without touching it. Romy was surprised to see tears in the woman's eyes when she raised her head. "Thank you. I know this has to be difficult for you, but I have to tell you, and this is totally off the record, how impressed I am with your strength. Not many would have survived a life such as yours with such a strong and healthy mind. You are a truly admirable woman, Ms. Sarika."

Jace leaned close and kissed Romy's cheek. "You have no idea, ma'am. But you're right. She is admirable, and truly amazing."

They left the cabin and Romy felt lighter than she had since she'd fled the compound. Finally, her mother would have justice. She, Romy, would have justice.

There were more questions. They asked, she answered what she could, and then it was okay to leave. Everyone had been very kind, cognizant of her feelings and some of the convoluted emotions that seemed to strike out of nowhere. She thanked everyone for their patience. Jace left his contact information. They made a couple of stops on the way back, but basically they were all silent during the drive to the cabin.

Romy actually felt sad when John Salazar dropped them off. He'd been so kind, and his wife truly had been generous, to give her such wonderful clothes.

She knew she'd see John again and would get to meet his wife. They'd have to return for the trial, but that wouldn't be for many months. And the reverend would be in jail until then, and probably for a long time afterward.

Romy opened the door for Jace, who had his hands filled with bags of fast food and a package of raw beef and chicken for the wolf. She turned and waved as John Salazar drove away, and then it was just the four of them again—Gabe waking up from a nap on the tumbled bed, the wolf staring at them from his bed in the corner, Jace with his arms loaded with food, and Romy, who felt as if her life had just begun.

She took the raw meat from Jace and cut it up into big chunks, and since she'd noticed the wolf preferred his meat at room temperature rather than cold from the refrigerator, she stuck it in the microwave for just a few seconds. As the smell of the meat filled the room, the wolf came to his feet, but he didn't leave the bed.

"He's got excellent manners, doesn't he?"

Jace glanced at the beast staring at the bowl Romy was carefully filling and laughed. "Better manners than Gabe. You put that much raw meat in front of Gabe's wolf and he'd probably take your arm off trying to get to it first."

"I find that hard to believe. Gabe's much too nice."

"Nice? She thinks I'm *nice*? Crap, Jace. Where'd I go so wrong?"

126

Laughing, Romy carried the meat to the wolf. His muzzle was soaked with saliva, but he still waited until the bowl was on the floor in front of him before attacking his meal.

Romy sat at the table with the guys and took the food Jace handed to her. Tacos, a burrito, and a carton of orange juice. At least she recognized this meal, though what a couple of the women at the compound cooked didn't look exactly the same. She bit into the taco and it crunched, but it was absolutely delicious.

Jace set his taco on a napkin and focused on Gabe and then Romy. "What do you guys think of leaving today? It's still early. We can head north toward the area where the pack should be about now. It's not that far. The wolves move around this time of year, with winter coming. I think our buddy in the corner can keep up with us if we don't push too hard."

Romy glanced at the wolf. She hated to think of turning him loose by himself. Already she recognized the value of the pack; the bond she felt with Gabe and Jace was growing stronger by the day. She worried the wild wolf might bond to them rather than his own kind. "Is it his pack that we'll be looking for?"

"I hope so." Jace was watching the wolf too. He sat there, alert and attentive, almost as if he knew they discussed him. "We need to get him settled with a pack before winter comes. It's hard to know what pack a wolf is associated with when they're not tagged, and he hasn't been."

"Nor are you gonna be, eh, buddy?" Gabe walked across the room, flopped down next to the wolf and rubbed between his ears. "Ya know, as relaxed as he is around the three of us, I'm sure he recognizes the wolf in us. Did you see how he watched Salazar? Like he wasn't sure whether to attack or hide."

Romy laughed at that. "And indecision won out. He went back to sleep."

Jace took her hand in both of his and squeezed. "That's because he trusts us to protect him. Right now, we're his pack. He's intelligent enough to know that we'd never let anyone harm him."

She looked into his dark amber eyes and nodded. Did Jace have any idea the effect he had on her? "Just the way you and Gabe are my pack. Is that what you're telling me?"

"Yeah. Exactly the same way." Jace grinned and Romy realized she was smiling right back at him. He was such a beautiful man. Good inside and out. So was Gabe, though for whatever reason her heart didn't stutter in her chest when she looked at Gabe, not the way it tripped all over the place around Jace.

But that was okay, because she knew Gabe didn't feel for her what

Jace did. He cared and he loved her in his own way, but when Romy looked at Jace she saw her future. Saw the man she could already imagine being with for the rest of her life, and it was such a good feeling.

"Did we decide?" Gabe wandered back over to the table and grabbed a tortilla chip. "Are we leaving today?"

"Romy? What do you want to do?"

Would she ever get used to having her opinion matter? "I'm ready when you guys are. My back is healed, John's got your contact information in case he needs us, the wolf looks like he's ready as long as we keep the pace slow enough for him. So yes, I say we go."

"Me too." Jace stood and started gathering up the remnants of their lunch. "Gabe, do you want to settle up with the manager?"

"Headed there now. I'll ask him to restock the place and charge it to me. I think we cleaned out Stef's beer and wine reserves."

"And all the frozen meat." Romy grabbed a towel to wipe the table clean. "What about laundry?"

"Why don't you guys strip the beds? Management will take care of sheets and towels and stuff. I just don't want Stef to get the bill for all the food and drinks we've used. Back in a minute."

Jace dumped the bags in the trash and caught Romy's attention. "Are you really okay with this? We travel as wolves and sleep as wolves. Generally we stay in caves we're familiar with, or forested areas where we can feel safe, but we won't have any modern conveniences. I never really thought of it with just Gabe and me. We've never had a woman with us before."

"That's good." She leaned close and kissed him. "I'm looking forward to it. Everything I've done with you so far has been an adventure." Memories flooded her, and with them amazement at how much had changed in only three days. Just three days ago she'd thought she was going to die, had mentally prepared herself for death. Now, everything was new.

She was new. A shapeshifter. A woman capable of sexual fulfillment. A woman with a future. An immediate one that didn't include indoor plumbing. Laughing, she kissed Jace again. "Give me a few minutes. I'm going to take a shower before we go. I really love that shower!"

• • •

The wild wolf fell right into line with them. Gabe took the lead with Romy on his heels, then the wolf and Jace at the rear. Gabe's nose was so much better, if there was a pack of wolves in the area he'd pick up the scent first.

So far nothing, but it was a gorgeous late summer day, and they were making excellent time. Jace loved watching Romy. He knew she wanted to stop and explore, but she'd stayed on course for the past couple of hours.

Until now. She skidded to a stop and raised her nose.

What is that I smell? It's like ambrosia!

He sniffed. *Deer. At least a couple of them.*

I'm starving. Is that my hunting instinct?

Look at the wolf.

Their wild companion was drooling and walking slowly off the trail, head down, nose twitching as he slowly stalked into the soft breeze. In the direction of the scent.

C'mon, Gabe. We need to teach Romy how to hunt as part of a pack.

He'd done this hundreds of times, but never with a fledgling wolf. Now, every step took on greater significance, but he was fascinated by Romy's instinctive movements. The fact she moved in absolute silence, that she watched their wild brother. The wolf looked directly at Romy. She hesitated, and then she moved around to the left, remaining downwind but gaining distance on the animals.

As if by unspoken agreement, Jace and Gabe hung back to see how Romy and the wolf would do on their own. The wild wolf had taken on the lead role. He moved through the thick underbrush without a sound. Romy was just as quiet, though she was in a more open area where stealth was necessary. Her black wolf clung to the shadows.

I see them, Jace. Half a dozen deer. The bucks have shed the velvet on their antlers, though a few have bloody strips clinging. That's what I smelled, I think.

It's your hunt, Romy. You and our wild brother. Good luck. She heard soft laughter in her mind. *Slide your travel bag off over your head. It will get in the way when you go after the deer.*

Thank you. I hadn't even thought of it. I'll leave it when I get closer. Where do I aim for the kill? The throat seems logical, but I don't want to be wrong.

Go for the throat and use your body weight. With luck you can break the animal's neck before it falls. The kill will be quick. Clean. Not as painful for your prey.

• • •

Romy had never thought about the act of killing a living creature. She'd always loved to watch the deer that occasionally leapt the fence and got into the garden on the compound. Of course, one of the guys would inevitably show up with either a bow or a rifle and shoot the poor beast. It was, after all, fresh meat.

But now, thoughts of sympathy for the wild things weren't even on her radar. All she wanted to do was make a clean kill and feed. They'd run for miles today. She knew the wild wolf was hungry. It was also depending on her to make the kill.

For whatever reason, Romy understood the beast. She didn't think Jace or Gabe really accepted the animal's innate intelligence, but it was well aware they were shapeshifters and understood that the three of them were only looking out for him and hoping to reunite him with his pack. And he accepted that, right now, of the two of them Romy was the stronger.

Romy circled, staying low and moving as silently as a wraith. Finally she found a narrow trail she could pass through without brushing noisy shrubs or stepping on crackling dry grass. She glanced between berry brambles and a twisted river willow.

The deer were so close she had to fight to keep herself in one place where she could figure out the best line of attack. She crouched there in the weeds, studying the animals. They were so beautiful that she hated to think of actually killing or eating one. Then she saw an older doe. The animal stood alone, off to the side closest to Romy. She seemed to be shivering. Tiny flies circled her muzzle, much thicker than the swarms around the other animals, and Romy knew this was to be her target. Killing a perfectly healthy animal was something she didn't think she'd ever want to do, unless it was a matter of life or death for a packmate.

The wild wolf had moved around to the far side of the meadow. Somehow Romy knew he wanted to let his scent scare the deer toward Romy. She moved closer to the meadow, with a clear shot at the animal she'd marked as hers, dipped her head and let the light travel bag slip to the ground. Free of her small burden, she crouched low in the dry grass.

A sudden burst of gray out of a thicket on the far side of the meadow sent the small herd running in Romy's direction. Could she do this? Kill a deer with teeth alone?

They raced through the closely cropped grass and then into the narrow trail that would lead them directly to Romy. She waited, forcing her wolf to be patient. Finally she saw the old doe coming across the meadow, running slowly and awkwardly, as if she were in pain.

Romy didn't give herself time to think about the animal's pain or lack thereof. She lunged forward, leaping into the air, grabbing the long, slim neck between powerful jaws. The sound of snapping vertebrae was sharp in her ears as she slammed her prey into the ground on the other side of the trail. The rough landing knocked the air out of her, but Romy managed to rise to her feet, instinctively guarding her kill.

The human side of her mind wanted to race around the meadow

screaming about her success. Her wolf merely wanted to eat, but the wild wolf stood just beyond, staring. She was vaguely aware of Jace and Gabe standing close by, also watching. The wild wolf finally acknowledged the two men. He gazed over his shoulder and snarled at them and then stalked past, his legs stiff and ears laid back against his skull.

Romy ripped into the soft belly. The wolf stopped near the kill, growling low in his throat. She ignored him as the rich, warm scent of blood teased her nostrils, as the taste of it exploded in her mouth. Then something—some inner sense of herself as a wolf?—made her pause. Whining softly, Romy backed away from the carcass, lowered herself to her belly and turned her head, exposing her throat. The wolf stopped growling. He walked up to her, sniffed noses and licked a drop of blood from her muzzle. Then he tore at the animal's haunch, ripping through hide into muscle and meat.

Romy rose, shook herself, and began to feed. As her wolf gorged itself, her human mind was fascinated by her feral instincts, the fact she'd recognized the wild wolf as the one who had first scented their prey and had known to cede the kill to him, that she'd immediately known that the scent of game was a good thing, and how to circle the small herd and keep to the shadows.

That when she'd leapt for the escaping animal, she'd instinctively known to grab the throat beneath the doe's jaw and use her weight to bring it down. She would have known it without Jace's reminder.

Jace? She'd totally forgotten about the two of them. She raised her head and spotted Jace and Gabe. Their travel bags lay on the ground in front of them, but they hadn't moved.

Jace cocked his head to one side. *We're waiting for an invitation.*

You're invited. She went back to feeding. The two males approached, each of them going low, belly to the ground, as they got close to the deer. The wild wolf ignored them. So did Romy. Formalities completed, Jace and Gabe tore into the warm body and began to feed.

Romy raised her head a few moments later, licking blood from her muzzle, then tilting her head to try and reach a few drops scattered across her chest. The wild wolf had moved away. He'd rubbed his bloody muzzle in the dry grass to clean himself and now rested in the shade of a large cedar. Jace and Gabe were still eating, but it was obvious they were just about done. Romy wasn't ready to leave. This was her first kill as a wolf, she'd been successful, and she chose to savor the event. It was important, though she wasn't quite sure why.

She was full and the sun was going down, but still she lingered.

A few big black ravens sat in the tree limbs overhead. Their raucous calls echoed off the low hills as they waited impatiently for the wolves to leave. Ignoring them, Romy glanced up and saw turkey vultures already circling, also waiting for whatever meat the four wolves might abandon. The late afternoon sun was low in the sky and long shadows stretched across the forest and meadow. Before long, porcupines and raccoons, coyotes and other creatures of the night would be claiming whatever they could of the carcass.

Sighing, Romy backed away from the remains of the doe. It was time to leave and give the crows and vultures a chance before night fell. Time for lesser creatures to feed. She was a wolf. This was her kill, and wolves fed first.

Romy? Gabe raised his head. His muzzle was bloodstained, his eyes sparkling. *I have to tell you that was a magnificent first kill.*

Jace didn't speak, but he walked over to her and licked the remaining drops of blood from her muzzle. Then he shifted, as did Gabe, both of them standing tall for a brief moment before looping their bags over their necks and shifting to wolf again.

Shift, Romy, and you'll shed any remaining blood. Jace trotted a few feet down the trail, grabbed her travel bag and brought it back.

Romy shifted and picked the bag up off the ground before slipping it over her neck. Then another shift and she stood beside Jace and Gabe. *What now? Do we travel until it's dark?*

Not tonight. Jace shot a quick glance at Gabe. *There are some small caves not far from here, and if no one else has moved in, they'll make a good place to spend the night. It smells like rain, and I'd rather be some- place dry.*

I second that. Gabe sniffed the air. *That doesn't happen often.*

What?

You smelling rain before I do. But you're right. I think it's going to pour, if you want my opinion. And those caves are still a few miles away. He trotted over to the wild wolf and nudged him with his nose. The wolf yawned and lurched to his feet, but he didn't look happy about having to move again.

He's tired, Romy said. *We've gone a long way today. He's still not at full strength.*

Jace glanced at the wolf and gazed steadily at Romy. *Does he speak to you?*

Not really. Not in words or images, but in feelings. I know what he's feeling, what he needs. He's tired, but he won't leave us. We just need to take it slow for him.

Jace didn't say anything, but the way he looked at her was different, as if he might be seeing more of her than he'd seen before. She wasn't sure what that meant, but it left her with a good feeling. A sense that between her first kill and her relationship with their wild brother, she'd stepped further into the Chanku world.

Maybe that's what it would take for Jace to love her. Maybe she merely needed to learn the rules of being Chanku. So far she'd just been winging it, and maybe that wasn't enough. She knew he wanted her, but love? That was an emotion Romy wasn't at all sure of. How did anyone know if what they felt was romantic love or merely an attraction? She'd never experienced either. Not until now, but nothing was clear to her. Nothing but what she felt, what her senses told her as they trotted through the woods, headed for a place to stay the night.

• • •

The cave Jace had been thinking of was only a few miles from the site of Romy's kill. They were almost there and he still couldn't think of the right words, the way to tell her what she meant to him, what she'd shown in her every move and action. How impressed he was with her amazing adaptation to this totally new life. At the very least, he should have said something to her after she brought down that doe with an absolutely perfect charge, the way Gabe had with his open and honest approval of Romy's hunt.

Jace still hadn't said a word. How could he tell her that his heart was too full, his mind so overwhelmed by her beauty, her unbelievable transition from human to wolf and the honesty that seemed to shine in everything she did, that he'd been utterly incapable of speech. She epitomized the ideal Chanku bitch—strong of mind and body, open to new experiences and accepting of whatever the Fates might hand her.

Sometimes, when he looked at Romy Sarika, he felt as if she were so far beyond him that he wasn't deserving of her love. And in that same breath, he'd be praying to the goddess, asking for guidance to win that love.

Eve, of course, wasn't answering. Either she wanted him to figure it out on his own or she didn't think he was the right one for Romy. He hoped it was the former.

Jace? That's it, isn't it? It looks different since we were here last. Gabe stopped at the bottom of a rocky cliff. There was a crevice in the rock that led into a narrow canyon.

Water flowed down the middle, a small stream Jace knew was spring fed. He dipped his muzzle into the cold water and lapped up enough to ease his thirst. Romy took a drink beside the wild wolf. When she raised her head, water drops sparkled against her dark muzzle. Jace forced himself to look away. Instead, he gazed around the area, trying to see what had changed.

Gabe was right—it was different from the way it had looked on their last visit. The sun had set about an hour ago, but there was still enough light to get a good view of the area. He finally spotted the opening to the cave just inside the canyon. It was partially hidden behind a boulder that had fallen sometime over the past year. Trotting through the narrow cleft in the rock, Jace climbed up the rubble-strewn bank to the place where the boulder had landed. It appeared to be completely lodged in between a larger rock and the face of the cliff.

It's not going anywhere. I'll check to see if the cave's empty.

It was. Empty and dry, and large enough for the four of them to rest comfortably, protected from the storm drifting in from the west. Wind was picking up and leaves swirled through the canyon. Thunder rumbled in the distance, and Gabe, Romy, and the wolf climbed the hillside and then followed Jace back inside the cave. He lowered his head and let his bag slip to the ground.

Romy sniffed around all the corners and behind a couple of rocks. Then she lowered her head and slipped her travel bag to the ground, found a fairly smooth spot, circled around a couple of times and lay down. Raising her head, she sniffed the air and then looked toward Jace. *It's actually warm in here. Why is that?*

The opening faces south, so it probably warms up during the day. The storm is coming out of the northwest, so we shouldn't get any wind or water inside. It's small enough that our body heat might warm it.

The wild wolf had taken a spot close to Romy. Jace studied them for a moment, the two of them lying so close together, and realized that there was absolutely nothing about Romy—or any of them—that would differentiate them from wild wolves. He wondered what Romy felt when she and the wolf were communicating, because they had to be, on some level.

Gabe entered the cave. He'd been scouting the area, making sure there weren't any dangers nearby. *The wolf pack has been through here recently. I think we're a day or two behind them. They generally stick to the forest between Bend and Eugene.*

Romy? Do you think he might be able to tell you if this is his pack Gabe scented?

She stared at the wolf for at least two or three minutes. Jace wanted to listen in, but he didn't want to upset the wolf if there was any actual communication taking place. Finally, Romy looked at Jace. *He said it doesn't matter. We're his pack now.*

13

Gabe shifted and pulled on his pants and shoes. "You guys okay with a small campfire? There's plenty of dry wood out there, but once the rain hits it won't stay that way for long."

"I'll help." Jace grabbed his pack and dressed. "Romy, do you mind staying with your buddy?"

Not at all. I'm warm, dry, and comfortable. You guys go be manly.

"Spoken like a true woman. C'mon, Gabe."

She watched them leave. She couldn't help but appreciate their perfect forms, the strong muscles and tall, lean bodies. Nor could she help wondering what the night would bring. Wondering and anticipating, with her daylong arousal simmering at a low, slow burn.

Though neither of the guys had said anything, she knew if they were as aroused as she was, they'd all be doing more than just sleeping tonight. But as wolves? That didn't feel right to her, at least not if it was the three of them. Somehow, the idea of having sex in her wolven form should only happen with Jace. She wasn't sure exactly why, but for whatever reason Romy knew she was right.

In the meantime, she lay all curled up next to Wolf, who appeared to be perfectly happy keeping her warm and not entirely alone.

· · ·

"Do you think Romy will want both of us?"

Jace paused, arms loaded with firewood, and stared at his buddy. "I'm more worried about you. Are you healthy enough? I don't want you reinjuring yourself."

"I'm fine," Gabe said. "My neck and shoulder were a little stiff this morning, but the run today appears to have worked that out." He stared toward the rising moon, waning now as it rose slowly in the east. "I don't want to rush Romy. Does she really know what we're like? What we're used to doing with each other?"

"She saw us together the first night she was with us and didn't seem to mind a bit when both of us brought her to climax." Merely thinking about that night, how it felt when he'd realized she was watching with such avid interest, made him hot. "And last night she was right in the middle of things. I think she's smart enough to figure it out." He laughed, remembering his shock when she'd cupped his balls in her hand. "All we can do is ask, Gabe. But if she doesn't, I can certainly take care of whatever you need. You'll never have to be alone or do without if I'm around. You know that."

Gabe shrugged and then adjusted the heavy load of branches he carried. "It's always been just the two of us on this trip. I'm not sure what my role is now that we have Romy."

Jace laughed at the confused look on Gabe's face. "You don't have a role any more than I do. We are who we are, and Romy is who she is. I love her. I still can't believe how I feel about her, but I do. It's happened a lot faster than I ever expected, but I think I knew from the moment I realized she was Chanku that she was meant for me. Of course, convincing her of that minor detail might take a while, but . . ."

"I dunno about that. I've watched the way she looks at you. She's at least very intrigued."

"One can only hope. Let's get back to her. At least we don't have to worry about a meal tonight."

Gabe was laughing when he said, "Yeah. That was a pretty amazing first kill. We don't want to mention what a fiasco mine was."

"Or mine. It's probably a guy thing, but why did we both try to bring down the biggest bull elk in the herd? Definitely not smart. Not smart at all."

• • •

Romy glanced up as the guys walked into the cave. She'd shifted and put on her pants and halter top, but the air was cool and the idea of a campfire was more than appealing. It was almost entirely dark, but there was enough moonlight peeking between the clouds to allow her to see Jace and Gabe's silhouettes as they stepped inside. Wolf growled and she put a restraining hand on his shoulder.

"Be still," she said, and he relaxed beneath her touch.

Jace dropped his wood against the wall opposite Romy.

Gabe did the same. "I'll get the fire going," he said.

Jace nodded and walked over to sit beside Romy. "If you get thirsty, the creek below us is spring fed. Our bags are waterproof, so I can fill one if you think you'll want a drink during the night."

"I'll be fine." She stroked the wolf's thick coat. "He has a name."

"The wolf?" Jace touched her cheek, turned her face to his. "He told you his name?"

"Not in so many words, but when I asked if there was something I could call him, I saw an image of a wolf in my mind. I said, 'Is Wolf your name?' and he whined. I took that for a yes."

"Wolf it is." Jace ran his hand over the animal's head and scratched behind his ears. Wolf groaned and sprawled across Romy's lap for more. "He's not nearly as wild as I thought he would be. Feral wolves really can't be tamed. I don't get it."

"He's not tamed at all." Romy stroked the thick ruff of fur around the back of his neck. "He's part of our pack, and the same rules apply. You are the alpha wolf, therefore you may scratch behind his ears. I'm the alpha bitch, and I think I can do anything I want." She laughed as she stroked him. "He's still a wild wolf, still a predator, but I must admit, I felt perfectly safe while you and Gabe were gone. He was alert the entire time, listening and watching the cave entrance."

"That's good to know."

"It is." She sighed and stared at the cave entrance and the falling rain for so long that Jace began to fidget.

"What's wrong, Romy?"

She turned and gazed into his dark eyes and sighed again. "I've been thinking about something that I probably should have thought of before."

Jace frowned as he stared at her in that way he had, as if she were the only person in his universe. "Why does that sound so foreboding?" He smiled then and tapped the end of her nose with his fingertip.

She couldn't meet his gaze. Not with this on her mind. "We've done nothing to prevent pregnancy. I didn't get pregnant all those years with my father, but I figured it might be him, not me, with the fertility issues. I don't know. I was their only child, but I don't want to be pregnant right now. I'm not ready to be a mother."

"You won't be. Not until you choose to have a child."

How could that be? Frowning, she stared at him. The women at the compound were always worried about getting pregnant. They knew that their children tied them to the men, whether they wanted to stay or not, but all Romy said was, "I don't get it. Pregnancy isn't always something you choose. It's something that happens when you have sex without birth control. That's how the men controlled the women in the compound."

"When did you start eating the grasses?"

"Before my mother was killed. Probably when I was about four or five. Why?"

"Then you were already making the physical changes from human to Chanku. That's why your father couldn't impregnate you. A Chanku female has total control of conception, and you can only get pregnant in your wolven form. Probably why you were your mother's only child. She got pregnant before she started eating the grasses. Once we get to Montana and you have a chance to meet other women in the pack, they can explain it to you better than I can, but I know that when women decide to have a child, it can only be with her bonded mate, and she has to consciously choose to release an egg. Since only bonded mates have sex together as wolves, a child can only be conceived when a male and female mate in their wolven form and the woman releases an egg. I'm not aware of any accidental pregnancies."

Gabe laughed. He had a good fire going and the cave was already feeling warmer. He got up and walked across the small space to join them. "There are, however, occasional surprise conceptions."

Jace grinned and punched Gabe's shoulder. "Only your mother would have the balls to put one over on Anton."

Romy looked from one to the other, totally perplexed. "What happened?"

"My dad was perfectly happy with his three children. He had Lily, our older sister, who is so much like Dad it's scary, and then Mac and I came along. Mac's my twin brother, but I think we were such a handful that Mom didn't really get to enjoy our toddler years at all. She was too busy trying to keep us from killing ourselves or each other."

"Or Lily from turning you into a couple of frogs." Jace grinned at Romy, who knew she must look totally confused. "Lily is a more powerful wizard than Gabe's dad," he said, "and Anton is pretty amazing."

Wizard? Jace hadn't just called their pack alpha a wizard, had he?

"Yeah, well, Mom wanted another baby, and this time she wanted just one. She popped out an egg without discussing it with Dad first."

"Your father was not happy. I remember my mom was so pissed at him because he went around in a huff for weeks when he found out your mom was pregnant."

Gabe sighed. "Ya know, it's not that he didn't want the baby. He's such a control freak that he didn't like the choice being taken away from him, even though there was an ongoing argument between him and Mom about the times he'd made decisions for others and taken away their choice. He's a good guy, but he tends to narrowly focus on a desired result."

Laughing, Jace said, "That's putting it politely."

"Hey . . . I'm trying to be diplomatic. He is my father, after all. Anyway, Romy, he wanted Mom to himself, and then Lucia came along, and a few month later the fire wiped out the entire compound, and—"

"Fire? What fire?" Romy hadn't heard anything at all about a fire.

"It was about the time that the world found out about shapeshifters. There was a huge forest fire that burned through our valley and destroyed all the buildings, including my mom and dad's house. We hid out in the caves beneath the house, where we were safe until the fire had burned through, but I still remember coming up out of that cave."

"Yeah," Jace said. "The stairs used to lead into the kitchen, but we went up the stairs and there was nothing but blue sky and burned trees."

"And the stove and refrigerator. I still remember my mom staring at the melted kitchen appliances and trying so hard not to cry, but she held Lucia and looked straight at Dad and said we'd rebuild, better than ever."

"Did they?" Romy couldn't imagine having a lovely home and then losing it. She'd never had anything but the tiny cabin with her father, but it was the only home she'd ever known. The odd thing was, she'd loved it when her mother was alive. Then it was perfect.

After she died, it wasn't anymore.

"They did." Gabe grinned at Jace. "They built a beautiful new home, bigger and better than the one before, and then cottages and cabins for all the other members of the pack. Before the fire we'd been spread all over the country, with pack members in Maine and Colorado, down in San Francisco and up in Montana."

"But afterward," Jace said, interrupting Gabe almost as if they'd practiced the telling of this tale or had told it many times before, "everyone decided to live together in Montana. Eventually, Anton's business interests in San Francisco expanded to the point where Lily moved down to take over. A lot of the younger members of the pack are working in various Chanku companies around the globe, but the center of pack life is still in Montana. I imagine it will always be there, since we've gotten legal standing, sort of like Native Americans."

"Yeah, Dad's finally got his own fiefdom where he gets to be the feudal lord."

Jace had, at some point, taken hold of Romy's hand, and it was the most natural thing in the world to hang on to him, as if the connection between them was stronger than merely two hands holding. "Do you think he sees himself that way?" she asked. "As a feudal lord of his subjects?"

"Dad's an interesting character. You can't really describe him with any single trait or even by his flaws. He looks out for people. He's not perfect, but his goals are clear. He wants every person with the Chanku genes to learn about their heritage. He hates the thought of people like you going for their entire lives without knowing the connections to pack, to bonded mate, or to our goddess." Gabe sat, legs akimbo, and rested his chin on his fist.

"The most important person in his world is Mom. I've never seen a love truer than theirs. Jace's parents have an amazing bond as well, but Mom and Dad have been through a lot over the years, and they've always come through things stronger, their mating bond tighter than ever. But when Mom got pregnant with Lucia, knowing he really didn't want more children, it was the first time I think she'd openly defied him."

"What did he do? Was he horribly angry? Did he beat her?" Romy had always felt that her father hadn't wanted her, until he had no one else to fuck. Then he figured she'd do just fine. Her mother had said he'd beaten her when he found out she got pregnant.

"Oh, Goddess, no!" Gabe laughed. "He did what he always does with anything that concerns Mom. He caved. And he adores Lucia. I mean, Lily will always be special, mainly because she just is, but Lucia is Dad's baby."

"A gorgeous twenty-six-year-old baby, but still Anton's baby. We'll have to tell you Lily stories when we've got a longer night." Jace squeezed her hand. "I don't think anyone can find fault with Gabe's big sister. Her best friend is the goddess."

"Your goddess? Eve?" That was so far beyond belief that Romy didn't even think to disagree.

"Yep. They actually visit on the astral, in what Lily refers to as *Eve's when and where*, whatever that means."

It meant more than Jace could ever understand. Romy didn't think she'd ever felt further from him, not since the moment she'd met him, but now the distance between them yawned like a great bottomless chasm. She couldn't look into his eyes. Not with her thoughts swirling like water going down a drain, only it felt as if her dreams were disappearing as well.

She knew her voice was barely audible when she said, "It means you guys live in a world that's totally different than the one I know. I don't know anything about living with wizards and goddesses who speak to you as if you really matter. I don't know how to live in that kind of world."

"Sweetheart, there's nothing to know, nothing that matters beyond the fact that you already are part of our world, for better or for worse. You're Chanku now, Romy." Jace held both her hands and she couldn't have been any more aware of the heat in his touch and the burning emotion in his eyes.

"You'll meet our pack alpha. Anton Cheval is Gabe's dad. He's a brilliant man and a powerful wizard. You'll meet his daughter Lily and her mate, Sebastian, who are even more powerful than Anton. Then there's my mom, Liana. She was our goddess for thousands of years before she screwed up so badly that my dad's first mate was killed before it was her time to die. Eve, my father's first bonded mate, ended up trading places with my mother on the astral, which made Eve our new goddess and Liana—eventually—my mother."

He grinned at her. "I know, it's really confusing, but my mom, who was once a goddess, is just a really terrific mom, very much in love with my dad, me, and both my sisters. Their names are Eve and Phoenix." Jace raised her hands in his and pressed a kiss to her knuckles. "We're all special in our own way, Romy, but none is as special as you. They are going to love you, and they will all honor your bravery."

He leaned close and kissed her, but his steady gaze never left her face. He looked directly into her eyes and it felt as if he saw clear into her soul. As if he knew things about her she'd still not discovered.

"Jace is right, Romy." Gabe looped his arm around her shoulders and gently squeezed. "You will fit in with our pack so perfectly. I promise you that." Then he did something she hadn't expected—Gabe leaned close and kissed her. This wasn't like his usual peck to her lips—this time he kissed her the way Jace did, with firm pressure from his lips, the soft slide of his tongue. One hand slipped into her hair and cupped the back of her skull as he gently directed her. Then he pulled back and licked his lips. "Is this okay, Romy? May I kiss you?"

Her hands were still linked with Jace's hands, and she was aware he had moved closer, but she focused entirely on Gabe. "Yes." Turning to Jace, she gazed into his dark eyes, and then realized she was focusing on his mouth. "How do you feel about me kissing Gabe?"

"I love Gabe, Romy. I love watching him kiss you, watching you kiss him. At some point, I hope you'll want to make love with both of us, but not until you're entirely comfortable with the idea of two men loving you at the same time. Do you think that day will ever come?"

Romy shivered, but she knew it wasn't from fear. No, it was definitely expectation and probably a lot of arousal added in. Gabe and Jace at the same time? Why did that sound so absolutely decadent and yet unbelievably appealing? Granted, they'd both made love to her the night before last, and last night she'd managed to insinuate herself in between the two of them, but to actually make love? The three of them? To be an active participant? Knowing both Gabe and Jace wanted her, but wanted her as a part of the love they felt for each other? What did they want her to do? She knew how to make love to Jace and it couldn't be too much different with Gabe, but . . .

"Romy? Look at me."

She raised her head and once again was looking directly into Jace's eyes.

"Don't block me. Please? I'm glad you're open right now, because it lets me see all the confusion you're feeling. Don't think. Just let it happen. Gabe and I will show you. We won't hurt you, but we will give you more pleasure than you've ever known. Will you trust us to do that? Can you trust us?"

She nodded. What else could she do? She was already so in love with Jace she could barely trust herself not to blurt out the words, and she felt so much affection for Gabe that if not for the feelings she had for Jace, well . . . *oh*. She looked at Jace again, really looked, and realized he was still listening.

Listening to her convoluted thoughts, but instead of being embarrassed or angry, he was smiling. There were tears in his eyes, and his hands were trembling, but the way he was looking at Romy, the way he made her feel was . . .

"Goddess, Jace. I can feel it, the way you and Romy connect. It's almost scary."

Wolf whined and crawled closer. He rested his muzzle on Romy's knee and gazed at her with soulful eyes. She reached out and stroked his head, rubbed behind his ears, almost afraid to look at Jace again.

He tipped her chin up with his forefinger. "I don't think time will change the way I feel about you, Romy. It will make it stronger, if anything, but don't feel confused about loving me, because I've known from the beginning that's what I've felt for you."

Gabe had moved away, and Romy was vaguely aware of him in the background, but Jace was pulling her into his arms, stroking her hair, kissing her lips, her throat, the sensitive spot behind her ear. Kissing her and whispering words of love, promises of forever.

And while her heart soared, there was still a spot in the back of her mind reminding her that she'd only known him three days. Three days that felt like a lifetime and yet had passed in barely an instant.

Was it possible to make a lifetime commitment after only three short days? She didn't know, but there was no reason not to keep learning more about this amazing man. Learning about Jace, loving him, and maybe learning to love the woman she was fast becoming.

• • •

Jace lifted Romy in his arms and stood with the sound of her laughter ringing in his ears. "I'm too big," she said, but he just shook his head and carried her easily to the thin blankets Gabe had spread across the sandy floor of the cave. They were part of the emergency gear he and Gabe carried in their travel bags, lightweight yet designed to insulate and protect when holding in body heat was essential. They definitely weren't designed for comfort, but they were the best they could do to keep the sand out of places no one wanted it.

Still holding Romy, Jace lowered himself to the blanket, crossed his legs and settled her in his lap. She looped her hands over his shoulders and turned to study him. There was something almost mesmerizing about the way she watched him. He knew she wasn't used to men being kind to her, but that wasn't everything. He didn't fully understand her, even though her thoughts were often an open book to him. For now, she was blocking, but he was okay with that. She needed to learn to guard her thoughts or life among the pack would be unbearable. For a woman not used to the mindspeak all of them grew up with, it had to be a horrible shock to have her private thoughts suddenly so public.

"Not really," she said. Then she laughed. "You're open to me, and it's getting easier all the time for me to read what you're thinking."

Jace felt his skin flush hot and then cold. He slammed his shields shut and then, embarrassed, lifted them again. He wanted to be open to Romy. He really didn't want there to be secrets between them. Not ever. Instead, to cover his embarrassment, he kissed her.

Romy's arousal was a living, breathing entity, set free by that single kiss. He realized she'd been holding herself in check, unsure what he and Gabe wanted.

"Only you, Romy." He licked her upper lip, nipped the lower one, and she opened to him. "I want to show you so much. Both of us do, but we don't want to frighten you."

She kissed him and then once again leaned back so she could get a better look. "Do I look scared?"

"Nope. Not one bit."

"Good." Then she reached for the hem of her shirt and pulled it over her head.

Her breasts were full, the areolas a dark rose and her nipples ruched into tight buds, revealing her arousal. Gabe knelt behind Romy, reached around and palmed her breasts, holding them for Jace to lick and nip. Jace drew one taut bud deep between his lips. Romy groaned and arched her back, thrusting her breasts forward, but Jace lifted her, turning her easily so that her back was to him, holding her breasts in his palms, and it was Gabe's turn.

He sucked her right nipple and then her left. Groaning, twisting her body to give Gabe more access, Romy cried out as he kissed his way down her rib cage and then tugged at the waistband of her pants. She lifted her butt, helping him, and Jace made sure that when she dropped back down his palms cupped her buttocks.

He kneaded her muscular cheeks and used his fingertips to explore the crevice between, slipping over her perineum to her damp sheath, fully aware that Gabe had reached her sex at the same time. When he felt Romy's body begin to shudder, he knew that the first of the climaxes he and Gabe had planned for her tonight was just a stroke, a lick, a touch away.

· · ·

Gabe's touch was different than Jace's, but the result was every bit as effective. His tongue had barely connected with her clit when the first orgasm raced through her, a shock of sensation leaping from breasts to womb to clit and then deep inside again, rolling and roiling through nerve endings already sensitized by a day running as a wolf.

She was gasping for breath, still trying to see past the stars and spots blinding her, when Gabe stroked deep inside her sex, sweeping his fingers through the thick fluids filling her vagina. But then he did something that surprised her, though she'd learned not to be shocked by anything either of these men did. He dragged her feminine fluids with his fingertips and then rubbed them over her anus, a slow, sensual sweep of tissues she'd never thought of as sexual.

That opinion immediately reversed. All her muscles clenched in response.

Jace had a grip on her bottom, though, and his fingers were holding her cheeks apart while Gabe swept more of her fluids from one opening to the other. She didn't understand, but it felt so good she wasn't about to complain.

Then Jace did the same thing, trailing his fingers through the moisture that had gathered between her legs and spreading it around her bottom. He was swirling that tiny opening with his slick fingertip and the sensations were amazing.

"I want you to trust me, Romy. This might hurt at first, but I promise it will get better. Will you let me?"

Confused, she glanced over her shoulder. She was well aware of Jace's erection pressing against her spine, but the look on his face, the absolute need he didn't even try to hide, had her wondering what he was asking her. And then, she realized it wasn't important. She would do anything for him. No matter what. "Of course I will. Anything."

He didn't speak. Instead he bowed his head and took a deep breath.

Then he rubbed her bottom opening again. Her first thought was that it was embarrassing to have him touching her there, but again, it felt so good, and this was Jace. The one who had saved her life.

She leaned forward, giving him better access. Whatever he was doing was making her so wet, and he was taking those fluids and using them to lubricate her bottom. She knew now what he intended. Some of the women had talked about this, and their reactions were mixed.

Some loved it, others hated it. From the way Romy's body was beginning to react, she had a feeling she was going to be part of the "love it" group. Jace wrapped one arm around her waist, holding her, and with his other hand he dragged the tip of his penis from her vagina to her bottom, paying particular attention to that tight little opening.

She'd thought she might be embarrassed. She had no idea it would feel this good. He pressed against her with the thick crown of his penis, and she did what felt right and pushed against him. He pressed forward, she pushed back, and after a momentary burning flash of pain, he was in, slipping through that taut muscle, sliding slowly, deeply, inside.

"Ah, Romy. I was so afraid I'd hurt you. Are you okay? Have you done this before?"

"Never. Honestly?" She groaned as he slid deeper. "I thought it would hurt, but it doesn't. Jace, this feels so good."

"What's Gabe doing?"

"Staring at us like he's going to explode."

Jace laughed. "He just might. Tilt forward and he can enter you at the same time."

Romy slowly turned and stared at Jace. She knew her eyes had to be as big as saucers. "This is how you both plan to make love to me? At the same time?" She really hadn't meant for her voice to squeak, but it did.

Jace just grinned at her. "Trust us, it works. We've done this before."

"Says the man with his cock up my butt."

"Gabe! Romy did it! She said cock!" Jace might be laughing, but Romy noticed it didn't affect the size of his erection. She tightened her muscles around him, loving it when he groaned.

"I knew there was hope for her." Gabe cupped her face in his palms and kissed her. "I promise to be careful. Okay?"

She nodded. Jace leaned forward, and Gabe slid beneath her thighs so that both she and Jace were straddling his legs. Jace pulled out a bit, and she wanted him back, now, but then Gabe was slipping into her vagina, his thick, hot cock slowly forcing its way deep inside. She knew he felt Jace as he entered her. Had to feel the thick, hard shaft inside her dark passage, the one she'd never really imagined as something sexual, but it felt so good, so absolutely amazing to have both men filling her, both of them equally aroused, the two of them driving her arousal higher with each careful thrust.

But then she let herself go. Let the sensations rule, and Gabe and Jace seemed to know the moment she'd set all of her inhibitions free.

They drove into her, in and out, the two of them synchronizing their thrust and retreat so that the sensation was constant, and it wasn't at all painful. Not in a manner that would make her want to escape. No, this pain was amazing, a part of her arousal, of her desires, and her love for Jace, even her love for Gabe.

And as the two of them loved her, Romy knew a contentment she'd never expected.

And the beginnings of a love that would transcend time.

14

Three weeks later, northeast of Spokane, Washington . . .

Romy'd slept like the dead that first night in the wild, totally relaxed and unafraid of sleeping in a dark cave. She'd awakened at dawn, curled up in a furry pile with three other warm wolves, convinced this was the most comfortable way in the world to spend an otherwise chilly night.

They'd made good time, checking on the various wolf packs roaming through Oregon and on into Washington. Jace had explained that while wolves now enjoyed full protection under the law—since killing one would be murder if it were, in fact, not a wild wolf but a Chanku running in wolf form—they were still regularly hunted in secret, often by those who actually hoped they were killing Chanku.

Thus the need for their yearly survey. The packs seemed healthy, though with a few losses. There were always those hit by vehicles on the busy roads or shot by ranchers angry over losing livestock. Acceptable losses, to a certain extent, but frustrating just the same.

The loss of any wolf by anything other than natural death was a tragedy, in both Jace's and Gabe's eyes. And now, in Romy's as well.

Wolf had become her shadow. If they'd come across his pack over the past three weeks, he'd neglected to let them know. Romy, Jace, and Gabe were his pack.

It was midafternoon on a day in late August when they shifted and dressed under cover of a dense copse of trees in a small community northeast of Spokane, Washington. They'd stayed in hotels whenever possible, but it had been almost a week since their last brush with civilization. Romy was ready. She missed her showers, even though shifting left each of them totally clean.

It just wasn't the same, though she was perfectly happy with their nightly sexual encounters under a starry sky. She didn't care where they were when they made love—it was always wonderful. With Wolf standing watch, it was relaxing, too, knowing they didn't have to remain on full alert. On the other hand, two men and a big bed sounded pretty good.

"What about Wolf?" Romy tangled her fingers in the wolf's thick fur at the back of his neck. Some of the places they'd stayed in hadn't been too happy about their unusual "pet."

"Put the leash on him. This place advertises that it's dog-friendly. Let's hope they aren't limiting what part of the *canidae* family that covers." Jace dug into his almost empty travel bag and found the leash they'd picked up a couple of weeks earlier, when it appeared their four-legged companion was sticking with them.

Romy knelt and showed the leash to Wolf. He sniffed it, gave her a disgusted look, and held still while she slipped it around his neck. There was no collar and the leash was fashioned with a breakaway link that would give way if he tugged harder than usual.

Wolf was wild. Not a pet. He stayed with them of his own free will, something Chanku honored. Free will was everything. Romy figured she understood that better than most.

She stood and held the leash as they walked across the parking lot to the hotel office.

Gabe held the door. Romy, Wolf, and Jace walked in ahead. Romy found a place in the lobby to sit with Wolf while Jace got them a room.

She was staring out the window, idly running her fingers through Wolf's thick fur, when she realized a young woman was staring at them. After a few minutes, while Romy did her best to ignore her, the woman said, "Is that a wild wolf?"

Romy clenched Wolf's leash. *Jace? What do I say?*

Tell her the truth. It's no secret what we are or that we can heal . . . only the telepathy is not openly discussed.

Romy glanced up at the attractive young woman. She stood far enough back to feel safe, but she was obviously intrigued by Wolf. "He is. He was shot by a hunter, my friend healed his injuries, and he's stayed with us of his own free will. I think he's decided we're his pack."

Her eyes lit up. "Are you Chanku? Is the wolf Chanku?"

Smiling, Romy ran her fingers through Wolf's fur. "I'm Chanku." The moment the words passed her lips, Romy sat straighter. She'd never told anyone of her new reality. "So are the two men registering." She nodded toward Jace and Gabe. "But this guy is all wolf."

"Do you mind if I sit?"

Romy shrugged and gestured toward the empty chair on the far side, away from Wolf. "He really isn't tame, and I'd hate for him to think you were a threat to me. He's very protective."

The woman laughed. "I'd rather he not think I'm a threat either." She held out her hand. "I'm Sandra Watson. I'm a reporter for *Northeast Washington News*. We're up here doing a story on the expansion of the wolf population in the northeast part of the state. We're very proud of our wolves."

Romy took her hand for a quick, firm shake. "Romy Sarika. You might want to talk to my friends. They're doing an annual survey of wolf populations in the northwestern states."

"I'd like that. Do you think they'd be willing to speak with me? My crew's here for another couple of hours. I'm staying until tomorrow morning. It would be wonderful to get something straight from the wolf's mouth, so to speak."

She blinked and then smiled brightly. Romy didn't even have to turn around to know that Jace and Gabe must be headed their way.

"Hello." Jace, with Gabe beside him, walked across the lobby. "I'm Jace Wolf, this is my partner, Gabe Cheval. I see you've met Romy."

"Just now." Sandra stood, and the look she gave to both of the guys had Romy biting back laughter. It was nice knowing she wasn't the only woman who thought they were absolutely gorgeous. But she had to admit, she loved knowing she was the woman who had them in her bed.

"Romy told me you're doing an annual survey of wolves in the northwest. I'm up here reporting on the growth of the wolf population in this part of the state. As I told Romy, we're very proud of our wolves. I'd love to get your take on things."

"Sounds good. There's nothing more we like to talk about." Jace glanced at Gabe, who seemed more than a little interested in the reporter.

Gabe added, "We're just getting ready to check into our room. When and where would you like to meet after we get settled?"

"Half an hour? Outside, on the patio? And can you bring your buddy? He's gorgeous."

Jace glanced at Gabe and then nodded. "We can do that. Where is the patio?"

Sandra pointed to a set of double doors that led to the back side of the hotel. "You can't miss it. Just look for me and two guys with cameras and a microphone. It's nice to meet you."

• • •

"I'm glad that's over." Romy flopped on the bed. Wolf, after only a moment's hesitation, jumped lightly up to join her. "I really didn't like her asking me about life at the compound."

"I'm sorry." Jace sat beside her. "I should have thought of that possibility, but you can't fault a reporter for doing her research. You handled it really well, though. Enough to answer her questions but very few details."

"I figure they're all going to come out in the trial. I'm dreading that. I wish it had never happened. I just want all of it to go away."

Jace sighed. "I do, and I don't. If not for the evil reverend, I might never have met you." He took her hands in both of his. "I don't want to imagine my life without you in it. I love you, Romy. I hope that someday you'll love me enough to agree to be my mate. Will you at least think about it?"

She glanced at their linked hands. "I've been thinking about it. A lot." She glanced out the window, unwilling to see the questions in his eyes. She was such a coward. "Jace, I have to admit, I'm afraid. Mating is forever. I don't want you to realize, somewhere down the line, that you made a horrible mistake in choosing me." She turned to him, blinking back tears. She didn't want to cry. She'd never cried during all those long years. She wasn't going to cry now, when her life was so amazing. They'd had three wonderful weeks together, weeks that were the best time in her whole life, but how could she expect it to last?

If they mated, if they made that promise meant to last a lifetime, she was certain he'd grow tired of her. Before long, he'd realize it was a mistake. She didn't deserve someone like Jace, a man so good, so strong and steady and absolutely gorgeous that he was perfect. Not someone as horribly damaged as she was. A good life with a man so perfect wasn't for her. But how to explain what a coward she was to Jace, a man who was so brave, so open and honest about his feelings? How was she going to make him see the ugly truth. "Sometimes," she said, gazing at their linked hands, "I feel like I'm broken, as if the years I spent as my father's whore, the . . ."

"No. Don't say that, Romy. You were not your father's whore. Never that. You were his daughter and he was a bastard for treating you the way he did. You were just a little girl, Romy, and he was a sick and twisted fuck. Nothing that happened was your fault. You are most definitely not broken. Never think that. You're strong and smart and so brave."

He smiled and pushed her hair out of her eyes. "We should all be as broken as you, Romy Sarika. You amaze me." He kissed her, and she knew he tasted the salt from her tears. They fell steadily now, but no matter how she tried she couldn't hold them back.

"I'm not going to push you, sweetheart. I promise. When you're ready, all you have to do is let me know. In my heart and mind, you are already my mate."

Wolf faced the door and growled. Jace put his hand on the beast's shoulder. "It's okay, Wolf. Just Gabe. He's back from the store." He kissed Romy and then opened the door for Gabe. His arms were loaded with bags and the scent of hamburgers and fries filled the room. Jace grabbed the beer and bottle of wine and took them to the small refrigerator while Gabe spread their meal out on the table. Then he unwrapped a package of freshly ground beef and put it on a paper plate for Wolf.

Romy quickly washed her face and hands. She managed a smile as she walked back into the kitchen area of their suite, but she was still rattled from the conversation she'd had with Jace, the fact she'd actually voiced the fears that had been plaguing her over the past three weeks. Jace held a chair out for her.

"Thank you." She loved the little courtesies he performed so easily. Once she sat, Romy took a good look at their meal.

"What is it with you and hamburgers and fries, Gabe?"

"Comfort food." He pointed a fry at her. "Makes me happy. So does Ms. Watson." He shot a grin at Jace. "I saw her on the way to the burger joint. She asked me if I'd like to come up to her room and talk some more about the survey. I, of course, said I'd be happy to help her with her story."

Jace almost choked on his hamburger. "Like you really expect to get much talking done?"

Gabe shot a grin at Romy and then slapped his hand over his heart. "Jace? How can you say that? I'm willing to suffer a few hours of Ms. Watson's charm, all for you. It's a hardship, but I can handle it because you and Romy could use a night alone for a change. Or at least a few hours."

Jace turned to Romy and there was no laughter in his voice when he said, "Yeah, Gabe. I think I'd like that. A lot."

Romy couldn't look away. Not with Jace staring at her so thoroughly she felt as if he could see every thought, understand every worry. Gabe got up and went after a beer. He brought one back for Jace, sat it in front of his buddy, and when Jace didn't respond, sat back in front of his dinner.

Romy took a deep breath, shook her head to clear her thoughts. She refused to think about hours alone with Jace. What surprising things he would think of to entertain her. To make love to her. It was never just sex with Jace. It was always making love.

She took a deep breath and focused on something she could handle. Like dinner and their survey. "So," she said. "What's our plan tomorrow?" She took the top of her burger and squeezed catsup all over the meat. Anything but make eye contact with Jace again.

After a long pause, Jace finally answered, but she could feel his questions battering at her mind. She kept her shields tightly in place.

"As we told Ms. Watson, we've connected with the packs west of here, and now we need to check on the ones northeast of Spokane. We should be able to make it to Huckleberry in the next couple of days."

"Good," she said. "That's good." Even though she had absolutely no idea where or what Huckleberry was. Instead of asking, she concentrated on her hamburger.

Jace stared at her for a long, steady moment out of time. Then he softly sighed and turned away from Romy. He shot a grin at Gabe.

And for the rest of their meal teased him unmercifully about the lovely Ms. Watson.

• • •

Within the week they'd reached the northernmost part of Washington. The only drawback to searching this isolated area was the spotty cell phone service, but they'd checked in with John Salazar as they'd promised to do, and everything was still moving along, albeit slowly. The reverend remained in jail along with a few other men from the compound, and prosecutors were gathering evidence to file added charges against them.

There were a number of wolf packs in this part of the state and the survey was going well. The pack at Huckleberry had added a couple of pups this year, though three years of drought and cold, dry winters had been hard on the older animals. They'd run across similar situations with the other packs. A few new young but a high mortality rate among the elders, and most of it from purely natural causes. There'd been little sign of poaching, and ranchers had finally put in strong enough fences to protect their livestock, so the number of depredation permits issued was way down.

Sort of a good news, bad news story, as far as Jace was concerned.

He, Romy, and Gabe sat on a rocky outcropping, watching three wolf pups playing in the meadow below. Wolf lay in the sun nearby, resting but always alert to their surroundings.

Romy sat with her arms wrapped around her knees, staring at the pups. "It's good to see them playing like that, but I can't help but wonder if they'll survive the winter."

Jace took Romy's hand and squeezed her fingers. "In nature, it really is survival of the fittest. They're strong and healthy now. If they can find enough food, they'll make it, but we had about four good years with mild winters and wet springs. Plenty of green grass and browse for the deer and elk, and perfect conditions for the packs to grow large and healthy. Then the weather changed again, and after three hard years of drought and below-average temperatures, there hasn't been enough food to sustain the wolves' preferred prey. When the deer and elk start to die off, there's a huge impact on food for the predators. It's tough, but more of them will die when there's not enough to eat."

"I wish there was a way to help." She leaned her head against his shoulder.

He wrapped his arm around her waist. "We've learned that when you feed animals and keep them alive through hard times, it upsets the natural balance. Mankind has messed with nature for way too many years. All we've done is make things worse. These little guys look perfectly healthy. That's the best we can hope for. C'mon, we need to get moving."

He stood and offered a hand to Romy and tugged her lightly to her feet. "Gabe, move it. We're just a couple of miles from that really nice cavern. If we get a move on, we can get settled before dark."

"It's going to be a full moon tonight." Gabe lay stretched out on a flat rock, eyes closed, soaking up the warm afternoon sun. "Should be gorgeous. You sure we need to leave now?"

"Now." Jace laughed. "C'mon, Romy. He can catch up. I want to get going."

Grumbling, Gabe stood and brushed the sand off his butt. "Okay, but Romy? You really have to make this worth my while. I hope you understand that."

Laughing, she curled one hand under his chin and tapped his lips with her forefinger. "Ah, Gabriel. I always make it worth your while."

Gabe stared at Jace, frowning. "Jace, my friend. Please note. We have created a monster."

They shifted and headed toward the cavern. Jace led, with Romy on his heels and Gabe behind her. Wolf traveled off to their left, keeping to the woods and scouting for other wolves. He'd started scouting wide just east of Spokane, and the tactic had worked well. He was often the first to scent the packs as they moved from one territory to the next.

It was perfect. Absolutely perfect. The woman he loved, the man who'd been closer than a brother, who would always be both friend and lover, the three of them running with their wild brother beneath the perfect blue skies of an August afternoon. He couldn't ask for more.

Except that he really wanted Romy as his mate.

She'd come around. He knew that might take time, and he had time. All the time he needed.

Jace! Gabe's mental shout slammed into Jace. *Something's hit me . . . something's . . .*

He spun around just in time to see Gabe stagger and fall.

A fletched dart protruded from Gabe's throat.

Shit. Romy, Gabe's been darted. Jace felt the sting in his right shoulder, the harsh burn of chemicals plunging into his system. *Crap. They got me, too.* He stopped and twisted, nipping at the dart sticking out of his shoulder. He caught it between his teeth, yanked it free.

It was too late.

Run, Romy. Run! You're the only one who can save us. His vision shattered into blotches of gray and black. He couldn't see Romy. Couldn't tell if she got away or, Goddess forbid, if she'd been shot. He had no idea who had attacked them, or why. Frantic, he tried to keep his feet under him, but there was no up, no down. No day or night.

Then the rough ground came up to meet him as his legs folded and he hit the dirt.

• • •

Romy didn't hesitate. She raced for the trees to the left of the trail, running north of where they'd been attacked, calling out to Wolf to stay hidden. She'd sensed him coming closer the moment Gabe cried out. Who would do this? Why? She knew there were people who hated Chanku, but to shoot at three wolves on an isolated mountain trail? Were they just hunting wolves or were they hunting Chanku?

The only way to find out was to watch who came after Jace and Gabe. Once deep in the woods, she turned and circled back until she was directly opposite where Jace and Gabe still lay in the trail. Quietly she worked her way into a thick tangle of blackberry vines, oblivious to the thorns raking her coat. She'd found a narrow trail that gave her access and a fairly clear area where she could crouch and remain hidden.

The guys were barely a dozen feet away, but she knew she was entirely hidden.

Wolf slipped in beside her, silent as a wraith. They touched noses and he whined softly.

Quiet. Wait, she said. He seemed to understand simple commands, thank goodness. Now he hid close beside her in the dark tangle of brambles. They waited.

For many minutes, they waited. Neither Gabe nor Jace moved. She tried to make contact, but they were both unconscious.

Or dead. No!

She couldn't think that. They were merely unconscious from the drug, and she would continue trying to connect. Wolf whimpered softly and she glanced up in time to see two men creep out of the rocks high above the trail. They stayed to the shadows and scanned the forest. Romy knew they looked for her, but she couldn't see who they were.

Their voices carried, though.

She recognized at least one of those voices. The hackles rose along her spine and she bit back her growl. She couldn't let him see her.

That bastard was supposed to be in jail, had been the last time Jace spoke with John Salazar. So what in the hell was Franklin Ambrose Smith, otherwise known as the Reverend Ezekiel, doing in northern Washington? It was definitely him, but who was the other guy? As if she'd asked, he stepped out of the shadows. It looked like one of the older men from the compound, one she'd always been afraid of because of the way he watched her. As if he'd wanted her, even when she was small, though it took a long time for her to recognize that look in his eyes as something sick. Brother Gordon had been fond of many of the little girls. She'd known him to take in two young sisters when their parents died, but that had been years ago.

She had no idea where the girls had gone. She figured they'd escaped.

Which made all of this terribly clear. The men weren't hunting wolves and they weren't merely hunting Chanku.

No. They were hunting Romy.

And Jace and Gabe had just become innocent victims of killers.

She watched the two of them climb down the hillside. Brother Gordon held one of those big compound bows, the same kind the men had used when they came after Romy. He held it in one hand and hung on to trees and boulders to keep from sliding down the steep hillside as he followed the reverend. Small rocks clattered and bounced ahead of them, falling all the way to the trail below, and she heard the reverend curse. For a man of God, he had a really foul mouth. He'd always acted so holy, so pious at the compound. Hands folded at his waist, words from the Bible—mostly misquoted—peppered throughout his speech.

They finally made it to the bottom and walked toward the bodies of the two wolves lying in the trail. The reverend hung back like the coward he was, while Gordon walked close enough to kick Jace hard in the back.

The wolf didn't move. "Out like the dead. These guys aren't going anywhere."

"They're still alive, though, right?" Ezekiel got in his face. "You didn't kill them, did you?"

"You're the one who got the tranqs. You tell me."

"Damned coward." Ezekiel got closer, touched his hand to Gabe's chest. Then he did the same to Jace. "They're alive. Which one's Romy?"

"Neither, you idiot. They're both males. She must have been the one that took off into the trees." He gazed toward the forest, but he was look-ing north of the spot where Romy and Wolf were hidden.

"Don't call me an idiot. I'm the one who found the buyer for these abominations."

"Money you'll have good use for in prison, right?" Gordon laughed.

"Don't laugh. And you are an idiot. There's enough money offered for these guys that the good reverend will be able to disappear forever. But we still need to find the bitch. I promised a breeding pair, and that's what we're going to give them."

"Well, you'd better hurry before these two decide to wake up. Shock collars around their necks will keep them from shifting."

"You're sure about that?"

"Makes sense. They try to escape, we hit 'em with a few volts of cur-rent. They can't shift with the collars on."

"So how do we get Romy?" Ezekiel had pulled two heavy collars out of his backpack. He slipped the travel bag off of Jace and affixed the col-lar. Then he did the same to Gabe.

"She'll show up. She's not going to leave her buddies. They're pack animals. She'll show up before too long. We can set up camp against that boulder. With the mountain behind us, the only way to get to these two is across this open area."

Romy?

Gabe! Don't move. Pretend you're still unconscious.

What happened?

Reverend Ezekiel and one of his men hit you and Jace with tranquil-izer darts. They've put shock collars on both of you. The guy said you couldn't shift with a collar on. They're planning to camp against the rocks so that my only way to attempt a rescue is to come across an open area.

Jace? You waking up yet?

Slowly. I'm listening. Romy? We can shift with collars. That's old and incorrect information, what we believed before we knew we could become other kinds of predators.

He and Gabe had showed her one night. Gabe had turned into a bear, and Jace had become a puma, and then he'd shifted again and become an eagle.

The collars won't stop us, he said, *though I'd prefer not to get shocked.*

What do you want me to do?

Stay where you are until it starts to get dark. The moon won't be up until later, probably around ten or so, so we've got time. That will give us a chance to get the drug out of our systems. I'm too loopy right now to shift.

How did they shoot us? Gabe asked. *I didn't hear a gun.*

Compound bow, just like the ones they hunted me with.

Did you see any other weapons? Rifles or handguns?

No. But they're both carrying packs. They could have anything in them.

We'll play it safe, then. Gabe? I think both of us are going to remain unconscious at least until the sun sets. Get some rest, Romy. You're going to need your energy.

I love you, Jace. And she did. Why had she been so afraid to tell him before? What if they didn't survive? What if it was too late?

I love you too, sweetheart. Don't worry. We'll get out of this.

Yeah, Gabe said, *and with any luck, the reverend and his buddy won't.*

15

Finally, the damned sun was down. It took every bit of willpower Jace had not to attempt what could only be a fruitless attack on the two men holding them prisoner. Not while they were still chained to a tree stump, wearing shock collars. Hours ago the men had dragged both Jace and Gabe across the rough ground and secured them without any shade or water. Luckily, the temperature in late afternoon had only reached the eighties, but thirst would become a serious issue if they were held much longer.

The only time he'd experienced this level of anger and frustration was the day they'd found Romy, but now he had someone to focus on. Someone who, for whatever reason, now wanted Chanku alive. After the attempts to kill Romy, it made no sense to him. None at all.

The reverend had pulled out an ugly-looking handgun and placed it beside him where he sat on a fallen log. He'd also opened a bottle of expensive bourbon. It appeared that he and the muscle he'd brought along were celebrating their hunt.

A bit early, in Jace's estimation, though the gun made him nervous. He needed to make sure Romy was aware of the danger. He glanced at the dark purple sky and the deep shadows that now filled the area between here and the forest.

It was almost dark enough to put their plan into motion. *Romy? Where are you?*

In the rocks about three feet above Ezekiel. Wolf's closer to Gordon. I wasn't sure if you were conscious or not. Are you okay?

Jace felt his stomach tie into a knot of pure terror. Terror he couldn't let Romy sense. *Other than totally pissed off, I'm fine. Wolf knows to wait?*

He does. What are you going to do?

We'll shift into eagles. Our smaller skulls will allow us to slip out of the collars, but we'll be slower getting away as birds. Plus, it might take us longer to shift. Whatever drug they used is still in our systems. Gabe couldn't pull his dart out, and he's not recovering as quickly as I'd expected. I must have pulled mine out before I got a full dose.

Gabe hadn't moved. Neither had Jace, other than surreptitious glances to figure out where they were, where their captors were, but his inactivity had been by choice. He wasn't sure about Gabe, who'd been unusually quiet for longer and longer periods of time. With any luck, the two men would think he and Gabe were still unconscious. He hoped that, when the time came, Gabe was capable of shifting. So many things could go wrong. He reached for Romy again. *Ezekiel has a handgun. It's on the log beside him.*

I see it.

Good. You and Wolf will need to keep both of them focused on anything but us while we shift and get out of range. The compound bow is cocked and loaded with another dart. Gordon's practically got it in his lap, and I don't think he's as drunk as he wants us to think he is. Just don't let either of them get a shot at you. Be careful, Romy. I hate like hell putting you in danger like this, but I also know you're tough enough to get us out of here.

Let us know when you're ready. I'll go for Ezekiel. Wolf's going to take Gordon down.

A little bit longer. I want it darker. We'll have a better chance.

Waiting seemed to last forever, but the shadows deepened. Jace watched the men through narrowed eyes. *About ready, Gabe?*

Hold up. They're coming this way.

Shit.

"I don't understand why they're not coming around yet." Gordon knelt in front of Gabe. "It's been almost five hours. That stuff is supposed to wear off in less than an hour. Hits 'em hard and then it's out of the animal's system."

"I'll try the shock collar. That should wake them up." Ezekiel walked back toward his pack beside the log.

Gordon glanced his way. "Just one of them, and don't hit him with a full charge. I don't want to risk killing either of them, but as long as we've got one male, we're okay. Wish we knew where the bitch went. These two are only part of our ticket out of here."

Now, Romy!

But Ezekiel already had the controls for the shock collar. Gabe shrieked, an inhuman cry of pain. His wolven body arched and convulsed.

Jace prepared for his own shock, when Romy leapt from behind the boulder and grabbed Ezekiel by the throat. The man screamed and went down.

Gordon went for his bow but Wolf met him before he could reach it, launching his sinewy body straight at the man. His jaws connected around Gordon's throat, ripping and tearing as the big man grabbed Wolf around the middle and tried to pull him off.

Jace shifted. The eagle pulled his head free of the collar and then took human shape. His fingers flew as he released the catch on Gabe's collar and dragged the stunned wolf away from the fight.

Romy and Wolf seemed to be handling everything here. Gordon looked like he was unconscious. Ezekiel was lying limp and bloodied beneath Romy's attack.

The men were no longer a threat, but Gabe wasn't breathing.

• • •

Romy backed away from Ezekiel's body when it was obvious the man was no longer breathing. Hard to, with his throat ripped out and the bones of his neck exposed. She stood there, blood dripping from her jaws, legs spread wide and head hanging low, breathing hard and fast as she brought the bloodlust under control.

She'd killed a man. Again. And it shouldn't be so satisfying, but this felt pretty damned good. Slowly raising her head, she glanced around the dark campsite. Wolf was standing over Gordon, but that man also appeared to be dead. She took another look at the reverend to make sure he was through misquoting the Bible and then trotted across the ground to stand beside Wolf. He turned and looked at her, whining softly.

He knew killing humans was a bad thing. How could she convince him that killing this one was okay? Finally, she merely licked some of the blood off his muzzle and then sniffed the body. This one would never hurt another little girl, thank the goddess.

Where were Jace and Gabe?

Then she remembered. Gabe's scream, his body convulsing as she attacked. But that was all she recalled. She hadn't seen Jace shift. She'd been too intent on killing a man. She hadn't seen him and Gabe escape, but they were gone.

Jace?

No answer. She went over to the spot where they'd been chained and found their scent. It reeked of fear, frustration, and pain. Nose to the ground, she followed. It was almost entirely dark now, though the eastern sky glowed with the rising moon. It hadn't crested the mountains, but in another hour it should be really bright.

She walked around the large boulder on the north of the campsite and found them. Gabe was still in his wolf form, lying still beside Jace. Jace, human and so beautiful, sat beside the wolf with both his hands twisted in Gabe's thick fur. Tears rolled down his face, gathered in the rough beard covering his chin.

He didn't notice. He was inside Gabe, healing him. Only Romy sensed this was more than a mere healing. Gabe's life hung in the balance. The combination of the drug and the shock collar must have been too much.

Gabe's chest barely rose and fell.

Romy wanted to scream. She wanted to cry out the injustice of this, that a man who had done nothing but try to help her live should be lying here near death. It was her fault. All her fault, but screaming and crying served no purpose. Instead, she slowly walked around Gabe's body and lay beside him, sharing her warmth. Hopefully some of her life force. She'd give it all, whatever Gabe needed to survive. Anything. Willingly. With joy if he lived.

She was only vaguely aware of Wolf joining her, lying close beside her with his muzzle on Gabe's shoulder. She focused her mind not on Gabe and Jace but on their goddess. Would she answer Romy's plea? Carefully, with great respect, she called on the Goddess Eve.

• • •

This wasn't what she'd expected, this pristine, surreal world with light filtering through trees of an unbelievable green and a silvery mist sparkling against an azure sky. Romy was walking through ankle-high grass too green to be real, wearing a robe of pure white silk. At least it felt like silk, the way it shifted and flowed over her skin.

She really didn't know. She'd never felt or even seen silk before. So many things she'd missed. So much yet to learn. She stopped walking and ran her hands over the fabric, fascinated by the quality, the sleek feel of it. But that wasn't why she was here, wherever here was. She paused and glanced about her, only mildly curious when she really should be questioning everything she saw.

Except it was right. Exactly the way it should be. She felt a crackling of energy in the air, as if lightning were about to strike, and turned to her left. A column of light glowed, and before long a beautiful woman stepped out of the light. Without even wondering, she knew this was Eve. The woman who had been mated to Jace's father, the one who had died too soon and become their goddess.

As Eve walked toward her, Romy went to her knees and bowed her head. The soft laughter she heard wasn't ridiculing her. No, she had the feeling Eve was laughing at herself.

"Please, Romy. Stand. There is no need to bow to me. I may exist here in this amazing place out of time and space, but I'm just like you. Like any of the other Chanku who live and toil on the earthbound plane."

She took Romy's hands and tugged her to her feet. "Come. I've been wanting to meet you."

Romy followed her. They stopped by a small pond of the most perfect teal blue. It bubbled and frothed, but Eve waved her hand over the surface and the water calmed. A face appeared, and she realized it was Jace. His eyes were closed and his fingers held strands of bright fire that he wove with infinite care.

"What is he doing? What is that?"

"Jace is weaving together the strands of Gabe's life force. They were torn apart by the strength of the shock collar. Gabe still hovers near death, but Jace will save him. You offered part of your life force to save Gabe." She sighed. "I took it without telling Jace. He doesn't realize he is weaving some of your strands together into Gabe and I fear he will be angry with me when he finds out. He loves you too much to want you to risk yourself that way. Even for Gabriel."

Tilting her head to one side, thinking long and hard about what Eve said, Romy finally asked, "Do we have to tell him?"

Eve laughed. "Oh, yes. There are some things we never hide, and that is the truth of our actions. I will confess to Jace, and so will you. He must not feel any guilt for what he does, because your life force, my intervention, and his actions are going to save Gabe's life."

"The collar wasn't supposed to kill. That's what the men said."

"No. It wouldn't harm a wild wolf or a human, and generally not even Chanku. They would feel pain from the shock, but Gabe had a serious reaction to the tranquilizer. It didn't affect Jace the same way, but Gabe was hovering close to death when the collar shocked his heart and caused it to fibrillate. Jace tried CPR, but it wasn't enough. That's when he went inside Gabe and controlled the rate of his heartbeat internally, but he couldn't have kept it going."

She shrugged and Romy thought she actually looked guilty. "Not until you made your offer and I took you up on it, even though I was certain you really had no idea what you were offering. I transferred part of your life force to Gabe through Jace's hands. He'll know when he finally emerges from his trance, but I'll have you back in plenty of time so you can explain that it was a gift freely given. Not something he or I took from you. I hope he's not upset with either of us. Especially you. Romy, you are such an amazing young woman. You have much to offer as a member of the pack. I'm thrilled you've found your way to us."

Romy gazed at the goddess. She'd never seen a more beautiful woman. Tall and lean with long blonde hair that almost reached her ankles, and her eyes were fascinating, swirling in colors of blue and gold, green and gray, a hypnotic spin that made Romy feel sort of dizzy.

"Actually, Romy, that dizziness is weakness you feel, but you'll gain strength as your life force rebuilds. Right now, you probably feel as if you've given a large blood transfusion. That's why I brought you here, to share a bit of strength with you so you can hunt when you return. Both Gabe and Jace will need to eat as soon as Jace finishes healing."

She raised her head and frowned. "Return now, Romy. You'll have your full strength back in a very short time, and I'm giving you a bit of mine as well to speed things along. Your gift saved Gabe's life tonight, but I think his father is anxious to speak with you. Tell him the truth. He needs to know what you've done."

She leaned close and kissed Romy's forehead, and the touch of her lips sent a burst of energy through Romy. She closed her eyes at the sweetness of the rush. When she opened them, she was a wolf once again, lying beside Gabe with Wolf next to her. Jace was still caught in his trance.

She raised her head and sniffed the air, hoping to find game close by.

Romy? Is this you?

So startled by the strange voice, Romy jerked her head around and looked to see who was speaking. Then she recognized him. It was Gabe's father, and he sounded frantic. *Mr. Cheval?*

Yes. It's Anton. Is my son dead? Tell me! I have to know. Is he . . .

No. No, he's not dead. Almost, and it was really scary, but he'll be fine. Jace is healing him now, and I was just with the goddess, with Eve. I think we were on the astral, and she told me Gabe would be fine, that my life force helped save him.

Your life force?

She felt rather than heard his sigh.

Maybe you'd better start from the beginning. Tell me what happened to my son.

Just a minute. She checked on Jace. He seemed to be withdrawing from his trance, and Gabe was resting easier, but she needed to find game. They had to eat and rebuild their strength. *Mr. Cheval? I promise I will tell you everything as soon as I hunt. Eve told me I need to have something here for them to eat when they both come out of wherever they go when Jace heals. Do I just call your name?*

This time she was certain she heard laughter. *That will work just fine. Go. Find fresh meat and take care of my son and his friend. But I expect to hear from you. I know you'll tell me the whole truth. As I said before, Gabe and Jace tend to leave out the details.*

I understand.

She knew the moment he was gone. Romy told Wolf to stay and guard the two men. Then she trotted out along the trail, beneath the brilliant light of the full moon. The scent of game was rich in her nostrils, and she had a feeling this was something else she'd need to thank Eve for.

• • •

Jace's nose twitched at the rich aroma of fresh blood. He raised his head, blinking slowly at the brilliant slash of moonlight cutting across the ground where he sat. Gabe slept soundly in front of him, and Wolf was resting his chin on Gabe's shoulder, staring at Jace.

He didn't see Romy, but there was a beautiful buck lying in the sand not three feet away. The belly had been torn open but the entrails were intact and hadn't spilled their contents onto the meat.

So exhausted he trembled, Jace shifted and went to the buck. Nothing had been eaten. Romy must have delivered this meal for him and Gabe. He had no idea where she was, but he wasn't about to ignore her gift.

After a moment, Wolf joined him, and the two of them fed steadily, tearing away huge pieces of still-warm meat. Whenever he'd done a long, involved healing, hunger became a living, breathing entity, but he quickly filled his empty belly. By the time he'd eaten as much as he could, Gabe was stirring.

Jace went to him, touched noses with the wolf. Gabe blinked, his eyes still unfocused, his breathing shallow, but he was no longer dying. *I almost lost you, Gabe. Don't ever do that to me again.*

I don't plan on it. What happened?

I'm not sure. You were really quiet coming off the drug, and then that bastard got you with the shock collar. Your heart stopped.

Oh, is that all? Shit. No wonder I feel awful . . . except? Where's Romy?

I'm not sure. She brought fresh meat. You need to eat something, get your strength back.

So does Romy. Gabe slowly struggled to his feet. *You weren't the only one to save me, bud. She gave me part of her. Something. Not sure, but I can feel it.*

Shit. That was Romy? I thought it was from Eve.

I think Eve helped. We need to find Romy.

No, I need to find Romy. You need to eat. Wolf? Keep an eye on him for me, okay?

Wolf crawled closer to the carcass and watched Gabe.

Romy said he can understand us. I think she's right. Eat. I'll find her.

He raised his nose to the air and ended up back at the campsite. Romy sat on a boulder, a lovely human woman staring down at the two mangled bodies lying in the dirt. She wore her pants and halter top, but she looked like she was a million miles away.

Jace sat there, still in wolf form, and admired her. There was nothing about Romy he didn't love, but the fact she'd been willing to give up part of her life force to save his friend, that she'd been smart enough to figure out how to do it . . . the woman was amazing. Definitely more than he should ever hope for, but he wanted her as he'd never wanted anything or anyone in his life.

He shifted. Then he found his bag near the chains and collars lying in the dirt and slipped on his pants and shirt. After a moment, Romy raised her head and smiled at him.

"You found the buck?"

"I did. Thank you. Gabe is eating now. Wolf's keeping an eye on him."

"Good. I've been talking to his father. Anton was worried sick. He said Gabe just winked out and his dad thought he was dead. He couldn't find him, couldn't reach you, and even Eve wasn't answering. So he called me. I filled him in on everything that's happened over the past couple of days. He said he saw the newscast with all of us being interviewed. Sandra gave our intended route. That must be how the reverend found us."

"That makes sense. But he was in jail when I talked to John."

"Anton said the news last night mentioned that he'd made bail. It shocked prosecutors, because no one thought he had any money. Anton's going to look into it."

"Good. If there's anything to discover, he'll find it. I'm surprised Eve didn't answer him. She's usually pretty good about getting back to Anton when he's got questions." As he talked, Jace was climbing up the rock to Romy. He finally reached her perch and sat beside her. The trail, the meadow and the dark forest spread out before them, all bathed in moonlight. There was something mystical about this night, and he wondered where the spirits of the two men who'd died here had gone.

Hopefully nowhere good.

"Eve probably didn't answer because she was busy with me. I was on the astral tonight. We talked."

Jace slowly spun around and gaped at Romy. "On the astral? When? Why?"

She shrugged and looked away for a moment. Then she turned back to him. "When I realized how serious Gabe's condition was, I prayed to Eve. I offered my life force if it would save him. She took me up on it, but she only took a little. She said it was like donating blood for a transfusion, but it's not something easily done without her help. I offered, she passed it to you and you put it inside Gabe. You did an amazing job tonight, Jace. She showed me what your healing looked like, as if you were weaving strands of fire. You truly saved his life."

He was going to have to do some serious thinking about all this. Romy was giving him a lot more information than he'd expected. Or that he knew how to deal with. "I thought it was Eve's strength I was using. I had no idea it was yours. Thank you, Romy. Thank you more than I can possibly express." He wrapped his arms around her and drew her close. Her arms slipped around his waist, and they sat there for a long time.

An owl hooted, bats squeaked overhead, and the moon moved across the sky, but Jace felt as if he needed nothing more than Romy Sarika in his arms. Romy, and the knowledge that Gabe was safe, even if he did have a little bit of Romy keeping him alive.

A few minutes later, Romy's stomach growled. Jace chuckled. "You didn't eat, did you?"

She shook her head. "No. I was so excited about actually getting that buck all on my own, I couldn't eat."

"C'mon." He held out his hand to help her down off the boulder.

Once they reached the bottom, she stared at the two corpses lying in their own blood and filth. "We need to call John."

"No cell service. I'll have Anton get in touch with the authorities. We'll have to hang around here for a while."

"This time you talk to Anton. I'm going to eat." She slipped off her clothing and stuffed everything in her pack. Then she shifted and, with a glance over her shoulder, walked around the boulder to where Wolf and Gabe were feeding.

Jace watched her go. He wanted her. Not just for now, not merely for tonight. Forever. Convincing Romy was going to be the hard part. Or maybe not. He had a feeling that somehow things had changed tonight. Romy seemed stronger. More sure of herself.

Maybe more open to love? One could only hope. In the meantime, he had a couple of bodies to deal with, and he knew just the man to handle things.

Anton? Got a favor to ask . . .

• • •

Luckily, John Salazar managed to get on the same helicopter flight with the members of the FBI who arrived early the next morning. Anton had contacted him first.

166

Jace and the others had left the entire scene untouched. Wolf had spent the night guarding it against scavengers, which had infuriated the local critter population, but he was obviously proud of himself when the sun rose to an absolutely pristine crime scene.

The men lay where they'd fallen, their throats ripped out, blood soaked into the coarse sand. The chains and shock collars were still in place, the compound bow loaded with its dart, and there were two ATVs they'd left behind the rocky outcropping. Each ATV was loaded with camping gear and carried collapsible cages designed for restraining large animals.

There were three of those.

Jace, Gabe, and Romy stayed out of the way while the team members collected evidence. Photographs were taken, video shot. The bodies were tagged and bagged, as was each piece of evidence. They answered a lot of questions, all recorded, but no one seemed to fault them for the bloody deaths. They also had to shift and give samples of their wolf hair and saliva for DNA testing. All part of the investigation, but there was no talk of arrest or charges. At least not against Jace, Gabe, Romy, or Wolf.

Chanku protected their own, and they'd all been under attack. Besides, Wolf had taken down the biggest threat, a man armed with a compound bow, while protecting the others. No one was going to fault a wolf protecting himself or his pack in his natural habitat. Now, though, he waited across the open area, close against the forest in the shade of the trees. Obviously he wanted nothing to do with so many humans, though there was definitely human interest directed toward such an intelligent animal who'd chosen Chanku as his pack.

By midafternoon, everyone was gone. The campground where the killings had taken place was as pristine as if a crime had never been committed. The plastic gloves and crime scene tape had been removed, the illegal fire pit carefully deconstructed.

Gabe was exhausted, and Romy wasn't in much better shape. Jace convinced them to travel the few miles to the cavern where he'd hoped to stay . . . was that just last night? So much had happened, and he figured the cavern would be a good place to spend a few days to get their strength back.

"It's not a five-star hotel, but there's a hot mineral pool inside and fresh spring water close by the opening outside. It's warm and dry, and John said there's more rain expected tonight."

Gabe raised his head. He'd stayed in his wolf form most of the day. *Well, that changes everything. If it's supposed to rain, I want a roof.*

"I want that hot mineral pool." Romy kissed the top of Gabe's head. "Give me a minute to change."

16

Romy stopped at the entrance and just stood there, staring at the bands of color winding across the rock walls of the huge cavern. "Wow." Laughing, she turned to Jace with both hands on her hips. "I was about ready to wring your neck when you said I'd have to climb up to this damned thing, but this is gorgeous. How'd you know it was here?"

Jace stepped close, spun her around to face the beauty once again and rested his hands on her shoulders. "Years ago, Gabe and I were teenagers, and my dad and his, and Stefan Aragat and his son, Alex, wanted to look into buying property here, mostly to preserve it. We didn't fly. Instead we turned it into a cross-country trip, traveling as wolves, hunting along the way. It was the most amazing trip we'd ever taken, and when we found this cavern it felt as if we'd stepped into something magical."

"Anton thinks it might even connect to the caverns at the Chanku holdings in Montana," Gabe said, "but no one's ever had time to explore the entire system. We know it flows over into Idaho, but not how far beyond that area."

"So, did they buy it?" Romy tilted her head back far enough to see Jace's eyes. Goddess, but she loved his beautiful eyes.

"Of course." Jace laughed. "Wait until you see the hot tub this place comes with." He took her hand and tugged. Romy followed him into the depths of the cave. It was darker here, though there was still some light coming in through the opening. Jace stopped and retrieved a lantern from a small shelf carved into the wall. "Here. Hold this."

She took the lantern while Jace dug around a bit more and came up with a box of old-fashioned wooden matches. One strike and the tip flared. He lifted the glass and lit the wick, rolled it to a height that appeared to satisfy him, and replaced the glass. Light danced on the walls and threw shadows over Jace and Gabe's faces. Wolf sat on the ground between them, staring at the men as if they were both a bit nuts.

Gabe took the lantern and they walked around a couple of bends until the strong scent of minerals and increased humidity led them through a narrow crevice.

The pool was everything Romy could have hoped for—hot, but not uncomfortably so, bubbling with a fizzy effervescence that tingled over her skin and eased muscles she hadn't realized were sore.

They'd found a smooth shelf of serpentine where they could recline in comfort with the water bubbling across their chests. Romy figured she could stay like this forever, or at least until she got too pruny to move. She was already too relaxed.

Gabe dragged himself out first. "I don't want to push it. Any longer and I won't be able to crawl out by myself." He leaned over and kissed Romy, then planted an equally sound kiss on Jace. "Thank you. Both of you. I don't think I've said that, but please don't think I'm not aware of all you did to keep me alive."

When Jace started to say something, he held up his hand. "Nope. This time I get the last word. And now I'm going back near the entrance, where the sand is soft and I can see moonlight. I'll sleep there." He snapped his fingers. "C'mon, Wolf. You're on guard duty again tonight, but mine's the body you're watching."

Wolf shot a quick glance at Romy. She waved him off. "Go. You're such a good boy. Keep an eye on Gabe. Jace worked too hard to save him, and I'd hate for him to get eaten by a bear."

"I'd hate that too." Grinning, Gabe tossed off a salute and he and the wolf left.

Romy lay there in the churning water, her head resting against Jace's chest. She was warm and safe and clean, and so much in love she hardly remembered a time without love.

It had been almost a month to the day since Jace had saved her life, and yet it was difficult to remember life before him. Her memories of her mother were fresh and true, but when she thought of the years of abuse, she realized those memories had faded, almost as if they'd all been a horrible nightmare, the kind that disappears in the light of day.

Jace was the one who'd finally chased them away. He'd given her the strength to believe in herself and enough love to sustain both of them until she could find her own way. And he'd told her, not that many days ago, that when she was ready, all she had to do was let him know.

She was definitely ready. There was still the trial to face, but she wouldn't be doing that alone. She had Jace.

There was so much to learn about the realities of her new life, but again, she had the perfect teacher.

Jace.

He'd taught her how to shield her thoughts, no matter how much he might want to know what she was thinking. He'd shown her excitement and adventure; he'd protected her and encouraged her. He'd taught her what love was about, purely by example—the selfless, all-consuming love between longtime friends, the respectful, honorable love he felt for his pack and their leader and the goddess he served, and the powerful, passionate, and enduring love he showed Romy in everything he said, every action he took, every thought he had.

A love she returned without any doubts at all. There was no one else she could imagine as capable of love or as deserving of her love as John Charles Wolf.

Slipping out of his loose grasp, Romy floated in the warm water, sliding over him, coming down with her legs locked around his thighs. She kissed him, a warm exploration of lips and teeth and tongues. And then, with her arms looped over his shoulders and his holding her lightly at her waist, she pressed her forehead to his.

"You told me that when I was ready, I should let you know," she said. "Jace. I love you. I'm ready."

• • •

They left their clothing and bags in the cave near Gabe. He was almost asleep when Jace knelt beside him. *Romy and I are going to run. Wolf will watch over you. We'll be back soon.* He didn't mention they were planning to mate. He didn't want Gabe to tell him it was too soon, or that they should wait until they'd known each other longer.

I love you, Jace. And I think I love Romy just as much. She's perfect for you. Claim her before she figures out you're not the perfect god she thinks you are. He snorted in the wolf equivalent of laughter. *I'll be here when you get back.*

I love you, too, Gabe. And you're right. I'm not going to give her time to change her mind. Thank you. He brushed his hand over Gabe's head and then leaned over and kissed the big wolf on the nose. Gabe growled.

Grinning, Jace stood and took Romy's hands in his. "Are you ready?"

She kissed him. "I said I was. If you want me to change my mind, it's too late."

"All I want is you, Romy. Forever."

Should he tell her, he wondered, that forever for Chanku was, quite literally, almost forever?

They shifted, the two of them at the same time, as if their mating link were already forged. Romy left the cavern and scrambled down the rocky slope with Jace close behind. They paused together at the bottom and sniffed the air, searching for any hint of danger, but the only smells on the night air were the ones that belonged here. Then Romy nipped his shoulder and took off for the forest, less than a hundred yards away.

They chased each other through deep woods and moonlit meadows until Romy stopped to drink at a tiny spring bubbling out of what looked like solid rock. Ferns grew lush around them, and while the trees were dark and close around, the tiny meadow where they stood was bathed in moonlight.

She turned and glanced over her shoulder, silently inviting him to mount her, but Jace simply stood, taking a moment to admire the scene before him. Drops of water glistened along the short hairs on her muzzle, and her eyes sparkled in the moonlight. Her coat was such a true black that it appeared almost blue in the silvery light.

Finally he approached her. Romy didn't play any games. She didn't nip or try to run. Instead, she waited with a calm dignity that made him feel like an awkward teen. This woman might be younger than he was in years, but she'd experienced so many horrible things and had managed to come through them stronger than any woman he'd known.

And when he thought of the strong women he'd grown up with, Jace knew that wasn't an exaggeration, but he figured he did owe her full disclosure.

Romy? I said I would love you forever, but you need to know this— Chanku are almost immortal. We've got life spans that transcend any known number of years. Are you sure you want me forever? It's a really long, long time.

He actually heard her laughter. *Gabe told me how old your mother is, how old Igmutaka of your pack is. He told me about the ancient ones whose lives went back millions of years. I don't know if forever will be enough time to spend with you. I love you.*

Jace brushed her back with his paw and mounted her gently. He'd never had sex in his wolven form, but it was the most natural thing in the world to find her sheath ready for him, to fill her quickly, to feel the mating knot forming in his cock, slipping through her narrow opening and locking the two of them together.

As that tie bound them, the mating link almost audibly clicked into place. He was no longer Jace Wolf, no longer alone. He was Romy as an infant, as a child, as a growing girl. His admiration for her grew as he saw the horror she had lived with all her life. Not merely sexual abuse but the mental abuse a sadistic father wielded against his daughter.

Twenty years spent punishing her for what he saw as her mother's desertion, a woman the man had wanted to control more than he had ever wanted to love. And yet Romy was love. She was everything Jace had never imagined, more than he'd ever hoped for.

And she was perfect. Absolutely perfect.

• • •

It was strange, when she thought about it, but Romy'd asked Gabe what to expect in a mating bond, not Jace. She really couldn't ask Jace. That just seemed so, well . . . presumptuous.

Gabe had told her about the physical things that would happen, how the male wolf had a penis like a dog's and there would be a big knot that formed inside her that would essentially tie them together until the process ended. That she would experience the sensations with her wolven body but with the mind of a woman, just as Jace would remain mentally all man when their minds linked.

And that was the best part, Gabe said. When they suddenly knew everything there was to know about their mate. When their minds linked on a level so far beyond basic communication that there was really no way to describe it. All Gabe knew was that those who were mated said it was the most perfect experience they'd ever shared, and that once the bond clicked into place she would never be alone again.

Romy wondered if that was the thing that appealed the most. She'd been so alone, so isolated for most of her life. An unwilling receptacle for her father's seed, a helper to the women in the kitchen, a shadow trying to remain invisible whenever possible. Then she realized that no, it wasn't the idea of finally having a pack. It was that she'd have Jace, forever.

She braced her legs to take his superior weight, thrilled with a penetration that was similar and yet unlike anything she'd ever felt, and tensed, just a bit, when she felt the knot forming inside and wondered just how big it was going to get.

Then their minds linked, and Romy forgot entirely about the physical aspects of mating. How could she think of something so mundane as a physical response when she was traveling the corridors and tunnels, the broad highways and narrow catwalks of Jace's mind? Of his memories.

She saw his parents and felt their love—for each other and for their children—saw the man she'd grown to respect without ever meeting him in person, Gabe's father, Anton. She met the rest of the pack, including Gabe's sister Lily and her new husband, and saw all the mischief Jace had ever gotten into—and out of—over his twenty-nine years.

She experienced his love for his students, his passion for teaching, for learning, for exploring everything and anything. And she saw exactly how he healed. How he went inside an injured body, whether human or animal, Chanku or not, and just *knew* what needed to be done.

And Romy knew as well. She would have his skills, and while she would need training, they were not beyond her. Those skills would give her an honored place in her new pack. A needed skill as their numbers grew.

She hadn't thought it possible, but the more Romy learned about this man she loved, the more she loved him. He was strong and brave and true, his honor and integrity were without question, his love for her unshakable. He was everything. He was perfect.

And he was hers.

• • •

They shifted at the same time, the moment the link was complete, but they were still connected and it was such a perfect segue into making love in their human forms. Jace sat back on his heels and pulled Romy over him. She locked her heels behind the small of his back and wrapped her arms around his neck, and kissed him.

"I love you," she said. "You're absolutely perfect. I don't know what I was afraid of."

Her hot sheath pulsed around his shaft and he bit back a rather unseemly whimper. "I was never afraid. Fascinated, overwhelmed, surprised and excited, but never afraid." He kissed her slowly, methodically, and thought he would never grow tired of this woman. She would always surprise him, always drive him to be better, to be stronger. "I knew from the moment I realized you were Chanku, before I even saw how beautiful you are, that I wanted you. That I would never be happy without you. I knew you were absolutely perfect for me."

He thrust harder, driving into her while holding her close against him, and because of the mating link he knew when her climax was approaching, felt the first tiny tremors and shocks rocketing through her—their—system.

The hot slide of his cock inside her passage, the rhythmic clenching of her strong inner muscles—what she felt, what he felt—all of it spiraling inside his mind and body, shared and duplicated as the sensations bounced from Romy to Jace, from Jace to Romy.

His mated friends had tried to explain it, but without much luck. Now he knew, and he knew just as well he'd never be able to describe the sensation.

They shuddered together, clenched muscles at the same time, relaxed as the peak passed through and around, leaving them loose-limbed and ready for bed.

"We need to go back." Romy nuzzled his chest. "I don't want Gabe to worry."

"I know." They shifted at the same time and trotted back along the way they'd come. The moon was beginning to dip behind the treetops and they paused in the middle of the trail with moonlit rocks on one side and the dark forest on the other. Romy lifted her nose to the sky and let loose with a long, mournful-sounding howl.

But it wasn't mournful at all. Not one bit. And when Jace joined in, his deeper song brought an answering cry from Wolf, sitting in the opening to the cavern. A couple of minutes later, Gabe wandered out and sat beside Wolf. He raised his head and his song joined theirs, until their voices echoed off the rocky cliffs and floated out across the forest.

After a moment, Romy went silent. The others did as well.

Then, to the north of them, another pack took up their song. And in the west, there was another, and more wolves to the east and south. The packs were healthy. Healthy and finally, after so many years, sustainable, their size ebbing and flowing as nature ebbed and flowed.

All went quiet. Romy carefully made her way up the steep hillside to the mouth of the cave, where Gabe waited. He met Romy at the top, touched his nose to hers.

Welcome to the pack, Romy Sarika. Jace has found the perfect mate. And you've mated a truly good man.

I know. She glanced over her shoulder at Jace, standing proud and strong behind her. *He's absolutely perfect.*

About the Author

Kate Douglas is the author of the popular erotic paranormal romance series Wolf Tales, the erotic SF series Dream Catchers and StarQuest, as well as the DemonSlayers series. She is currently writing the next book in the Spirit Wild series. The first book in the series, *Dark Wolf*, is available now, and look for *Dark Moon*, coming in February.

Kate and her husband of over forty years have two adult children and six grandchildren. They live in the beautiful wine country of Sonoma County, California, in the little town of Healdsburg.

Write to Kate at kate@katedouglas.com. She answers all her email. Connect with her on Facebook at www.facebook.com/katedouglas.authorpage or on Twitter @wolftales.

15659195R00106

Made in the USA
San Bernardino, CA
02 October 2014